THEGRIEFKEEPER

THEGRIEFKEEPER

Alexandra Villasante

G. P. PUTNAM'S SONS

G. P. PUTNAM'S SONS
an imprint of Penguin Random House LLC, New York

Visit us at penguinrandomhouse.com

Library of Congress Cataloging-in-Publication Data
Names: Villasante, Alexandra, author.
Title: The grief keeper / Alexandra Villasante.
Description: New York, NY: G. P. Putnam's Sons, [2019]
Summary: After escaping a detention center at the U.S. border, seventeen-year-old
Marisol agrees to participate in a medical experiment hoping to keep her and her
younger sister, Gabi, from being deported to El Salvador.
Identifiers: LCCN 2018018251 | ISBN 9780525514022 (hardcover)
| ISBN 9780525514039 (ebook)
Subjects: | CYAC: Sisters—Fiction. | Illegal aliens—Fiction. | Emigration
and immigration—Fiction. | Deportation—Fiction. | Grief—Fiction. | Human
experimentation in medicine—Fiction. | Lesbians—Fiction.
Classification: LCC PZ7.1.V548 Gri 2019 | DDC [Fic]—dc23
LC record available at https://lccn.loc.gov/2018018251

Printed in the United States of America.
ISBN 9780525514022
1 3 5 7 9 10 8 6 4 2

Design by Dave Kopka. Text set in Mercury.

Para Isabel y Herosilda
Nos queremos

Chapter 1

We believe in luck. The good kind and the cruel. The kind that graces and the kind that cripples. The kind that doesn't care what you deserve.

My mother cleaned for a wealthy couple in Colonia Escalón, in the time before our bad luck. Mrs. Rosen liked my mother because she spoke English and because she would play mahjongg with her. After Mamá had scrubbed the toilet and the bidet the Rosens never used, she would make tea, and I would help Mrs. Rosen lay the clicking tiles facedown on the table.

I was allowed to watch them play, as long as I was quiet. After Mamá would inevitably lose, she would joke about La Mala Suerte that followed her through life.

"Oh, Maria, don't give a kneina hura," Mrs. Rosen would say. "Don't call bad luck down on yourself."

But that's not how luck works. She comes when she comes, with an open hand or a fist. You never know which one.

"What does *priceless* mean?" My little sister leans close and whispers her words into my neck. She says the English word the way you would in Spanish, "prees-less." Her accent is still terrible. I whisper back, voice almost a sigh, because we're not supposed to talk in this room.

"It means without a price."

Gabi narrows her eyes at me in annoyance. It is very odd to see my mother's expression on my twelve-year-old sister's face.

"I know *that*," Gabi says, exhaling like she's talking to una tonta. "But what else does it mean?"

I dart a look at the closest metal doors. The two guards are talking. Not looking at us.

"*Priceless* means it's so valuable, you can't pay for it. You can't replace it. Ever." *Like you*, I think, then wish I hadn't. If I let myself worry about how little I can protect Gabi, I will scream.

"That doesn't make any sense. Why did that guard say a joke was priceless?" She points to one of the guards, and I immediately push her hand down. I don't want their attention on us.

"I don't know," I say distractedly. Lunch is almost over. We eat fast so we can have a few minutes together before Gabi goes to her classes and I go to mine. She's in an advanced class because she knows so much English. I sit alone with a guard in a small room meant for babies because there is no one else here in my grade. The guard gives me worksheets to do and books to read. I never take the ones in Spanish. I want to show her, and the people I know are watching on the video cameras mounted on the thin walls, how good an American I can be. The guard doesn't let me use the computer.

But today is different. After I take Gabi to her class in one of the trailers parked inside the walled courtyard, my guard—her name tag says REYNOLDS—takes me through the longer hallways that lead, I think, to the exit. I panic a little, thinking that they will push me out the door, or take me somewhere without Gabi. I take a deep breath and tell myself to steady my voice. I want to be respectful and not show fear.

"Where are we going, ma'am?" I ask Reynolds.

She slows her stride and looks at me with an expression that seems to say, *I forgot you could talk.*

"Your interview," she says curtly before picking up her pace again. I knew it was coming. The first night at the border, I knew to say we were asking for asylum. Now they want to know why, to ask questions. I'm ready. I have the right answers. I pat the front pocket of my jeans, find the envelope where it has been since the day we left home, then hurry to catch up with Reynolds.

Reynolds doesn't interview me, but she does guard the door. I sit at one of the chairs at a small table and wait. There's nothing personal in the room. Not a plant or a picture or even a cup with a funny design. It's a room that doesn't give anything away.

A woman in a business suit, tall like my tía Rosa and with a messy blond bun, bustles in and sits across from me. I love the word *bustle* because there isn't a word exactly like it in Spanish.

"My name is Mary Schoenbeck. You can call me Mary. I will be conducting your interview. Do you need an interpreter?"

If I needed an interpreter, how would I understand her enough to ask for one? There was a time when I thought I could be an interpreter, working for the government or the UN. Now I only want us to be allowed to stay.

"No, ma'am. I speak English fluently."

This surprises the woman enough that she looks up from her stack of folders. "Good. That makes my job easier. Your name is Marisol Morales, correct?"

I nod.

"Please speak your answers aloud," she says, pointing to a recording device on the table.

I clear my throat. "Yes."

"Marisol Morales, this is what is called a credible fear interview. You have claimed that you are seeking asylum in the United States of America due to your belief that you are in physical danger of torture or death." She barely takes a second to breathe. "You're seventeen, correct?"

"Yes. March. Twenty-seven." I spent my birthday somewhere between Guatemala and Mexico. Even Gabi forgot to say feliz cumple.

"All right. Tell me, in your own words, why are you seeking asylum in the United States?"

My words. My words want to jump out of my mouth, out of my heart. I have been keeping them inside for weeks.

"We." I stop. Then start again. "My brother, Pablo, was forced to join a gang. La Mara Salvatrucha."

Even though the recording device is on, Mrs. Schoenbeck scribbles in her notebook.

"After that, our father was threatened. He had to pay money."

"Even though your brother was in the gang?"

I stare at her.

"I mean, wouldn't he get some kind of break? A sort of discount for friends and family?"

I look into her eyes to check if this is a joke I don't understand. But I don't see a smile on Mrs. Schoenbeck's face.

"It was a different gang. Barrio 18."

"I see," she says, like she thinks that I am lying.

"There is nothing like a break for friends or family. When Papá could no longer pay, he went to San Salvador to find better work. He used to work at the Pepsi factory." Before he was fired in disgrace for coming to work drunk. Before he gambled and drank and wasted away all our lives. Tía Rosa said not to mention that.

I keep going with my story. It's a map to follow—first one place to land, then another. I follow the story so I don't get lost. "He was gone for two weeks. Then we got a letter that said he would not be coming back. And if we did not pay his debts, we would see trouble."

"Who was the letter from?" Mrs. Schoenbeck asks.

I shrug. "It wasn't signed."

"Do you have it with you?"

"No. Mamá burned it. And all the other ones."

"How many were there? Can you remember?"

"There were five." Pablo said not to worry. It was Barrio. Salvatrucha would take care of it. He and Antonio, Tato y El Negro, and all the others would protect us.

"And what did you think that meant?"

"I thought Barrio meant to hurt us. To kill us if we didn't give them money."

"But why? Why you specifically?"

Follow the story. Follow the map. "Because my father was in debt."

Mary Schoenbeck rubs the back of her neck, and suddenly I

want to do the same, to release the tension from my neck and shoulders. I didn't even realize I was hunched forward. I sit a little straighter.

"So, this was extortion. Nothing personal."

I feel sick. Every word she pulls out of me makes my throat ache. "Can I have some water?" I ask. That's something you can do when you don't know what else to do with your hands. Hold a glass of water. Reynolds leaves the room and almost immediately comes back with a cold bottle of water.

"Yes," I say after a long gulp. "If we didn't pay, Barrio would kill us." I'm glad Gabi isn't here. I'm not sure she could stick to the story. I would be worried about it coming out the wrong way.

Mrs. Schoenbeck reads over her notes, flipping the pages back, then forward again. "So, um. Your father is . . . missing? Dead?"

I shake my head, then shrug. Mamá thinks Papá left us. That he has saved himself, a selfish man who abandoned his family. But I think he was *made* to disappear, like a terrible magic trick.

"I don't know. He never came back."

"And you don't know where he is?"

"No."

"All right." She takes out the forms I completed when we arrived in Pennsylvania, four days ago. The I-589 form that asks for asylum. She writes a note in the margin of the first page. I wish I could read upside down.

Mrs. Schoenbeck circles her fingers in the air, a sign to continue. "Go ahead. Your father disappeared—mysterious circumstances."

"Yes. Then Pablo got in trouble with the leader of his gang, Antonio."

She sits up, her eyes catching mine. "Got in trouble how?"

I squirm. I know I have to stay with the story. But it's so difficult talking about this part. It is the most difficult part. The least true part.

"Because Pablo wanted his girlfriend."

"Whose girlfriend?"

"Antonio's girlfriend. Liliana."

"Ah, okay, so there was a love triangle."

"Yes."

Mary Schoenbeck exhales loudly. "So, first there was a gang—Barrio 18—that threatened you because of your father's debts. Then another gang's leader, Antonio, was upset because of a girlfriend. And that's why he threatened you and your family?"

The way she talks about it makes it seem so silly, so small.

"Yes. We got death threats."

"What kind?"

"Notes on the door. Strangers coming up to my mother on the street, telling her to watch out. One time, a window was broken at the salon where Mamá and I worked."

I close my eyes for a moment and see the image of my mother wringing out the sponge in the bucket, scrubbing at the words painted on the side of our house: *¡Putas de mierda!*

"Go back a bit," Mrs. Schoenbeck says. "What was the date your father disappeared?"

I am suddenly so tired that I want to cry, which is useless. Tears can't help us. I answer all her questions, though she repeats them using different words two or three times. I answer her like I am a machine. All the dates I had practiced with Tía Rosa, the map I have to follow.

"And what was the date that you were detained?" I snap my attention back to Mrs. Schoenbeck.

"*We* were detained," I say.

She stops writing and looks up. "Excuse me?"

"We. I am here with my sister, Gabriela. I'm her guardian. In loco parentis," I say. I immediately wish I hadn't. If she knows that means *in the place of a parent* in Latin, then she thinks I'm showing off. If she doesn't know what it means, then she'll hate me for knowing something she doesn't.

"Yes, I understand." She scribbles more notes. "What about Pablo. Why didn't he come with you?"

Her question, even though I expected it, makes me pause. I don't think of my brother. That is the rule I made. Pablo's memory weighs on me, all the time.

"He was killed. By the gang. It's only Gabi and me now." I push down the urge to say "Gabi and I" because sounding the way real people talk is important in learning a new language. I learned a lot from watching satellite TV in Mrs. Rosen's kitchen.

"Where is your mother?"

"She is staying with my tía Rosa. Rosa Morales. A hidden place north of San Miguel." *I am too slow, mijita. I cannot keep up with you and Gabriela. I will stay with Rosa until it is safe to leave. Then I will make my way to Mrs. Rosen's house. We will be together again, te lo juro.*

After more questions that go in circles, Mrs. Schoenbeck puts down her pen, folds her hands, and leans forward. This is the moment.

"When you were first interviewed at the detention center in Texas, you declared that you are seeking asylum in the United States of America." It isn't a question, but I answer anyway, aware of the recording device.

"Yes. For me and for Gabi."

"You claim that you and your sister's lives are both threatened by violence and death by gangs in your country. And that officials, the police, and the government are corrupt or unable to protect you—is that correct?"

"Yes."

That is what I was told to say. Those exact words. Words are like keys. Only the right ones will turn the lock.

Mrs. Schoenbeck rubs her eyes under her glasses. "I'm having trouble understanding the nature of the threats against you both."

"It's the gang. They are threatening us. They want to kill us." Maybe my English isn't as good as I think it is. But I don't know how to be more plain.

"I understand, but *why*?"

When I don't answer, she continues. "What is the nature of these threats? Are they political? Religious? Based on ethnicity?" She is reading from a list, I realize. I don't know how to answer. Tía Rosa didn't tell me about this. A cold feeling spreads through my arms and legs.

"I have letters," I say.

Mrs. Schoenbeck looks over her glasses at me. "You have documentation to support your claim?"

I pull the envelope from my pocket. It's warm and wrinkled and slightly stained. I put it in a plastic bag because I knew we'd be crossing water, walking in rain. For all that we passed through, it's in one piece, and that's what counts.

I watch her peel apart the plastic bag and take out the envelope. It seems like she's doing it slowly on purpose, though I know that's probably not true.

Mrs. Schoenbeck reads the letter from my teacher. I don't have to ask what it says since I helped Señora Marquez write it.

"Marisol," she said, "help me. It takes me twice as long to write in English as it does in Spanish. I don't want to seem *ignorante*."

To Whom It May Concern,

I am writing to inform you of the plight of Marisol and Gabriela Morales. Both girls were students in my school, the American Academy for English Studies, which has recently closed due to violence in Ilopango. I have known the Morales family since before the girls were born and know them to be good, honest, hardworking people. Due to an unfortunate incident involving Marisol's older brother, their family has come under the bad influence of the Salvatrucha gang. Their father disappeared and their brother, Pablo, was recently murdered. Everyone in Colonia Santa Lucia knows that the rest of the family has been put under a sentence of death. The sisters in particular have been threatened with murder and worse.

There is nowhere else they can go.
I am at your disposal to answer any questions
and vouch for the girls' honor and morality.

Sincerely,
Señora Ermeregilda Marquez

There were parts of the letter that I didn't like. "Honor and morality" made me feel itchy with shame. For myself, of course, not Gabi. And I winced when Señora Marquez added "with murder or worse" because the only thing worse than murder is watching someone you love be murdered.

Mrs. Schoenbeck's eyes return to the top of the page to reread the letter. Then, she unfolds the second envelope. This one is printed from a computer. The envelope, stamped with both POR AVIÓN and AIR MAIL, had made its way from New York to my mother and now back to the United States again.

To Whom It May Concern,

I am writing to give a character statement
for Marisol Morales. She is the daughter of my
longtime employee and friend Maria Espinosa
Morales. My husband and I lived in San Salvador
for nearly ten years. My husband worked
with Democracy International during the last
elections. When the election-monitoring mission
was over, we chose to stay, even though Howard
had retired. We thought the elections would bring

*changes, improvements. However, we watched
with concern as the situation in the country
continued to destabilize and gang influence
increased. We left eighteen months ago, afraid for
our lives when our driver was abducted in front
of our apartment complex and held for ransom.
Despite our paying the ransom, his headless body
was found in Parque San Jose a week later. I
believe that Marisol is being targeted by the local
gang and that her life is in danger. Marisol is not
an immigrant so much as a refugee, and as such
is seeking asylum.*

*I am now a widow of considerable means. I
am willing to act as a guarantor to Marisol. What
is more, I am willing to have Marisol live with
me at my farm in upstate New York, and I am
willing to support her so that she does not become
a burden upon the state.*

I enclose my address and contact details.

Sincerely,
Mrs. Howard J. Rosen

I didn't know what Mrs. Rosen would write, only that
Mamá had asked her for help and Mrs. Rosen had responded
with this letter and the money necessary to pay the coyotes
who brought us past the border. I knew we would get caught,
though Gabi hoped we'd be able to sneak ourselves all the way
up to New York. She was counting on my English being so good
that we'd be mistaken for Americans.

Mrs. Schoenbeck frowns. "This letter from Mrs. Rosen mentions you but not your sister."

I say a bad word under my breath. I don't know enough curse words in English yet, but I know plenty in Spanish.

I point to the date of the letter, written at the top of the first page. "Mrs. Rosen did not know, when she sent the letter, that Gabi was in danger too. It was before the letter from Señora Marquez, do you see?"

She does not answer. I want to fill Mrs. Schoenbeck's silence with words so badly, I nearly bite my tongue. The story of everything that happened to us before Pablo died, before Papá disappeared. How far back would I have to go? How many litros of words would I have to spill to tell a story that would convince her, convince all of them? When did our bad luck, our mala suerte, begin?

"Americans are stupid."

"They're rich, anyway," I said. I was ten, and agreeing with my brother was the price I paid to hang out with him.

"Rich and stupid," Pablo said.

"There have to be some poor Americans somewhere." And smart ones, like Amber's best friend, Aimee, on *Cedar Hollow*. But Pablo hated that I watched American TV shows.

He snorted. "They think they're poor if they have only four pairs of sneakers."

I tried to keep my breathing from turning into panting. I trailed behind Pablo, not wanting to lose sight of him. I couldn't let him slip away like he usually did.

"Slow down!"

"¡No seas mantequita!" he shouted over his shoulder, speeding up. *Don't be butter.* When he wanted to make sure the insult stuck, he'd say it in Spanish. I wasn't soft like butter, though, and he knew it. I ran faster to match his long strides.

We were the only kids in our neighborhood who really spoke English, thanks to Mamá and because Mrs. Rosen paid for us to attend the American Academy on weekends. The kids in the neighborhood thought we were gringos and stuck up. Pablo thought so too, and it burned a hole in his stomach. But I insisted on talking to him in English as much as I could. I didn't want to lose it by not practicing.

"¡Basta!" I yelled. He stopped, then leaned into the chain-link fence, waiting for me to catch up. When I finally reached him, my hands went to my hips, a replica of our mother's stance.

"Why are you hurrying? Why can't we just walk?"

"Because Flaco y Tato are waiting for me, and if I'm late because of my baby sister, I'll never hear the end of it."

"I'm not a baby."

"Yeah, you're not a baby. Gabi is the baby. You're the brat."

"Come on, Pablito." I let a little tremble lace my voice. I knew how to play the little sister.

"Fine!" He hooked his fingers high up on the metal links and dangled his feet, stretching his long brown body, like a hanging chile or a ham.

I laughed. "You look like un jamón."

"Well, you still look like una trucha," he snapped.

I was stung and furious. I wanted to come up with a really good respuesta—I just needed time to do it. Mamá always said I had beautiful eyes, like my abuela. But Pablo had started calling me trucha when I was five because my eyes were so big in my tiny face. The name stuck with his friends. What's funnier to seven-year-old boys than calling someone a trout?

Before I could insult my brother the way he deserved, his friends arrived.

"We came to find you. You're always late," Tato said as Pablo gave me a look that said *see?* and *peste* all at once. Pablo's friends were all there, slapping hands and teasing each other. El Flaco, who wasn't skinny, El Negro, who wasn't black, and Tato, the one who was really good at fútbol. There was a new, older, taller boy too. I stared at him like you'd stare at a lion in a flock of sheep.

"Hey, Pablo, this is my primo, Antonio," Flaco said.

My brother acted cool, nodding his head in Antonio's direction. But he couldn't keep his eyes off the older boy's shoes.

They were new. Blindingly white and clean. Expensive. American. They must have cost a million dollars.

The boys moved away and I followed them, despite the cloud of dust they kicked up with their shuffling steps.

"Who's this?" Antonio said, stopping to point at me. I felt smaller than I had a minute ago. As small as our youngest sister with her dolls and tea parties.

"My sister Marisol." Pablo shrugged. "I have to watch her."

Antonio gave me a look, like he was trying to see what I was made of underneath my skin. I felt like a bug, the kind in the folding cabinet that Señor Melo brings out for science, the dead and trapped kind.

"Muy guapa." Very pretty. And I was truly pinned to the spot. "Not so much today, maybe!" Antonio continued, and all the boys laughed. Pablo laughed the loudest. "But one day you'll be very pretty, Marisol." He leaned close to me, his head bowed. His teeth were the whitest I'd ever seen. He stroked his fingers down my cheek. I felt like it must be leaving a mark.

I started to cry. I didn't know why then, though I do now. I wonder at what kids can know without knowing. El Negro looked uncomfortable, and Antonio stared at Pablo, daring him to stop him.

Pablo shrugged. "Come on, it's a compliment," he said. It wasn't what I wanted. I wanted Pablo to shove the boy with the American shoes away. To tell him to leave and never come back. But he didn't.

Antonio winked at me before moving to the front of the pack, already the leader of the neighborhood boys.

That was the day La Mala Suerte came to my family. And she stayed, wearing us down, taking our money, my father, and my mother's health. Year after year until, in an abandoned locker room, dogs and guns making the same sounds of alarm in my head, we were trapped. My baby sister—no longer a baby—calling to me as if I could save her.

Chapter 2

Mrs. Rosen passed away.

I startle out of my chair a little. Was I asleep? Even after four days in this detention center, I crave sleep more than food. Every day Gabi and I were on the road, on a bus, hiding in a muddy hole, or walking along the train tracks until our legs were numb, I didn't sleep much. Someone had to watch over Gabi.

I rub my eyes and straighten up. "I'm sorry, I think I fell asleep." Mrs. Schoenbeck is standing at her end of the table. A different guard is by the door, and the door is open. How much time has passed?

Mrs. Schoenbeck doesn't sit or smile or ask me a question.

"Mrs. Rosen has died, Marisol. We just confirmed it."

Panic floods my chest—there's no room for air in my lungs. Mrs. Schoenbeck does not look into my eyes.

"But. But she wrote to us. She said to come." It was only a week ago—no, it was more than that. Everything is confused in my memory. Two weeks from San Salvador to the border. Two days in a detention center in Texas. Then a bus ride to Pennsylvania, where they gave us chaquetas because it is cold here in April. Almost a month since Mrs. Rosen sent the money. All that money. Gone. And now Mrs. Rosen is gone too.

"I'm sorry," Mrs. Schoenbeck says. I don't know if she is

sorry because Mrs. Rosen is dead or because we have come here for nothing. Without saying anything more, she leaves the room. It's a blessing, at least, that she hasn't said what I know must be true. There's no way we will be allowed to stay. We will be sent back home, and everything will be the way it was before. Only worse. Because I made it so much worse.

This guard—his name tag says WILSON—leads me back to my classroom and gives me a worksheet to do.

"Do you want something to eat?" he asks.

I need to be alone, so I break my rule—the one that says I should be as small and unnoticed as I can be, and not to bother anyone. "Yes, please."

As soon as he leaves the room, I cry. Quickly, to get all the tears out. I don't have time for more, but if I try to keep them in, they will pour out at the wrong time. I cry for myself, only a little, because I can't help it. Then I cry for Mrs. Rosen, who I didn't know I loved until I knew she was dead. And that's it. I grab a tissue from the desk. I can't cry for Gabi. If I cry for my sister, that means I've lost hope. I can't do that.

Wilson comes back with a glass of orange juice and a chocolate chip cookie. He notices my puffy, red face and asks if I want to go back to my room. If I needed any indication that we have failed, I need look no further than the pity in Wilson's eyes.

"No, thank you." I walk stiffly to the desk and start to fill out the worksheet on the periodic table, which I learned years ago, and imagine that each word I'm writing—*Antimonio, Arsénico, Aluminio, Selenio*—each element, is a brick. I can rebuild this dream. I can find a way to keep Gabi safe.

By the time I pick up Gabi at her classroom, my face is smiling and tear-free.

"Did you have a good day?"

"Yes!" She dances as we walk down the hall. I have to remind her to be more quiet. "I was star reader. Again." She smiles.

"Naturally."

"Yes. And Angela and Nestor called me a chupamedias and una culebra—how do you call it in English?"

"Um. Let me think. A suck-up? A brownnoser?" I look at her sharply. "Don't ask me why."

"Well, they said it behind my back but so I could hear it too. I ignored them."

"Good." Before dinner, we get an hour of exercise. The other children in the center go outside to play in the courtyard. But Gabi and I always go to the little trailer next to the kitchen, where most of the books are. It's not that we don't like the other kids. It's that they don't like us. They see us as different because we can speak English. Mrs. Rosen used to say that my English was good enough that I could be on TV in the States, if I were taller. Thinner. *Mrs. Rosen is dead,* I remind myself. There's no one here waiting.

At the trailer, I'm surprised to see Reynolds waiting for us. My body fills with panic, and I step in front of Gabi. *They're going to send us back. Right now. I don't know how to fight them.*

"Don't go to the dormitory after dinner. The asylum officer wants to see you again. Both of you girls." I don't move, as if being still can make me invisible.

"Okay? Marisol?"

"Yes," I say, my voice only just above a whisper. When Reynolds leaves, Gabi takes a book from where she's hidden it behind the bookcase. She settles in at one of the tiny tables that are too small for her and starts reading. She's been trying to read *Harry Potter and the Sorcerer's Stone* because it was the book Pablo and I loved most to read in English, but she struggles with some of the more complicated words.

"Why is this so hard?" she complains after a minute.

I look over her shoulder. "Well, English isn't like Spanish," I begin.

"I'm not stupid," she says sharply. I take a deep breath. Since we arrived in Pennsylvania, we have been fighting so much more.

"I just meant that Spanish is more simple, honesto—written like it's pronounced."

Gabi buries her head in her book. Her lips move, very slightly, as she sounds out the English words. I walk to the little trailer window, leaving her in peace to concentrate.

I wish I could escape into a book and forget what is happening to us. If the asylum officer says our form has been denied, do we go back the way we came? They could put us on a bus back to Texas, over the border again. Then, will they leave us in Mexico, unwanted baggage?

This trailer sits on cement blocks and is a little higher than the kitchen next door. I watch through the window as the women in white coats and paper hats make food. They might be talking, but I can't hear them over the clatter of metal pans. On the stove, huge pots hold boiling water and let out swirls of steam.

One of the women—she sweated through her paper hat and

has taken it off to fan herself—tosses the ladle she's been using into the sink and marches to the back door. I straighten up, all my muscles tense. She's not supposed to. I know she isn't, and so does she, because she looks over her shoulder at the other kitchen workers and at the door leading back into the main building where a guard sometimes stands. But no one is there now, and the woman swipes a plastic card in the lock. When the light on the door glows green, she uses a crate of oranges to prop the door open.

My hand goes to my jeans pocket, and I remember, all in a rush, that my letters are gone and that they will not let us stay. That we're only waiting to be sent back home. But the last of the money from Mrs. Rosen is still sewn into my belt, the stitches going right through the paper of a hundred-dollar bill so that nothing could shake it free. When I shower, I take the belt into the bathroom with me, holding it above my head so it stays dry. I keep the belt with me always. It's my last plan.

"Gabi?"

"¿Qué?" She's not paying attention if she's answering me in Spanish.

"We have to leave."

She turns to me, a confused expression on her face.

"¿Por qué?"

"Never mind why. We just have to. Now."

Her face is a storm of anger and fear. I think she will argue with me, and I don't know what I will do if she says no.

"Sí. Okay, yes, I mean."

She takes the Harry Potter book. I hesitate for a second, wondering if the beat-up paperback will slow us down or if it makes the situation worse if we've stolen a book. But the situation can't get worse, I tell myself. Which is always the wrong thing to say to yourself.

This is how I make decisions now. I ask myself, *What is the worst thing that can happen if I do this?* And if not doing it is even worse, then I do it. It becomes a question of which thing will hurt Gabi more. So, in the end, it isn't hard to choose to run away.

We walk out of the trailer and down the block steps to the kitchen doors. The kitchen workers are too busy to notice us. They assemble the huge metal pans of food at the front of the kitchen, where they will be put on carts and wheeled into the cafeteria. I hear the sounds of running feet and children's voices as they start to file into the cafeteria. If you didn't see the barbed wire on top of the metal fencing, you would be sure this was a school. Maybe it was a school once. Outside the back door of the kitchen, there is no fence, no barbed wire. Only a row of dumpsters and a road.

We crouch down low, Gabi in front of me, and head to the back door. A man's voice cuts through the clanging kitchen sounds, and my muscles tense up. This detention center is for women and children. The only men here are guards. Do we stop and turn back, or do we go on? I hear him laugh, teasingly. He's not paying attention. At the back door, I give Gabi two oranges from the crate and stuff two more into the pockets of my sweatshirt.

Outside, the cool air feels good on my face. I look down the road, so inviting and empty. But I decide against it. Anyone looking out the back door would see us walking down the road. Even if we ran. Instead, we wedge ourselves into the tight space between the building wall and the dumpster. Just in time, because the male guard, with sharp words, kicks the crate of oranges away and closes the kitchen door.

"It's disgusting," Gabi says, holding her nose. I put my finger to my lips, and she's instantly quiet. In a flash, we are back on the road, no longer safe.

I count three minutes in my head. That is long enough for the guard to have moved on to the cafeteria to watch the kids. I know this is a chance that won't come again. They don't count us at meals, only at bedtime. I push Gabi out from behind the dumpster, and we start walking, then running down the road, staying as close to the scrubby bushes along the side as we can. After fifteen minutes of running, we slow down.

She takes a minute to catch her breath. "Can we talk now?"

"No."

"That's talking."

"Will you shut up if I give you food?"

"Of course," she answers.

I pull out the cookie I saved from Wilson's snack. American cookies are giant, and Gabi loves chocolate. She breaks the cookie in half.

"Toma," she says, holding out half.

"No, I already ate mine," I lie.

We walk, Gabi in front. It's like we are back with the coyotes, afraid something will catch us. I imagine a thousand suns, a thousand eyes, a thousand hands behind me. It's like a fire growing at my back, and I have to walk away, fast, to keep it from consuming me.

I look at Gabi, nibbling on her cookie, making it last, and am thankful for one thing. She has this crazy amount of faith in me. I don't know where it comes from, or how I earned it. But when I tell her that it will be okay, that we'll make it, she believes me.

If we are lucky, so incredibly lucky that it couldn't be believed, we will find someone who can take us to New York, or at least in that direction. I know it isn't that far from Pennsylvania to New York, but is it hours or days? How much luck do we have? I don't know. Mrs. Rosen used to say, "I don't believe in luck, sweetie. I believe you make your own luck." Which sounds like she's saying two opposite things. She doesn't believe in it, but she does believe in making it. I never understood her. Now she's dead, Dios la bendiga.

"What's the plan?" Gabi asks.

I was so lost in my own thoughts that I forgot I needed to explain things to Gabi. But I don't want to. She was starting to relax, even smile. I let her believe that we were finally safe. Now it's all slipping away.

"We need to find a way to New York."

She lifts an eyebrow in question. I've always been jealous of her eyebrows—of all the silly things to be jealous about when you have a beautiful sister—but they are so expressive. Papá used to say that Gabi's eyebrows could tell a story with more drama than a telenovela.

"The asylum interview didn't go very well. We had to leave."

"But Mrs. Rosen was going to come get us. Won't she be mad we're not here?"

I can't tell her Mrs. Rosen is dead. Not yet. I can't see the fear make a home in her eyes again. I will tell her on the way. Soon. "We're going to where her house is, on our own." In her letter to Mamá, Mrs. Rosen said she was living with her eldest daughter in a place in New York called Rhinebeck. We'll go there and find Mrs. Rosen's daughter. Somehow.

Gabi doesn't argue or ask me questions I don't know how to answer. That's almost worse. We walk in silence for a few minutes more, until there is another road that crosses this road. There will be more cars on the new road.

"They won't figure out we are gone until bedtime. If we find a car to take us now—even if it's only going part of the way—we have a chance. Next car that comes, you hide and I'll see if it is okay."

Gabi nods. It's what we used to do at checkpoints with the coyotes, hiding from military patrols until the right car or SUV came to pick us up. When we hear a car coming, she flattens herself against the bushes. The first car that passes is too fancy; that means too many questions. Another car is driving too fast. When I see the third car, a mud-colored truck, I step out of the bushes and put my hand out, thumb up.

My father, years and years ago, used to tell us about the feeling of gambling. We knew when he'd had a good night; his face was flushed dark red with drink and excitement. He started by saying that, of course, gambling was bad, that we should never gamble. But his eyes were as bright as stars as he told us what it felt like to put money down on a number or a card game.

"El mundo se abre, and you can see everything you've ever wanted—so near at hand, you can almost touch it. The wheel spins, or the cards turn over, and then every possibility you imagine transforms, like magic, into one reality." His eyes glittered. Maybe he didn't realize, or maybe he didn't care, that he was making gambling sound so good. Like it was the only thing worth doing, the only thing making him feel alive. "It's like praying and knowing your prayers will be answered," he said before Mamá heard him and yelled at us, pushing us out of the kitchen and clos- ing the door behind us. Pablo and I stood there, looking at the closed door and hearing their argument. In me, a fear took root that I might gamble away things that I couldn't lose, the way Papá had been doing. In Pablo, I think, a different flower took root.

The mud-colored truck doesn't stop. Neither do the two other cars I think look okay. This is a gamble, I know. I can put my hand up and play, but I can't control what we get or don't get. Gabi peers over the bush, and in a moment she will come out and stand next to me. I know her so well. She is only good at listening for a little bit. Then she wants to do. I turn to tell her to hide herself again when I hear a car come to a stop. I forgot that my thumb was still out, that I was still gambling.

The window of a black car rolls down. A woman with dark hair and eyes leans over to look at us.

"Need a ride?" She has a little bit of an accent, and I'm try- ing to figure out where it's from and if it's a good thing or a bad thing, trying to process all the information and make the right decision. Only, I'm so tired. I feel thin as paper from keeping my fear from Gabi. My brain isn't giving me correct informa- tion about this woman and her nice car. But my body moves back, without the rest of me knowing why.

"Hi!" Gabi says, stepping in front of me. I grab at her sleeve but miss as the woman opens the passenger door.

"I like your car," Gabi says. It doesn't seem like a very special car to me, but Gabi loves cars. Mr. Rosen let Gabi borrow all his *Motor Trend* magazines, just like he let me borrow any book in his library. The walls of our room at home are covered with pictures of shiny, fast dream cars.

The woman smiles at her. "Where are you two going? I can take you part of the way if you want."

I hesitate, then look down the road. The sun will set soon. How long have we been gone? Are they missing us? We're not important, not anyone special or dangerous. But still, they will look for us, won't they?

I make a decision quickly—that's the only way to make it when you are running. I push Gabi into the back seat, then climb into the passenger seat. As she pulls onto the road again, I catch sight of a car behind us, black with darkened windows, and I freeze, convinced they have caught us, that I've been too slow.

The woman slows down, letting the dark car pass us. "Assho—jerk!" the woman yells with a quick glance at me and Gabi.

I settle into the seat, and the relief of being moved instead of moving is overwhelming.

"So, where are you ladies heading?"

"New York," I say quickly. "We are meeting our grandmother there."

The woman glances at her side mirror, and I wonder what she sees, if anyone is coming. "I can take you as far as New Jersey. Is that okay?" Even though the sun is starting to go down, the woman slips on dark, expensive-looking sunglasses.

"Are you rich or something?" Gabi asks from the back seat.

"¡Híjole!" I yelp. Why does she have to be rude now?

The woman looks at Gabi in the rearview mirror. "No. Why do you ask?"

"The car. The sunglasses. All of it is very expensive."

The woman laughs. "Not really. I only have a couple vices.

Cars are one. Chocolate chip cookies are another. I'm addicted to them." It's like she's read Gabi's mind. As crazy as she is about cars, Gabi will do anything for cookies—the American kind, not the galletas Diana we get at home. The first book I read to Gabi in English, borrowed from Mr. Rosen's library, was *The Lion, the Witch and the Wardrobe*. I teased that she was like Edmund and his Turkish Delight with her American chocolate chip cookies. I can't remember the last time I teased Gabi about anything.

I struggle to tell the lady our fake names—the entire story of our lives that I made up to distract myself as we walked on the carretera. It's a dream story about girls like us, if only we'd been lucky enough to be born in the United States. Some things are the same. That Gabi is fascinated with cars and loves to swim. That I love to read and won a prize at school for a short story. And then there are the lies that are too good not to tell. That we go to an American school. That our parents are legal immigrants with good jobs who go to school meetings and coach softball teams. I'm not even sure what a softball team is—I know it's like baseball, but what's different about it? Is the ball really just softer?

These are the questions I used to pester Pablo about all the time. He'd been to America once, on a visit with Tía Rosa when he was seven. I asked him every question I could think of, to store up the answer, ready for when I would go to America, so I would be prepared for anything.

But now, in the warm, expensive car of a stranger driving us all the way to New Jersey, I can only repeat the word *softball* over and over in my head until the road becomes a dark fuzzy line, and I fall asleep.

Chapter 3

I wake up with a pain in my neck and a feeling that I have run out of time. My face has been leaning against the window of the car. How are we in a car? Are we at the border? Will we have to stay the night in another shelter? Then I remember that we are in America. We made it. We only have to figure out how to stay.

I look behind me to see Gabi lying on the back seat, asleep.

"What time is it?" I ask the woman who picked us up. I remember that she told us her name, but I don't remember what she said.

"It's late. Go back to sleep, Marisol," she says. Her face is lit by the dials of the car. The heat is on, and it's comfortably warm. We seem to be the only car on the road, and the hum of the tires is soothing.

Then the bottom falls from my stomach as I realize I never told this woman our real names. I stiffen and pull back into the seat, but there is nowhere to go.

"Who are you?" I ask.

She glances my way before returning her eyes to the road ahead. "My name is Indranie Patel. I work for the United States government," she says, looking at me again. The panic in my eyes must make her speak faster. "There's nothing to worry about."

"You lied to us."

"We lied to each other. I believe you said your name was Mary and your sister's name was Jenny."

I won't cry. I refuse.

Indranie reaches over to touch my shoulder. "It's okay. I promise. We can help each other."

I'm shaking my head because I'm stupid. Why did I think we could get away? Now they will punish us for trying to escape.

"Hey, you know what?" Indranie keeps her voice low as she turns onto a big road. "I'm an immigrant too. I came here many years ago from India with my parents. I was only eight when I came."

I want to ask her if someone was trying to kill her in India. If her brother had been killed. But I already know the answer. There are immigrants and then there are *immigrants*, and some are easier than others. Gabi and me, we had so much more than the others traveling with us. We had English, and we had Mrs. Rosen and the money she sent. Now we don't have anything.

"Where are you taking us?" I ask. I pull at the seat belt that's digging into my neck.

"Listen. Don't panic. I only want to talk. I promise."

"Talk about what?"

"About you and your sister and what will happen next."

"Did you follow us from the detention center?"

She hesitates. "Yes."

"I am so stupid." I want to hit something, to scream. But it would be useless.

"Not true. You're smart. You're resourceful. And you're willing to take risks."

Risks, gambling. My father never talked about what happened when the gamble *failed*. Despite what I told Gabi, I knew we would probably fail. I just hoped that this time we could win.

I look back at Gabi, who sleeps on, undisturbed. I don't think we are in physical danger, and I don't know what to do next, but the urge to run is tremendo.

"Don't try to get away, okay? Please? We'll find you, but it will make my job a lot harder. And we have a proposal for you. A proposition. Do you know what that means?"

I scowl at her to show that it is a stupid question.

"When we get to our destination, I'll tell you everything you need to know. Just be patient."

I try to make my body relax as my mind spins with desperate plans that lead nowhere. Nothing I come up with helps me do the only thing I *must* do: keep Gabi safe. Until I can figure out how to do that, for today and for always, I have to wait. Wait and be ready.

Indranie stops at a place to get gas and coffee. She tells me I can go to the bathroom, but Gabi will stay in the car until I come back. She knows I won't leave without my sister. I spend a long time looking at my face in the cloudy bathroom mirror. This is the face they will look at today when they decide what to do with us. How can I make this plain face move their hearts?

When Mrs. Rosen still lived in Colonia Escalón, my mother would sometimes set curlers in her thin, gray hair. She would tell my mother, though I was standing right next to her, that I could be pretty if I lost a little of what she called "the puppy fat." And if I wore makeup. My mother would nod gravely as if taking all those suggestions to heart. I'd want to laugh because I knew there was no way of turning a plain brown bird, un gorrión, into a songbird. The only place where miracles like that happened was on TV. Then I'd drifted back into the warmth of the kitchen, where a TV was always on. Mrs. Rosen liked to hear the voices of Americans throughout her house. She said it made her less homesick. She didn't care what she watched, but I'd always switched the channel to SKY II so I could watch *Cedar Hollow*.

I learned how to curse and insult someone in English watching *Cedar Hollow*. Not bad words, really, but words like *Dammit!* and insults like *You worthless waste of space!* I learned that when there is a pretty girl, there will always be two pretty boys wanting to be with her. I learned that, at least on American TV, those boys would never follow her down an empty street at night to grab her. Only the villains did that. And the villains on *Cedar Hollow* were usually from out of town, so you always knew who they were, right away. And many of them wore black jackets.

The main character on *Cedar Hollow* was called Amber. She had blue eyes and golden blond hair that reached to her waist, as straight as a curtain. She was tan, like a peach that was ripe, but never too dark. The first night I watched *Cedar Hollow*, I sat at Mrs. Rosen's kitchen table with a little notebook, writing down, as best I could, all the words I didn't understand. Later, I would ask Mrs. Rosen to tell me what they meant. Soon, she got tired of answering and gave me a dictionary. Some words Mrs. Rosen didn't know, and weren't even in a dictionary, but I wrote them down and puzzled over them until their meaning became clear. The best part of *Cedar Hollow* was watching Amber.

She was a good person, but she made bad choices. Sometimes I'd want to yell at the TV, at her, but I knew that was silly. She was beautiful. So beautiful it made my heart race. But I was ashamed too, to be spending so much time thinking about a girl who wasn't even real.

I look away from the mirror, sick of my own reflection. Compared to Amber Brooks, my face is a disappointment. I have a tiny mouth, shaped like a fish looking for a kiss. My eyes are black, and there are pecas across my nose, a shade darker than the rest of my face. And unlike Gabi, my eyebrows are straight and don't express much of anything.

Indranie, sipping from a huge cup of coffee, pulls the car out of the gas station and onto an empty highway. The sun has started to come up, or, rather, all the light that comes up before the sun. The purples and blues and pinks. We cross a bridge, the rippling water reflecting the light of the sky. Ahead of us, a city, a centro of some kind, unwinds. Old buildings, new buildings, and clean, so clean the city doesn't look real. I sit up straighter as a building I recognize comes into view. A white dome.

"Where are we?"

"Welcome to Washington, DC."

We loop around the domed building. I have my hands against the window, making a smudge, I know, but I can't help it. I feel electric. In the capital of the United States? Maybe this is good news after all. No one would bring us here only to deport us. Whatever the proposal is, it must be important.

"Indranie?"

"Mm-hmm?" she answers distractedly, the road curving

into a circle of traffic as we cross another bridge, this time over other roads instead of water.

"What is this proposal?" I picked the shorter of the words she said, *proposal* and *proposition*. I know what *proposition* means, of course, but I don't want to say it incorrectly.

"I can't talk to you about it now. But it will all be explained when we get inside." We drive down a ramp under a large building with many columns. We're underground, in what looks like a parking garage. I shift my knees as she opens the glove compartment and takes out a badge to hand to the guard in the booth. They talk about a sporting team that lost last night and always seems to lose. The guard hands her badge back to her, and I hope to ask more questions, but Gabi inhales deeply, smiling and stretching.

She should look like me because we have the same hair and eyes and even the same lips. But Gabi is lovely, even having slept in a car all night. Fresh-faced and pretty, she's got a face that you want to kiss—that's what my father used to say. "¡Besos para todos!" he would say when he got home from a trip. Gabi would get the first and best kisses, then Pablo. I would get the last kisses, the half-hearted, tired ones.

Indranie opens the door, telling us that she'll have breakfast for us once we get upstairs. Every elevator we enter, every door we go through, Indranie has to put her badge in front of a scanner and wait for the red light to turn green. In a white room with a huge table and twelve chairs, we sit and wait for breakfast. When it comes, it's almost as big as the table. We ate well at the detention center. Three times a day and sometimes snacks. All the puppy fat I had left on the carretera, I started to get back.

But this breakfast is different. *Cedar Hollow* was sponsored by a restaurant called IHOP. A strange name: I hop. I could never figure out what it meant. But the commercials were amazing. A family of four—sometimes they were black, sometimes they were white—would sit at a table stacked with plates of food. Pancakes and sausage and tocino and fruit and whipped crema. And every person would have at least two drinks, so there was never a chance of them getting thirsty.

"It's like I hop," I say as two men in uniforms push a cart of food into the room. We get two drinks too, one hot chocolate and one orange juice.

Indranie laughs at our expressions, then pours herself a cup of coffee. "Eat up, girls. We have a lot of talking to do today. And a lot of thinking."

I hurry to keep up with Gabi. When I'm finished, when I can't actually eat more, not when the food is gone, I ask for a cup of coffee. Whatever is going to happen next, I need to stay alert.

"Can I have coffee?" Gabi asks. I am about to tell her it isn't a good idea, but Indranie pours her a cup, passing her the milk and sugar.

The plates are piled back onto the cart and removed. Only the smell of the honey-brown syrup from the pancakes is left in the room. Gabi has wrapped some bacon in a tissue and put it in her pocket. I frown at her, but she ignores me and at least Indranie doesn't notice.

Indranie shows us to the bathroom, where we swipe at our teeth with a paper towel to try to make up for not brushing them.

"Why bother? It's not like anyone's going to kiss me."

"No seas grosera," I say. We're alone. Indranie waits for us outside the bathroom door. "Gabi. They have a proposal for us, una propuesta, ¿sabes?"

She goes still, wary eyes watching me in the mirror. "What kind of proposal?" Her question is as careful and slow as if she'd just uncovered a snake in the grass.

"I don't know yet. But it doesn't matter. If we can stay here and work, even for a little bit, it will make it better for us if we have to go back."

"Go back?" The fear in her voice is a knife in my side.

"No, no, we won't go back. I mean, maybe one day?"

"We don't need to go back. You said that Mrs. Rosen will help Mamá to come in a few months. Then we'll all be together, here. In America."

I push down hard on the secret of Mrs. Rosen's death. Now isn't the time to tell her.

"I know. But sometimes plans change, and we have to make the best of it, right?" Her eyebrows come together, a look I know well. "Let me find out what is happening and then I'll tell you everything I can. Okay?"

Gabi blows out her breath. "No, it's not okay. What happened in the interview? Why didn't we get—¿cómo se dice *asilo*? Did you tell them everything that happened?"

"I told them what I was supposed to tell them. What Tía Rosa said to tell them."

She frowns fiercely, crossing her arms—and she is a tiny version of my mother again. It makes me ache for home.

"This way might be better, faster than staying with Mrs. Rosen," I lie. "You trust me, right?" I ask.

"Of course. Don't be stupid."

"Love me?"

She tips her head to the side. "Depends. What day is today?" she asks, tapping her finger against her head like she's thinking. I know she's making a joke, but I don't actually know what day it is. It scares me in a new way, like I am losing control of even the smallest things.

"I don't know," I say, close to tears.

Gabi wraps her arms around me. Can it be that she has gotten taller?

"It doesn't matter. I love you today and every day. Even though you are una peste."

I laugh and hug her. *Peste* was what Pablo and I called Gabi. She was forever our little pest, our hermanita.

"Okay in there?" Indranie asks from outside the bathroom.

Forever is over.

# Chapter 4

What we are proposing," the man in the heavy sweater repeats. I am trying to listen, but I am fascinated by his sweater. Why is he wearing it now? It's not cold in this room, and usually large men are hot in spring, like the carnicero or the man selling paletas. The carnicero sweats even with the fan in his store on full power. I hate to think of him sweating on the lamb chops, the ground beef. I force my attention back to this man in front of me. My mind wanders when I'm nervous. I am very nervous.

"If I could interrupt, Dr. Deng?" Indranie says after his third repetition of "what we are proposing." She turns to me with a friendly smile. "You're a smart girl, Marisol. You showed resourcefulness and grit, not only in getting yourself and your sister to the United States but also in escaping the detention center. I'm not saying those were good choices, by the way. They were dangerous. I hope you know that."

I drop my eyes, hoping I look sorry.

"But you are strong and willing to take risks. You are also here illegally."

I flinch at the word. It doesn't matter that it's true. It feels like a smack in the face. Indranie wants me to know how few choices we have. As if I could forget.

"Even though your reasons may be good, you do not have permission to be here." She looks down at the folder in front of her, but I know she's not reading anything there that she doesn't already know. "Your case for asylum has been denied."

A pain pierces my stomach so quickly and sharply that I think I will fall out of my chair. I take a deep breath and look at Gabi. She sits up straight, hands tight around her empty coffee cup. I wish I could keep her from the room, send her somewhere safe. Pablo would laugh at me for trying to protect her in this way. "Es casi una mujer," he'd say. *She's almost a woman.* But I refuse to see her that way. She *can* have a childhood, if I protect her.

"Okay," I say as calmly as I can. "But there's some other form we can fill out? Something else we can do, right?"

Dr. Deng and Indranie look at each other.

"No," Indranie says.

My stomachache turns into a wash of acid.

"At least, not officially." Indranie's smile is sad.

Dr. Deng continues, "We're developing a biomedical device that, we hope, can help soldiers who have been in combat missions and who come back with PTSD—"

"Do you know what that is, Marisol?" Indranie interrupts.

I shake my head.

"PTSD stands for post-traumatic stress disorder," Dr. Deng replies. "When these soldiers are subjected to stressful events that impact their mental health, they are often unable to function when returning from combat duty."

I look at Gabi to see if she is understanding any more than I am. She is drawing on a notepad—a racing car with wings sits on a cloud. When she wants to focus, she draws cars. She catches me looking at her and pushes the drawing away, her expression guilty.

Dr. Deng continues, "These damaged soldiers are a burden to the VA system—"

"They are not a burden," Idranie says sharply. "They are the responsibility of the United States. Their well-being is not a burden." She's angry—I can tell. Dr. Deng can tell too.

"Yes, of course. What I mean to say is that the resources we use currently are not adequate to help these soldiers. More must be done." He turns to me. "Do you understand?"

I nod. I think I do understand. If a lot of American soldiers are coming back from war damaged, there must not be many Americans who want to go to war.

"You want me to be a soldier?" I ask.

Dr. Deng's shocked expression transforms into a wide smile. "No! Ha ha! Of course not! We don't have child soldiers." He pushes back a little on his wheeled chair.

"I'm seventeen," I say. "That is old enough."

"Marisol, what we need you to do is help us test a technology. Kind of like a medicine, one that would help our soldiers get better when their brains have had too much stress." Indranie, unlike Dr. Deng, doesn't use her chair on wheels to make a point.

"More than stress," Dr. Deng says. "They've had a severe traumatic episode, sometimes more than one. They suffer from overwhelming grief and shame, regret and anxiety. It makes it impossible for them to live normal lives. We've tried all of the approved treatments—talk therapy, EMDR, antidepressants, antianxiety, alternative medicine. But nothing works consistently. Until now." For the first time, his smile reaches his eyes.

I shiver. Now I know why he wears that heavy sweater. The vents in the ceiling have started to blow cold air over the table where Gabi and I sit on one side and Dr. Deng and Indranie sit on the other. Under the table, I rub my hands.

Indranie must see me shivering because she takes off her gray jacket and puts it on my shoulders. It smells of perfume and cigarette smoke.

Dr. Deng continues. "We call it the corticotropin transfer system, or CTS. It allows the chemicals, the stress factors—released into the body of a person suffering trauma—to be transferred to another person, a 'clean' subject without the same trauma burden. The memories of the trauma are intact—this is not some kind of mind eraser—but the feelings, deep depression, suicidal thoughts, and perhaps even homicidal thoughts that can be produced after severe trauma are greatly reduced. For the aggrieved person, in a matter of weeks it feels as if the trauma is in the distant past. Painful but vague. Remembered but distant."

"That's good, right?" I ask.

"It could be the difference between life and death," Indranie says carefully. She pours a cup of coffee, adding milk and lots of sugar. She puts the cup in front of me and urges me to drink. I can't think why she isn't cold. She's standing right next to me, and I feel heat coming from her, as if she has been running a long time, or sitting in the sun.

"We're in the last testing phase of the project. We've run all the tests we can without actually trying it on human subjects. The procedure works and it is safe," Indranie says.

"As far as we know," Dr. Deng counters, and it occurs to me that they are like a married couple, or a brother and sister. They are silently having a battle, right now, in front of us.

"What about me and Gabi? What is the proposal?"

Another flash of silent argument crosses between Indranie and Dr. Deng. Then, Indranie sits down next to me, pulling our chairs close until the wheels clink together.

"We want you to be the first person to try this. We want to test the CTS transference on you and another person. Someone who is suffering terribly and needs our help. Someone who wakes up from nightmares every night, has uncontrollable panic attacks. Someone's daughter." Indranie leans in close to me. I imagine, only for a moment, that I see tears in her eyes. But no, she is calm, a tranquil smile on her face. I know she desperately wants me to agree. But I can't understand why she thinks I have a choice.

"I'll do it," Gabi says before I can speak.

"¡Cállate la boca!" I spit. "You don't know what you are talking about."

Gabi turns to me. "Neither do you. And I can do things as much as you can."

I trip over words in my frustration. "Gabriela—"

Indranie puts a hand up, and we are quiet. "There's no need to argue. Gabriela is too young to participate. It has to be you, Marisol."

I can tell Gabi wants to argue, and I'm relieved she can't. I don't have the energy to fight with her.

"What happens to Gabi while I do this, this testing thing?"

"She would be with you, both of you safe in a comfortable house with everything you need. Gabi would even be able to go to a school. I know how bright she is."

"And after the tests? What happens to us?" I ask.

Dr. Deng answers. "The test period is one month. If we

hit all our targets and everything goes well, we'll know after thirty days if the transference project works as it's meant to. Then we will launch a pilot program, which runs for a year. We can then recruit more immigrants who want a chance to improve the science."

Who want to live here at any price, I think.

"But for you and your sister," Indranie says, taking my cold hand in her warm one, "it would only be a month. Then, I will be authorized to approve your asylum request." She squeezes my hand and smiles.

"Not just for you. But for Gabi and for your mother. You will all be able to live and work here. Isn't that what you've always wanted?"

Chapter 5

No. This isn't what I've always wanted. I didn't always want to leave my home. For a long time, it was enough to borrow books from Mr. Rosen's library and watch *Cedar Hollow* in Mrs. Rosen's kitchen. It was enough to joke around with Pablo, chase him through the streets, darting around the afternoon shopping crowd like silvery fish in water. We would walk around Parque Central, and he would tell me about his trip to America with Tía Rosa.

"What's the best part?" I'd ask him, like I always did.

"Everything is so clean. No one leaves garbage on the street."

I'd nod wisely. "You would be arrested if you dropped garbage on the street, I bet."

"Por supuesto," Pablo would answer, just as wisely.

"What's the worst part of America?" I'd ask. He always changed his answer. Sometimes it was missing watching his team play. Sometimes it would be missing Mamá and her pupusas. It would always be about missing home.

"One day we'll all go and you'll see. It's even better than that basura show you watch." He always insulted *Cedar Hollow*. Instead of arguing with him, I'd push him over, then run as fast as I could, laughing, until he caught me.

Those were good days, though I didn't know it at the time. I just thought it was my life. But once Antonio came, Pablo didn't talk to me as much. When Mamá started working a second job at the beauty salon, I watched Gabi at the Rosens', where it was safe. And Pablo went out without me all the time. I barely saw him, so I didn't notice the changes. Until Mamá asked me to find Pablo at el Club Atlético and instead I found myself stopped by Antonio at the entrance to the locker rooms.

"Que guapita que estás, nenita." He stood in front of me, cutting me off from my brother and his other friends.

"I'm not a little girl," I said. In the two years since Antonio moved to Santa Lucia, he had not stopped teasing me, making me feel small. Pablo would never say anything against him.

"No, and not pretty yet either. But you will be. I can predict these things." He brought his face closer to mine with every word he said. It was hard not to take a step back.

My brother called to me, "¿Qué quieres?"

"Mamá is looking for you. She wants you home. Now." I tried to make it sound like a command, but it only made Pablo and his friends laugh.

"Tell esa mujer that I'm busy," Pablo said, turning away from me like I didn't exist. Sometimes, I hated Pablo.

"Adiós, little sparrow. I can't wait to see you all grown up," Antonio said silkily.

I ran then, not caring how stupid it made me look, or how the boys laughed.

Good days. Bad days. Which is this going to be? I shake my head to chase the memories away. I sit at the gigantic table and sign a stack of papers as thick as my hand, trying to read a few words on each page. Eventually, I just sign my name and my initials wherever there is a blank line.

"This is for agreeing to a full medical checkup," Indranie says.

I sign.

"This one says you do not hold the United States culpable." *Culpable. Culpable.* Spelled the same. Means the same. Whatever happens to me, no one is responsible for it other than myself.

"This one says that you will not discuss the details of the CTS project with anyone."

I stop signing. "What about Gabi?" My sister is next to me, head down, filling the notepad with drawings. She looks like she is not paying attention, but I know she is absorbing every word.

"You two are a package deal."

Even Gabi looks up at that. At our blank expressions, Indranie explains, "You come together. There's no separating you two. You don't have to keep secrets from Gabi." Which is so far from the truth.

More signing, until . . . "This one is the first application for a green card. It's a long process, but if everything goes well, we'll be able to set you and your family up in no time." I sign my name, the black ink glossy on the page. My name doesn't seem important enough to mean so much.

Indranie walks Gabi and me down a long hallway to a giant space filled with desks and computers. I am surprised it is so empty until I realize it is still early.

She shows us to a smaller room. "This is Dr. Deng's office.

There's a TV, a couch, and even a mini fridge," she says, though we can see all that clearly.

"Where is your office?" I ask.

"I don't have one. Not anymore. I work from anywhere I'm sent."

Gabi hesitates by the door. "Won't Dr. Deng get mad if I watch his TV, or eat his food?" she asks.

Indranie laughs. "No. He knows you're here. And anyway, he almost never leaves his lab."

She turns on the TV for Gabi and even gets her a soda from the mini fridge. My sister's face is a mix of exhaustion and worry.

"I'm only a few steps away. And you'll be okay here. Just like the detention center." Safe, comfortable. For now.

"I know. I'm good," she says.

"Come on," Indranie says once Gabi is settled on Dr. Deng's couch drinking a Coke. "She's fine."

We take an elevator down a few floors to what must be Dr. Deng's lab. I barely have time to take in the details of the room before Indranie leads me to a small side room.

"Doing okay?" she asks.

I nod and try to copy her smile.

"Excellent. I'll leave you to get ready. Once you undress, put on this gown here—you can keep your bra and underwear on— and put all your belongings in this white bag. See? It has your name on it. It will all be returned to you."

I hesitate.

"I promise, no one will steal anything of yours. I give you my word as a government employee. I'll keep this somewhere safe."

"Will there be X-rays?" I blurt out.

She looks confused, as if that was not what she expected me to ask.

"Yes, a few. A CT scan and some other scans—all just to make sure you're healthy enough to begin the trials."

I've never had an X-ray. I know they show things, see through your clothes, right to your bones. But if I unpick the stitches on Mrs. Rosen's hundred-dollar bill and remove it from my belt, the only place I'll have left to put it is in my bra. Will the X-ray see it there? I know it's stupid to worry so much about the money. I don't know how much or even if it could help us now. And we have another chance. This experiment could be our bad luck, changing again into something sweet. But I don't want to let go of the last bit of our plan.

Indranie holds out the white bag to me. "Don't worry, okay? It will be all right. I'll be with you the whole time."

"Don't be with me. Be with Gabi," I say, suddenly incredibly scared.

"I'll be with both of you." She gives my shoulder a squeeze and leaves me to undress. I put my shirt, sweatshirt, and shoes into the white bag, then roll the belt into a coil and tuck it into my jeans before pushing it into the white bag too. Then I put the gown on. It opens in the front, so I wrap it around myself and tuck it under my arms so it stays closed. I keep my socks on. I hope that is okay.

Indranie walks me back to the lab, and the first thing I notice is how very cold it is. Dr. Deng sits in a chair on wheels—the only kind they seem to have in this building—and is rolling from one computer to another. A padded table sits in the middle of an already crowded room. This isn't what I thought a laboratory would look like. I thought it would be more like the ones on TV, with blinking lights and important-looking machines.

Dr. Deng motions for me to sit on the padded table, then motions again for me to lie. I push the gown down around my legs, as if that can protect me at all.

"This won't hurt, Marisol."

"Okay."

"It's usually the first thing people ask."

A nurse appears wearing a mask. I can't tell, without seeing her face, if she's frowning or smiling. My heart is thudding in my chest, even though I try to convince myself that everything is fine, that this is normal. I just have to get through one more thing to land in the safe place. That is what I told myself on the carretera, in the walks through the jungle. On the other side of this is safety.

Indranie stands next to Dr. Deng, her arms crossed tightly against her chest. She smiles at me as the nurse takes my arm.

"It won't hurt," she says.

It does hurt. Not a lot, but it pinches and stings. Then I feel a coldness spread through my arm, then a hot feeling through my whole body. It's nice because the room is so terribly cold. Now I can feel warm even without a blanket. I think about how wonderful that would be for people who do not have enough clothes or a house to live in. A medicine that makes you warm even when wearing only a hospital gown. And I think, *Maybe that's what alcohol is anyway, and why my father drank so much. To make himself warm.* And then I think that I am falling asleep, and I panic, as if I'm slipping off a cliff I didn't know I was standing on. Indranie is next to me.

"It's okay, Marisol. You can sleep."

When I wake, I'm still warm, wrapped in white blankets. I turn my head away from the blinding light above the table. A hot pain spreads from the back of my neck down my spine.

"How are you doing?" the nurse asks.

My throat is dry. I am careful not to move my head again, not to speak too loudly. "Okay," I whisper.

The nurse bends down close to my face. "You're going to be sore for a few days. Headaches are normal. Nausea and vomiting are not." She lifts my arm and injects something into the suero on my arm. *What is the English word for* suero? I think. I cannot remember. Maybe I never knew.

In a moment, I feel better, though my head feels as if it is floating, like a balloon, high above my body. The nurse unwraps me from the blanket, helps me sit up, and even helps me walk to the little room where my bag of clothes sits. Without a word, she leaves me to get dressed.

Though my head only hurts now if I move it too quickly, I feel slow and unfocused. I pull my belt from the white bag, uncoiling it to find the hundred-dollar bill exactly as I left it. I sit on a window ledge, a little dizzy with relief. After that, I put my clothes on, slowly, clumsily. There is a knock at the door. I wait. Then Indranie's voice asks, "Can I come in?"

"Yes," I say, tying my shoes.

Indranie is smiling. "You did great in there."

"I don't remember."

"I know. It's a pretty mild procedure—the implant is subdermal, but only just."

"I didn't know there would be an implant," I say.

Indranie smiles again. "Oh yes, it was in the paperwork you signed. But it's no big deal. Easy to remove. Though, it will ache. Does your neck hurt now?"

"Only a tiny bit," I say.

"Fantastic." She takes out her phone and shows me the screen. "I went to check on Gabi, because I know you worry. Just took this photo a few minutes ago."

I look at the photo of my sister. She is sprawled out on Dr. Deng's couch, blissfully asleep, an empty bag of some kind of potato chip next to her. I have seen Gabi asleep many, many times, from when she was an infant and would fall asleep sitting up to when she fought to stay awake with me on the journey here. Seeing her asleep, relaxed as a baby, is another relief.

"See? She's completely fine. I never thought she'd fall asleep with that much caffeine in her." Indranie laughs.

If you knew what that little girl has seen, what I couldn't keep her from seeing, you would be surprised she could sleep at all, I think. But I only nod in agreement. "Am I finished?"

"Not yet. A few more things today, okay?"

I nod again, then, because it feels so strange, I put my cold fingers to the back of my neck. There is a bandage there, square and stiff. Underneath it, I am healing. I can feel the herida, the skin hot and pulling. But what did they do to me?

Chapter 6

How did your brother die?"

"He died in gang violence."

"Was he murdered?"

"Yes."

"Did you see it?"

I have tried to keep my eyes on the pillow in my lap because I don't like answering this doctor's questions. But now I look straight at her. "Excuse me?"

Dr. Vizzachero slides her glasses onto her head. In a moment, she'll remember she needs them again, and pull them onto her face. I've seen her do this at least three times. She's always touching them.

"Did you see your brother die? I know it's a stark question, but I'm asking, Marisol, so I can gauge how much trauma you have already suffered."

When we sat down, Dr. Vizzachero said to call her Liz. So many Americans want me to call them by their first name. I sit on a leather sofa across from her, and Indranie stands next to the sofa, like a guard.

"No," I say, eyes back on the pillow. "I didn't see him die. His friend Tato came and told us the next day. Mamá went to get his body." As Dr. Vizzachero scribbles on a pad of paper,

I flick the fringe on the pillow in my lap. This is much more painful than the cut on my neck.

"How did you feel about your brother's death?"

Tía Rosa said I should tell them about Pablo, that it was important. Proof, she said. But I have to be careful not to tell them too many bad things. If they think I've had too much trauma, they might not let me do the experiment. So I don't mention Antonio or Liliana or anything else that hurt me before. I'm strong. I can handle it.

Indranie only said Dr. Vizzachero was a doctor, but she must be a psicóloga to be asking so many questions about how I feel. I'm exhausted. I want to see Gabi and sleep, not answer more questions.

Indranie interrupts the doctor as she asks the same questions with different words. "I think that's enough for today."

The doctor looks up from her notes. "Yes. Of course. I have enough information for an initial report."

"We'll need that report tomorrow, Liz. As soon as you can."

"Such a rush?"

"I'm afraid so. It's top priority."

"Well, I better call my husband and tell him to order pizza for the kids," she says with a sigh.

"Are we finished?" I ask Indranie once we climb into the elevator.

"For now. How's your neck?"

My hand reaches up to touch the bandage. Whatever medicine Dr. Deng gave me is wearing off. I feel the herida throbbing.

"It's okay."

"Remember to take your medicine for pain every four hours.

Dr. Deng doesn't want you to be a hero. You might be uncomfortable tonight from the implant."

"What does the implant do?"

"Well, it lets someone who is suffering transfer some of their grief to you," she says absently, looking at her phone.

"Yes, but how does it do this thing? Does it read that person's mind? Do I feel the same things they feel? How does it work?"

She looks at me, surprised. "No! I mean, of course it doesn't read anyone's mind. That's sci-fi stuff, Marisol."

The elevator stops and a woman in a raincoat steps in. She greets Indranie with a smile. "They say it's going to rain. I bring the raincoat, the rain boots, everything." She gestures at her colorful rubber boots, then her umbrella.

"And then, of course, it doesn't rain," Indranie says. "Never fails, Joanne. Never fails." As the elevator continues down, I catch Indranie's eyes.

"It's okay, Marisol. I'll have Dr. Deng explain it tomorrow. Don't worry. You're doing great."

In Dr. Deng's office, Gabi is awake and upset.

"You were gone so long." Her eyes ask me if I am all right. If *we* are all right. After weeks staying silent on the road, I can read the words on her face.

"I'm sorry. Are you okay?"

"Bored. I left Harry Potter in Indranie's car."

"Oh, there are lots of books upstairs. You'll have plenty to do," Indranie says, picking up the food wrappers and the empty soda cans. She puts the garbage in the trash can, making sure there's not a crumb left anywhere. "Come on, I'm tired. I bet you are too."

Back in the elevator, Indranie presses the button with PH on it. When the elevator doors open, the room we walk into is grander than anything I've ever seen on TV, and that includes *Cedar Hollow*. Several families could live in this apartment that Indranie calls the penthouse. I want to sink into the soft cushions of the sofa. Even the thick white rug would be wonderful to sleep on. Windows that go from the shiny white floor all the way to the ceiling surround the apartment.

"How do you sleep in the morning with the light coming in?" Gabi asks.

Indranie presses a button, and the clear glass of the windows darkens until I can't see the city below.

Gabi's mouth opens in amazement. "¡Qué chivo!" She grins. Indranie pushes the button again, the magic glass clears, and we can see the city—the dome of the Capitol and the river. The sun is setting, in almost the same colors as the sunrise, only deeper and somehow sadder.

We sit on high stools in the kitchen and eat noodles as Gabi tells us about the TV shows she's watched today. I'm happy to let her do all the talking as she describes telenovelas in English and the commercials to buy vacuums that are really robots and clean houses by themselves.

I can tell she's tired because she leaves noodles hanging from her fork, forgetting to eat. But she rallies to ask how my day was.

"It was good," I say, touching my bandage.

"That's it? Just good?"

"Yes. All is good."

I eat steadily, like it is my tarea, my task. When my bowl is empty, Indranie takes out ice cream. Gabi is thrilled, but I cannot eat any more.

Indranie scoops ice cream into a bowl for Gabi. There is crema, but there is also chocolate sauce and a small glass jar of cherries. Indranie opens the bottle of pills Dr. Deng gave me and hands me one.

"What's that for?" Gabi asks.

As if she is answering the question, Indranie turns to Gabi with a confidential look. "While your sister did very well today and is generally healthy, she's a bit anemic."

"What's that mean?" Gabi asks, her mouth full of ice cream.

"It means that Marisol wasn't eating as well as she should have been."

"That's because she gave me most of the food," Gabi says.

I push my empty bowl away. "No, I didn't. I just wasn't hungry."

Gabi uses her spoon to make her points. "On the carretera and in the detention center. And in the shelter en Tapachula. You gave me your food. I put the food back on your plate sometimes when you weren't looking. It was easy."

I'm surprised. That she noticed and that, without my knowing, she gave me food back.

"¡Traviesa!" I say, pointing my finger at her, pretending outrage.

"What does that mean?" Indranie asks.

"It means naughty, or tricky," I say.

"*Tra-vi-esa*. I have to remember that one with you girls," Indranie says.

"Marisol is the tricky one," Gabi says.

I snort.

"Why is she so tricky?" Indranie asks.

"Because she's always sneaking away when she doesn't think anyone notices."

My face burns, first with surprise, then with shame. I don't do that anymore.

"Mentiras," I say. *Lies.* I put on what I hope is a convincing smile.

Gabi jumps up. "If I were an inventor, I would take the robot vacuum thing from the commercial and fix it so that it could follow people around."

"That sounds like a great idea," Indranie says, still smiling.

"Don't let her have any more crazy ideas," I say.

Gabi demonstrates how the robot vacuum from the commercial could follow people around while clearing the streets of garbage at the same time. She's very funny, pretending the vacuum is chasing her. I remember how she used to make everyone in the family laugh with her imitations of our neighbors. Indranie laughs and claps at her performance. I feel my body relax in a way I have not felt in a long time. I know there is so much to do, so much we can lose. But for now, I'm not hungry and Gabi is happy, and there is a way to get Gabi to safety.

Indranie shows us to a bedroom with a huge bed that four people could sleep on. "Tomorrow, I'll buy some clothes for you girls, just to tide you over," she says. I nod sleepily and tell her good night.

When I climb into bed next to Gabi, thinking she is already asleep, she puts her hand on my arm. "I could have done it."

"¿Qué cosa?" I ask.

"The test. The thing they are doing to you. I would have done it."

I push her hair behind her ear, like I used to do when she was little. "I know. But I need to do it. It's better this way."

"Okay, but I will help," she says, yawning the last word.

"Por supuesto. ¿Qué piensas? I'm going to let you be una haragana?" She tries to shove me away, but I give her a good-night kiss anyway. I wonder if I'll ever be able to fall asleep with all the worry I have. Then I tell myself it doesn't matter how much I worry, only what I do.

"Do you know what a neurotransmitter is?" At first, I don't think Dr. Deng is talking to me. I sit on the padded table, dressed in the hospital gown again. There is a sticky bandage on my forehead, with wires coming out of it into a little box on my lap. The box looks like part of a toy, like for a remote control car or a video game. When he calls my name, I look up, embarrassed.

"I'm sorry. I didn't hear you. Can you repeat the question?" I ask.

Indranie stands behind Dr. Deng, her straight black hair loose and her face free of makeup. She looks younger and more tired than she did yesterday. "I barely know what a neurotransmitter is, Dr. Deng," she says, swallowing a yawn. "I'd be very surprised if Marisol does."

"All right," he says, rolling back a little in his chair. "I don't want to make assumptions." He turns slightly to look at a screen.

Indranie winks at me and whispers, "We wouldn't want

that, would we?" I return her smile as if I understand. I am used to doing that when speaking in English.

"Neurotransmitters are like messengers in the brain. They transmit across synapses from one neuron or nerve cell to another," Dr. Deng begins.

"What is the message they are sending?" I ask.

"Well, it could be lots of things. It could be pain, or it could be pleasure. It could be for a muscle to move, that kind of thing." He waves his hand dismissively, as if pain and movement are unimportant.

"When someone is experiencing anxiety, or grief or fear, or any combination of emotions triggered by a traumatic event, neurotransmitters are released. Specifically, at least for our clinical trial, these are corticotropin-releasing hormone, or CRH, norepinephrine, and cholecystokinin, or CCK, which in this case act as anxiogenic or panicogenic substances."

He turns away from me for a moment, so I sneak a glance at Indranie for a hint of what his words mean, but she is frowning at her phone.

"Conversely, also of import to our trials are the anxiolytic agents the body produces. Serotonin, I'm sure you've heard of," he says, adjusting one of the monitors he peers into. Beside me, Indranie muffles a sigh. I wonder if she's heard this before and finds it boring, or maybe, like me, she doesn't understand it.

Dr. Deng turns in his chair and rolls over to me. Under his white lab coat, he wears another heavy sweater, a mix of blues and greens and grays. When he peers into my face, I see little red hairs mixed in his white beard. He is bald, but I bet when he had hair he had a lot of light, maybe even red, hair. "But there are lesser-known neurotransmitters such as gamma-aminobutyric acid, also known as GABA. Unlike those other neurotransmitters that trigger adverse reactions in the sympathetic nervous system, serotonin and GABA have a calming effect."

"Okay, Dr. Deng. You lost me about three alphabet soups ago," Indranie says. "And while Marisol is definitely smarter than me, I'm not sure she is following as much as you'd like. So, can you break it down for us?"

Instead of answering, Dr. Deng lightly taps the bandage on my forehead. "How does that feel, Marisol?"

"I don't feel anything."

"Okay, good! And your incision?"

At my blank look, Indranie steps in. "On your neck, Marisol, the surgery. How does it feel?"

I run my finger along the line, a few centimeters long, of raised skin. Indranie removed the bandage this morning, saying in a few weeks' time, I'd barely have a scar.

"It doesn't hurt too much."

Dr. Deng smiles broadly. "Excellent! She's a very good candidate," he says, looking at Indranie.

"I sure can pick 'em," Indranie says with an expression that is almost a frown.

"To continue. There are three components to our experiment. The implant, which acts as a sort of receiver of those neurotransmitters, ah, those messengers that come from the donor."

I try to focus on Dr. Deng, but I am hungry. Indranie promised after this last test that we could have lunch. Gabi and I barely ate this morning. I was too nervous, and Gabi was angry that she'd be on her own again today, even though Indranie got the Harry Potter book out of her car. Gabi wants to go out and see Washington, DC, but Indranie says she'll be too busy to take her.

"What does *donor* mean?" I ask.

"Well, *donor* usually refers to someone who is giving something. Like a person who donates an organ or blood," Indranie answers.

"But this donor is giving me something they don't want, right?"

"Yes. Or, rather, something they are not able to withstand," Dr. Deng says.

Withstand. It's such a strange word. *With* = con and *stand* = pararse. But it doesn't mean *standing with*. Or does it? When something is very heavy, very painful, maybe *withstanding* means that you stand up, even *with* that pain? I don't know. Thinking about the word makes me feel both better and worse.

"The second component, the sister component, is the transmitter. It implants, also subdermally, into the donor patient. That device is responsible for relaying the anxiogenic material to the receiver," Dr. Deng continues.

"*Anxiogenic* means something that causes anxiety," Indranie says in a too-loud whisper. I think she is teasing Dr. Deng, but he does not seem to notice.

"And the third component is the CTS device itself."

Dr. Deng pulls a white box out from under the padded table. He opens the cover as if he is opening a present, or a box of chocolates. But there is only a circular white object, like a very simple pulsera.

"We call it 'the cuff,'" Indranie says in a teasing tone that I can tell from Dr. Deng's face he doesn't like.

"What is a cuff?" I ask. I thought a cuff was part of a shirt, but I don't think that can be right.

"It's not a cuff—that makes it sound ordinary," Dr. Deng sniffs, "when it's really an extraordinary piece of medical equipment." He takes the pulsera out of the box, and it opens on a hinge. It is glossy and white, thin and cold-looking. "The implants only transmit and receive information about the neural activity of one person to another—not much use on its own. But the CTS allows for that neural activity to be experienced by the receiver and alleviated from the donor. Not only that, but the anxiety-inhibiting neurotransmitters, like serotonin and GABA, as well as dopamine and adrenaline, although they don't work in the same way, of course—"

"Of course," Indranie whispers under her breath.

"—allow the donor to absorb the anxiety-inhibiting neurotransmitters from the recipient." Dr. Deng takes my foot in his hand. I almost laugh—it reminds me so much of going to Zona Rosa as a child to try on shoes. He opens the pulsera like a clamp and settles it around my ankle, closing it with a click. There is soft padding inside the cuff so I don't feel the cold sharpness of the metal.

"It's a polymer alloy clad in superlight metal sheeting. It should be comfortable. How does it feel?" he asks.

"It's okay. Fine," I say.

"Not too heavy?"

I swing my leg a little. I'm surprised at how light it is.

"It's good."

"Wonderful!" Dr. Deng exclaims, looking at both of us with expectation. I feel as if I should clap. Praise him like I would praise Gabi when she won a medal in her swimming competition. I expect Indranie to laugh or say something funny, but her face is serious.

"It's truly remarkable, Dr. Deng. The CTS device will ease a lot of suffering."

"Exactly!" Dr. Deng shouts as he rolls his chair back to his computer.

"Do I need to understand how it works for it to work?" I whisper to Indranie.

She slowly shakes her head. "I don't understand how the sun works, but it's there for me every day."

I lie down in what Dr. Deng calls a scanner, which is a narrow bed that slides into an open tunnel. I have to be absolutely still while in the scanner. The top of the tunnel is only a few centimeters away from my nose, and I feel like my chest is being pressed down, even though nothing is touching me. The scanner makes sounds like knocks on a door, and at first it makes me jump. Dr. Deng reminds me to be still. I concentrate on my feet, which are outside of the scanner. If my feet can be free, then I can be free too—that's what I tell myself.

I come out of the scanner and sit up on the table.

"Almost done. One more scan with contrast and that's it. Drink this." He hands me a thick, white liquid that tastes a little like paper. I lie down again in the scanner, but almost immediately, I know something is wrong. I turn my head, which feels heavy with stones.

"Dr. Deng?" Something about my voice must alarm Dr.

Deng because he gets up from his wheeled chair, moving quickly to me.

"What are you feeling?"

"Like I'm going to be sick."

"Okay, it's okay. It happens sometimes." He injects something into the suero on my arm. I feel cold for a second, then the nausea subsides.

"Better?"

I nod.

"Why don't I take Marisol to get a drink of water, Dr. Deng? I think we're done with the scanner for now, right?"

Dr. Deng nods absently. "She might have an intolerance to the contrast. But we may not need that additional scan."

"Whatever you say. You're the boss." Indranie helps me get off the table and gives me the pole to hold on to. It's a pole on wheels that holds a clear bag of whatever medicine is going into my arm. *Everything here is on wheels,* I think dizzily. I don't feel in danger of throwing up anymore, but I do feel strange.

She gives me a paper cup of water. It tastes like metal. I frown.

"Everything tastes funny at first. Keep drinking; it will get better." I finish the water and feel more like myself.

"We're going to run some tests, Marisol. But no more scans and X-rays today. Part of the test is to see how the device feels while you're wearing it. After a while, you should stop noticing it," Dr. Deng says. I put my legs together, and the pulsera barely touches my other leg. I can feel it, but it doesn't hurt or pull at my leg.

"At the same time, we'll be testing the receiver in your cuff."

"Is this what makes the feelings go into someone else?" I ask Dr. Deng.

Dr. Deng is not paying attention to me. He is watching a monitor above my head.

"Is the bracelet—"

"Call it the CTS," he interrupts. "Or the cuff, if you have to."

"Is the cuff the machine that makes, um." I try to put my words in order, to use the same words they used. "That transfers the trauma?"

"Your cuff is the receiver. The partner cuff is the transmitter, but they look the same."

There is so much I don't understand. I know Indranie has told me I don't need to understand, but I feel as if I should at least try. "Why does it go on my leg? Why isn't it on my neck or near my head? I don't have emotions on my leg," I say.

"You are full of questions, aren't you?" Indranie asks, her eyebrows raised.

"I'm sorry," I say, because I think I'm supposed to be sorry. "But I thought about it last night, how one person's grief could be passed to another person, and it seemed to make sense if the two people were wearing helmets or something."

Indranie puts her hand on my shoulder. "That would make sense, I guess. But this is how the technology is designed. And I don't know a lot of people who would want to walk around with helmets on all day."

She smiles, and it feels like a slap. I feel like I've said the wrong thing, made a fool of myself, and it makes me angry.

"Have you got any other questions for Dr. Deng? Let's see if we can stump him."

I only shrug.

"Well, I have a question for Dr. Deng. Can we go to lunch? I'm starving! And I bet Marisol is too. She's got a hangry look to her, am I right?"

"I don't know what you mean," Dr. Deng says coldly. I don't know what she means either, but I pretend to, so that I can be on Indranie's side.

"I mean, are we free to go?"

"Yes," Dr. Deng says, giving the cuff on my leg a quick look before going back to the monitor. I wonder what secrets the cuff on my leg is already telling him. Then I remind myself that I have the receiver. Someone else will have the transmitter. Someone else will give their secrets.

"Come on," she says. "You can change into your clothes, then we can find some lunch."

"What about Gabi?" We carry our trays from the cafeteria out to a little patio area. Indranie nudges me toward a long table where a young man, un soldado, in a dark green army uniform sits alone. I think he's going to say something when Indranie sits so near to him. But his eyes are closed, his head dipping down like he's falling asleep. I don't know why Indranie wants to sit here, unless she knows the man. Maybe she only feels bad that he's alone.

"Your sister has somehow convinced my assistant, Traci, to take her out for a drive in her Audi TT RS."

I sit down. "Is it safe?"

"Oh, she's safe, all right. Traci values her Audi more than her own life. They will be fine." And Gabi will be thrilled, driving in a fancy car through the streets of the capital. It seems incredible that we are here when only days ago, we were traveling in the back of a truck, facedown against rust and dirt, covered with old blankets.

"What is the date?"

"April eighteenth," Indranie says.

That's much later than I thought. I try to do the calculations in my head, but we took so many buses, walked so many kilometers, and stayed at so many safe houses, I couldn't keep track.

"And we've been here, with Dr. Deng, three days?"

"That's right. Why do you ask?"

"I don't know. It feels like so much time has gone by and not any time at all." Pink petals from the trees are raining down onto the stone patio. It's pleasant here, and I'm eating my favorite American food—grilled cheese with tomato and bacon. But suddenly, like I am someone's puppet, I feel my stomach shrink and pull. I can't eat. I'm cold all over, as if I can no longer feel the sun on my skin. Something is building inside me, a rolling ache. For a moment, I don't know what will come out, a scream or a laugh. Then I burst into tears.

Indranie watches as tears roll down my face. I must disgust her. Here she is, doing all these things for me and Gabi, and all I do is complain and cry. She must hate me. I wonder if Dr. Deng hates me too, then realize that he must. He only talks to me because I'm useful for his experiment. I scrub at my face with a napkin and blow my nose to stop the crying, but there's a well inside me that is overflowing. I try to stop, but I don't seem to be able to. An office worker takes her lunch to the trash and leaves. I am making her leave. I'm spoiling her time, making things worse for everyone.

"Take a deep breath, Marisol." Indranie watches me, but

not with disgust, at least I don't think so. She's got a little note-book out on the table, next to her untouched salad. "How do you feel?"

"Sad," I wail. "So sad and I don't know why." The tears come harder, the well endless.

"What else do you feel? It's important you tell me."

I suck air into my lungs to speak, but that only makes more tears. "I feel like something bad has ha-happened, something t-terrible, and I'm too late to stop it."

I stand up, making the table shake.

Gabi. I run for the door, even though my brain is telling me that she is fine, that she's not even in the building. It makes no difference. Nothing touches my panic. I blink and for a second I see bursts of red and yellow and hear a boom so loud that I lose my balance. Every blink of my eye brings more colors that hurt my head.

There must have been an explosion. I feel dust in my eyes, on my face, in my throat. It mixes with the sweat running down my body. I am on the hot ground, staring up at an orange sun.

Then I'm not. I'm slumped against the door to the outdoor seating. There is no dust, no orange sun. I pull at the door han-dle. I have to get to Gabi before everything collapses.

Indranie grabs my arm, but I push her away. Why is everyone moving so slowly? Don't they feel the catástrofe? The building is going to fall down around us.

She takes my head in her hands until I have no choice but to look into her eyes, listen to her urgent whisper.

"It's not real, Marisol. It's just part of the test."

Chapter 7

What?

"The feelings you're experiencing are not yours. They belong to another test subject. Someone who is wearing a transmitter cuff."

My thoughts are confused, running in many directions. "You said I was the first to do the experiment."

"You are the first to be the *receiver* in the experiment. Someone else has to be the donor, remember? You are still very important," she says, handing me another napkin.

"What happened to him? The other test subject? Why does he feel like this?"

The explosions of color and sound that made me panic a moment before are gone, like waking up from una pesadilla. My heart still beats like a frightened rabbit.

The tears finally stop and I wipe my face. I look up, expecting to see concerned faces or people staring. Either no one notices my crying, or they pretend not to notice.

"He doesn't feel like this, not anymore," Indranie says. "You aren't sharing his feelings—you're taking them away, at least for a little while."

When Dr. Deng explained the cuff, I understood what I was supposed to do, and it felt like a very small thing to do. Take someone else's grief. But I'm trembling with the feelings that still run through me. I can remember the heat, the echo of an explosion, but even that feels like a memory of a nightmare. I might throw up.

"What about the colors?" I ask, remembering the blinding reds and yellows that crowded my mind.

Indranie becomes still, and her back straightens. I have said something wrong.

"Did you *see* something? During the transfer, did you have visual input?" I don't know what she means, but I know, from the way she asks, that it's a bad thing. I make my English sound a little broken, as if I chose the wrong word.

"No, I am confused. I mean to say another thing."

"You're sure you didn't see or hear anything during the transfer?" Indranie's dark, serious eyes burn into mine.

"No, I'm sorry. When I am confused, my English is also confused." I smile to cover how much I hate admitting that. "Why is it that it came all of a sudden?"

"The transfer happens whenever test subject A—that's the donor—has a triggered grief event." We walk back to where we were sitting. The man who was at our table, the soldier, is gone.

"What's that mean?" Asking questions makes me feel less helpless, like a kite caught in a windstorm. And it leads Indranie away from her doubts.

She opens her notebook.

"When a traumatic thing happens to a person, it doesn't just happen the one time, or at least, that's not how the mind perceives it. There is the initial impact on the brain and nervous system . . ." She draws a circle on a blank page in her notebook. "Then, every time the person is reminded of the trauma, there are shock waves." She makes lines around the circle, like dropping a stone into a lake. The lines of the circle break apart and move out farther and farther until they disappear. Ondulaciones. I know there's an English word for that, but I can't remember it.

"Sometimes, those ripples," she points to the lines around the circle, "those can trigger another wave of grief or sadness."

Ripples. That's the word.

Indranie looks up from her drawing. "How do you feel now?"

My face is damp from my tears, and my eyes feel hot from crying. My chest feels scooped out, like the skin of an avocado. I search for the panic, for any trace of those bad feelings, for the sounds and colors. I don't find any. In fact, I feel a little like smiling.

"I feel good. That can't be right, can it?" I even feel hungry. I pick up half my sandwich. It's so good, even cold.

Indranie smiles, relieved. "It is right. And it's a relief that you experience those good feelings. Dr. Deng hypothesized— do you know what that means? It means he made a guess on what would happen when test subject B absorbed the grief event. He guessed that once the event passed, your own body would boost the 'good' chemicals, like endorphins and dopamine, to compensate, which is what is making you feel better now." She pauses, frowning at the table. "That won't always happen. The CTS device is designed to funnel those 'good chemicals' you are making back to the donor, completing the loop." She draws a circle of arrows. "Negative feelings travel to the receiver, triggering positive feelings to compensate; positive feelings travel to the donor, improving mood and alleviating suffering." She shows me the drawing. I have lost track of which part of the circle I am, but I don't mind.

I don't just feel better—I feel wonderful. Happy and positive. I'm sure this is going to be the fastest month ever. But I think of something that makes me stop.

"If negative things make ripples in the donor, will they make ripples in me? Will I keep having my own bad memories?" I have shut the door on many of my memories. I don't want the door open again.

"No. That's the best part of the technology. Grief is often triggered by memories. If you miss a beloved grandmother who has just died, thinking of her will trigger the feelings of grief and loss. The more you think of her, the more your memories of her come up, and the more the grief echoes and ripples, making you suffer more. But you, Marisol, don't have those memories of test subject A. You don't remember his mother or his war or whatever happened to him. So, you feel the emotions, but they don't lead anywhere. Does that make sense?"

"A little," I say. I decide I won't mention the sounds and colors, the dust and orange sun. It is the first test, and it may be nothing. If I mention it, and they are worried about it, they might take away this proposition. And what does it matter if I see or hear things along with the feelings? They are not my sights and sounds. I can ignore them.

I'm very hungry now, and I ask Indranie if I can eat her fruit cup. She pushes the fruit to me. "What happened to test subject A? Did someone die?"

Indranie crosses her arms, considering. "No. In this case, it was something else. I'm not able to say. When you start your monthlong test, you won't know what the cause of grief is there either."

The first taste of fruit, an orange in jarabe, is so bright and sour that the flavor pops against my tongue. It is delicious. "Do you know who my test person will be? Have you met him?"

Indranie looks away. "We have a few possible candidates we're speaking to. Not everyone is keen on the idea."

"Who wouldn't want their grief taken away?"

"It's not that, I don't think. Though I imagine some people believe that grief is necessary. And maybe it is for some. But we're talking about people who are not able to process their grief, their trauma, in a productive way. This isn't the normal, everyday kind of grief. This is the kind of grief that could destroy someone."

I can tell from her face that she isn't thinking of me or even of test subject A. Her eyes are focused on the pink-and-white tree blossoms, but I don't think she sees them.

"Will it destroy me?" I ask.

She snaps back to attention, sitting up straighter. She takes the plastic wrap off her salad. "No, Marisol. I will make sure it doesn't."

I feel a wave of something. Ansiedad, worry, something. I wonder for a moment if these feelings are mine, or if they belong to another person with a leg cuff. I wonder how I'll ever be able to tell.

"Are you having second thoughts?" Indranie asks. But she can't be serious. What is a little grief in exchange for safety?

"Absolutely not."

It's the middle of the night when Indranie comes to our room, turning on the light to wake us.

"Come on, girls," she says, shaking Gabi awake.

"What's happening?" I ask, sitting up.

"Come on, get dressed. You can sleep on the way if you want." She leaves the room, a sense of urgency in her movements.

We get up quickly, my body remembering how to move at a moment's notice. Clothes have been left out for us, but everything else has been packed. Within a few minutes, we're in Indranie's car, and her assistant, Traci, is driving. Gabi is disappointed we are not driving in Traci's fancy car.

I watch as Indranie looks at her phone intently, moving her thumb along the screen.

"Where are we going?" I ask. Indranie and Traci are so serious. Something must have gone wrong with the experiment. Maybe they don't need us anymore. Or maybe I've done something wrong.

"Please, just tell me if you are sending us back." The words choke out of me.

Indranie turns to me, her face surprised. "No, no, of course not. I'm sorry. We're trying to move fast—I didn't even think about explaining things to you." She pushes her black hair out of her face. It doesn't look like Indranie has slept at all. "We have a candidate for the test program. A donor. Someone your own age who has suffered a serious traumatic event. We have been asked to move fast because the donor is in distress."

"I don't know what that means," I say. I know the word *distress* means trouble, or more than that. Angustia maybe? Anguish? But still I think the word means more.

"It means that the donor is in danger of hurting herself."

Two years ago, on *Cedar Hollow*, Amber's best friend, Aimee, was *in distress*. She took medicine meant for her mother. She almost died, but Amber found her in time.

"Suicide."

"Suicidal, yes." She tells Traci to make the next left before facing me again. "This is going to be hard, Marisol. I'm not going to lie to you. We have you, a strong, capable person. But it's going to be hard."

"What if I fail?"

"You won't fail. You'll do just fine, I promise. Remember what we talked about? You will have the feelings but not the memories attached to those feelings. There are times in our lives when we feel things, when we're sad or feel sick, and we don't know why we feel them. This will be like that, except you'll know that they aren't your feelings at all. And that you're helping someone else."

"So she doesn't hurt herself?"

"That's it. You could be helping to save a life."

Chapter 8

There's a river here too. Or maybe it's the same river that runs near the Capitol. I can't tell how far we've gone, though we have been driving for more than an hour. Here, the river is surrounded by trees, not buildings. Black iron gates lead to a courtyard. We stop in front of an enormous house.

A suddenly alert Gabi climbs out of the car. I wonder how she can sleep at the strangest times, in the most uncomfortable places, only to be wide awake a moment later. Though my head is heavy with sleep, my chest buzzes with anxiety. I don't know how to feel.

The house is inmensa. Not even the houses in *Cedar Hollow* were as grand as this. White columns stand on either side of a wide door painted black, and a light hanging down, an old-fashioned linterna, casts a soft glow on us as we approach the door. A voice calls, "Ms. Patel?"

Indranie turns toward a separate building to the right of the main house. I thought it was a different house before, but now I see it's connected.

An old man waves us to this smaller house.

"In the carriage house?" Indranie asks.

"I think it is better, yes," the man says. "We can take care of them better here." Next to him is a tiny, thin woman in a bathrobe.

"This is Manolo Borges and his wife, Olga. They are caretakers here," Indranie explains.

"Señoritas," Manolo says with a nod of his head. As we pass through the door of what Manolo has called the carriage house, I hear Olga Borges say "pobrecitas" under her breath.

The carriage house is only small when compared with the other house. In reality, this house has two levels, large rooms, and a kitchen that still, at this late hour, smells like baking bread. I follow Indranie, who follows Manolo, up the stairs. Gabi is behind me, dragging her feet. I keep checking on her because I'm so tired. Anything can happen when you are tired.

Manolo opens a door to a bedroom with two beds. Gabi picks a bed, climbs in, and turns her back to us, as if sleep is the only thing she has energy for.

"That girl likes her sleep," Traci whispers as she places our small bags on the floor next to the bed.

"She was always una dormilona," I say. "A sleepyhead."

We follow Manolo out of the room. Once the door is closed, Indranie stops me. She hands me a cell phone in a bright red case. It has a horse on it and the word *Ferrari* written in yellow.

"I bet you can guess who helped me pick out the phone case," she says. "It could have been worse. It could have been a unicorn."

I smile.

"My phone number is right there." She shows me how to find her number. It's not hard. It's the only one. I don't know anyone else.

She seems to realize this and quickly types in two more numbers.

"Dr. Deng is here." She points to his number. "If anything happens with how you feel, if anything feels overwhelming or wrong, call Dr. Deng, and he will get you the help you need. You can always call me, but if I can't answer, call Dr. Deng."

I nod.

"And then you can call Traci in any emergency too. She'll know where I am, okay?"

I nod again.

"I'll come by tomorrow to see how you're doing."

"What?" She can't be leaving.

"I'm sure you're tired, Marisol. I'll leave you to rest."

"But you said it was an emergency. That someone's life is in danger. In distress. That's why we rushed here in the middle of the night." I thought I'd be starting right away. I made myself ready—as ready as I could ever be.

Indranie stops, her hand on the banister. She looks embarrassed. I wonder what she has to be avergonzada about.

"It's not that the danger isn't urgent; it is. But it seems like the donor is, um, stable for now. So not to worry, okay?" She smiles weakly.

"Okay," I say, because I'm afraid she'll think I'm being rude if I keep questioning her. I say good night and disappear into our room. I stand, listening to my breath rise and fall unsteadily. I hear Indranie's footsteps down the stairs and then the front door closing. And finally, Gabi's soft little snores.

I'm not alone. I have Gabi. I will be all right. I climb into bed with Gabi, even though there is a bed for each of us, and fall asleep feeling her breath in my ear.

I wake up with a feeling, tight in my chest, that something is wrong. It's like a bad dream that my body remembers, even though I can't.

Gabi stretches her arms above her head.

"Soñe que nos mudamos."

"We did move," I tell her in English. "It wasn't a dream."

"Oh," she says. "Where are we?"

"In a carriage house."

She blinks her owl eyes at me. "A house for carriages? You mean a garage? Wait. ¿Carruajes? Like in the old fairy stories?"

"Yes, *carriage* means carruaje, but I don't think it means that now. It's like a big house, but it's next to a much bigger house." I sit up and tie my hair back with the hair band I left on my wrist last night.

"Where are we?"

"Virginia," I say, which is what Indranie told me last night.

"Is that in Washington?"

I frown. "I don't think so. But it's nearby. They're starting the experiment. The real one. No more tests."

Gabi stretches out on her stomach, her head propped on her hands. "You're not scared?"

"No. Why should I be?"

"I don't understand how you do it. Nothing scares you. Not Antonio, not the coyotes, not this thing on your leg." I don't look at her. I don't want her to see how much everything scares me to death. "I would be a crying mess. Mantequita, remember?" she says with a shrug.

Mantequita is what Pablo called us when we would cry or show we were afraid. *Butter*, because we were soft. "No, you wouldn't. You're just as brave as I am. Braver."

She shakes her head. "I don't think so. You know what Mamá said before we left?"

I shake my head.

"She said you'd take care of me. I told her I would take care of you too, but she said no, leave that to you. She doesn't think I can do anything."

"You are her pequeñita. She thinks it's your job to be taken care of and to cause trouble." I smile. "You are good at that last part."

"So, my job is to be a pain?"

"Yes. That's your job. You are excellent."

She tosses a pillow in my face just as I grab her foot and pull. She shrieks like a cat whose tail has just been stepped on, and we laugh as we wrestle.

A knock on the door stops us. "¿Todo bien?"

"¡Sí!" we say in unison, then break into giggles.

"Good. We are having breakfast downstairs," a woman says. "Come down, okay, nenas?"

"Yes," I say.

"Sí," Gabi says, and I shove her off the bed.

Downstairs, there's a large table in the kitchen, which is so white and clean that it makes my tired eyes squint. Instead of the colorful cereal Indranie gave us in the penthouse, Olga Borges serves us enough cooked breakfast for a family of twelve.

There are scrambled eggs, rice and beans—Cristianos y Moros, Olga calls them—fried plantains, slices of white cheese, and lots of fruit. Manolo serves us coffee, half a cup, mixed with hot milk and sugar. Everything tastes amazing and a little like home. When we are full, Manolo leaves for work.

"Where does Señor Borges work?" Gabi asks Olga.

"Es jardinero. Trabaja aquí en la casa."

"Can you speak English to Gabi, Mrs. Borges? Please?" I know I sound rude. And Olga's face confirms that she thinks so too. She answers slowly.

"Of course I can. I speak English very well. I have been here for twenty years. Does Gabriela not understand Spanish?"

"Yes, we both do. But Gabi needs to practice. We want to sound American."

Olga's mouth turns down with distaste. "You sound American already. Maybe too much."

"Please?" I ask again.

"Yes, okay," she says with a shrug. She's a skinny woman with a face so wrinkled and brown that it's hard to tell her age. With her white hair in a neat bun, she's the kind of woman I would have seen every day on our street, wearing a faded dress and straw chanclas on her feet. But here she is wearing a large pink T-shirt that says FRIDAYS MAKE ME HAPPY and black leggings.

"Well, Manny is a gardener. He works here on the house grounds," Olga says.

"And you?" Gabi asks.

"I help in the big house. I clean, but not the windows or high things. I'm too old for that. A maid does that. I also cook for Rey because she is very picky now. She only wants *my* cooking." Olga grabs a kitchen towel and wipes down the already spotless counters.

"Who is Rey?" I ask.

"Rey is Mr. Warner's daughter." Olga takes in the confused looks on our faces. "This is Mr. Warner's house. He's a very important person. He has a big pharmaceutical company. Usually, he is in Washington. But he lives here with his family." Olga lowers her eyes. "Well, only Rey now. Pobre Riley, que Dios le bendiga," she says, crossing herself.

I don't know what to say. Is Mr. Warner the doncr who will give me his grief? Indranie said it was someone my age, so maybe it's his daughter, Rey. Gabi takes a plantain off my plate, and I push the rest of my breakfast toward her.

"What should we do?" I ask, wanting to change the subject. I want to know what our tasks are so I can plan the rest of the day for Gabi. I also want to make sure Indranie didn't forget that she said Gabi could go to school. I don't want her to be working in this big house and miss out on classes. I can do most of our work on my own, and if I can't, maybe she can do some in the morning before school starts.

"You girls? You should finish eating. Then you can go to the pool. It's heated," Olga says with obvious pride.

"To clean it?" Gabi asks, her nose wrinkling. I nudge her. I know she's not afraid of work and is probably just afraid that she doesn't know how to clean a pool. But we will figure it out.

"No, por supuesto que no," Olga says with scorn. "You go to the pool to swim, not clean it. We have a man who comes to clean it."

Gabi's face blossoms with delight. She loves to swim and hasn't been able to do it for many years.

"We don't have bathing suits," I say.

"Hmm. Maybe I can find something in Rey's old clothes. You can go to the pool later."

I've never gone swimming in a pool. Pablo and I would take Gabi to el Club Atlético for swim lessons that Mrs. Rosen paid for—she said it was important for a child to know how to swim. It was too expensive for Pablo and me to swim there, and we had already learned how to swim in the lake by Abuela's house.

We'd drop Gabi off to her lesson, then Pablo would hang out with his friends, ignoring me. They would spend all day at el Club, chatting with Liliana, who worked behind the bar stocking the glass bottles of beer and cutting lemons and limes for drinks. Pablo would talk to her, and I would watch her. She was beautiful in a way that made me feel uncomfortable, like I had mariposas en la barriga. She had dyed her light brown hair blond, like the girls in *Cedar Hollow*, and wore the same kind of makeup—a lot of it to make it look like no makeup at all. I remembered wondering if her skin smelled of limes, but I never had the nerve to ask Pablo.

"What about school? For Gabi?" I ask Olga.

She shrugs with her whole body. "That, I do not know."

When Gabi finishes breakfast, we go upstairs to change. I stand in front of the closet where Indranie has put the clothes she bought for us. The clothes are pretty—the kind American girls wear—and smell new. The jeans Indranie bought me are called "boot cut," which makes it sound like they were cut in the shape of a boot, but they aren't. The wide leg of the jeans hides Dr. Deng's cuff perfectly.

"What if you don't have boots? Do you have to wear jeans that aren't boot cut?" Gabi asks.

She's already changed into a soft blue T-shirt and jeans. Her piyamas are neatly folded on the bed.

"It's just the moda, the name of the style. It doesn't mean you have to wear boots with them. That's silly."

"Yes, but if you did have boots, you shouldn't need different jeans to wear them. That's the real silly."

"Silliness," I correct her. I scratch at the skin under the cuff, wishing I could take it off. I'm only allowed to take it off to shower and to put powder on my ankle so my skin doesn't get irritated. Other than that, it sits on my leg doing nothing. It doesn't even hum or make any noise. I have trouble believing it's doing anything.

"I wish I had boots," Gabi says, looking down at her blue-and-purple sneakers. "Black ones, like for riding una moto."

"Sure, Gabi. One of these days."

Once we're back downstairs, we ask if we can go outside and look around. I expect Olga to say "No" or "Wait to talk to someone in charge."

"Of course. Go wherever you want," she says. "But don't leave the grounds."

"How big can grounds be?" Gabi whispers as we walk out the door.

"I don't know. Let's find out." I take her hand, but I'm not pulling her forward or back like I did on the carretera, so it feels strange. After a few minutes, she takes her hand away to point at a bluebird sitting on a wooden gate that leads to a garden.

What I thought was the garden is only one part of a larger garden, with pebbles for paths and strong-smelling plants. Romero, salvia, menta, all herbs good for one thing or another.

If they had manzanilla, we could make a tea for stomachaches. At the end of this garden, there is another gate in the brick wall that leads to a much bigger area. Not even the Parque National is this beautiful, this green. The grass leads like a carpet to a long rectangle the color of the sky.

When we get closer to it, I realize it isn't sky-colored but reflects the sky. It's a pool of water, but it's not deep, so not a pool for bathing.

"This isn't the pool, is it?" Gabi asks dubiously.

"No. It can't be. It's too small."

"So, what is it for?"

"Maybe it's for birds?" I say, though it seems too grand even for American birds.

We have our jackets on, beautiful ones that Indranie bought us—mine is black and Gabi's is blue, and they keep us warm without being too heavy. I watch Gabi float a leaf on the water's surface, adding tiny rocks and sticks to see how many she can add before it sinks.

Then she wants to play al escondite.

"Gabi, aren't we too old for hide-and-seek?"

"Maybe *you* are too old, but not me." She squirms, shaking her arms and legs. "Dale, Sol, I'm bored." Even though I am enjoying the sun on my face, I agree.

"But don't go too far," I say, because the fear is never very far away.

I sneak up on Gabi in her hiding place, making her jump and laugh. When it's my turn to hide, I push myself behind a tall bush next to a high balcony of the main house. I hear Gabi calling for me, telling me I have to come out and save her from being attacked by a gang of black cats in top hats. She's trying to get me to laugh so she can find me. It's worked before, but I'm too well hidden now. I'll let her look for me a little longer.

Above me, I hear a sharp bang. I take half a step out from behind the bush and see the door that leads to the balcony slam shut. I hear breaking glass and step away from the bush to see better. A girl in a white nightgown stands frozen, barefoot, like in a novela. Her long blond hair tangles into hanging knots, and she wears a heavy leather jacket over her nightgown, like she's forgotten to get dressed or maybe had no time. Her face is a nightmare, a mix of despair and fear. She's standing on broken glass, leaning against the door to keep it closed.

"¿Qué pasó?" Gabi whispers. My already racing heart gives an extra-loud thump. She was so quiet that I didn't hear her coming.

"No sé. Be quiet. I don't want anyone to see us."

The door the girl leans against rattles, but she's putting all her weight on it, not allowing it to open.

There's yelling from inside the house, but I can't hear what's being said. From the far side of the garden where we walked in, there's more shouting. I don't want us to be found here, watching someone else's trouble. That is how trouble spreads. But I can't look away.

With a lurch, the girl pushes against the door one last time and runs for the balcony railing. Her foot is on the ledge, her hands gripping the iron. She only needs one good push to throw herself over—and right in front of us.

I grab Gabi and hold her head against my shoulder. I don't want her to see. The girl's nightgown catches, and she's pulled back a little. No, it's not caught, it's Indranie, grabbing at the white cotton gown and using it to pull the girl away. The girl's face is pure agony.

"Let me go!"

Memories of the carretera rush into my mind. Gabi's hand slipping from my sweaty one as we hung on to the side of a truck full of too many people. Watching a boy we had traveled with for two days fall off the truck like a dead leaf.

On the balcony, the girl struggles to free herself of arms, hands, to free herself into the sky.

"Rey, don't. Come on, honey, talk to me," Indranie says, pulling on the girl's jacket. Gabi pushes away from me. I think the girl is going to wriggle out of the jacket, tear the night-gown away somehow. She looks like a trapped bird. Traci steps onto the balcony and plucks the girl off her feet as if she weighs nothing. The girl's arms and legs swing and kick. We watch one bare foot kick Indranie in the face. And then the girl's eyes find mine, and it's as if *I* have jumped off the balcony. Her look makes me part of what is happening. Her face, her eyes—I can't bear to see them. I close my eyes.

"Sol," Gabi says after a moment or one hundred moments.

"¿Qué?"

"It's over."

I look back up at the balcony, at the broken door and the fluttering white curtains. I want to push the image from my mind, but it's stuck there, like a piece of cloth on a nail. I see the girl's face, her eyes so lost, and it's like she has a message for me, something I need to know.

No, it's not over.

Chapter 9

I urge Gabi back down the pebble path to the carriage house. In the hallway, there is a sign in English and in Spanish telling us to take off our shoes. Music blares in another room, and I can hear Olga singing "Lágrimas Negras," a song I have always hated.

"Come on," I say to Gabi, and lead her to the kitchen table. I get juice out of the fridge and pour us both a cup.

"What happened to that girl?" Gabi's voice trembles and she coughs to hide it.

"I don't know. I'm sure she's fine. You saw Traci. She got her safe."

"Did you see how she kicked Ni-ni?" She whistles, equal parts shocked and impressed.

Gabi started calling Indranie "Ni-ni" as a joke. Ni esto, ni lo otro—neither this nor that—because when Gabi would ask simple questions, Indranie would answer them in a complicated way. "It's not that it's hard or it's easy, it's just different" was a typical Indranie answer.

Indranie walks into the kitchen holding an ice pack to her face.

"Ni-ni! Are you okay?" Gabi asks.

"I'm fine," she says tiredly. "I'm tougher than I look."

She looks terrible. Her usually neat ponytail is half undone and her blouse is crooked, a button missing.

"Come on, girls, let's sit down and talk."

I give Indranie a little juice in a cup because I don't know how to make coffee with the machine they have here.

"I have to say, this is not the way I wanted this to go." Indranie takes a sip of juice and makes a face. Under the ice pack, her forehead is red and swollen.

"Was that girl the donor?" I ask, even though I'm pretty sure I know the answer.

"Yes. She had the transmitter implanted two days ago. She is not happy about it."

"And she tried to kill herself?"

Indranie doesn't answer.

"That's awful," Gabi says.

Indranie puts the ice pack down on the table. "You have to understand. People handle grief in very different ways. It isn't the same for everyone. Some people can manage with help, and others lock themselves into grief. Still others become stronger by it. And it isn't only grief. It's trauma. When Dr. Deng started this program, he wanted to help people. Victims of terrible assaults, soldiers who were damaged in body and in spirit. That's a kind of grief that is even more entrenched, when it is augmented by guilt and fear."

I don't understand all of Indranie's words, and I think that maybe she isn't really talking to us anymore.

"Why didn't I feel any of her grief?" I ask. That's been at the back of my mind. That I failed somehow in the experiment and that is why this girl nearly killed herself. If I'd been good enough, I could have made her feel less like dying.

"Rey won't wear the cuff. The transmitter won't work without the cuff. She's refusing point-blank to participate." Indranie sighs, tilting back in her chair.

"Why would she do that? Why would she rather die than feel better?" Gabi asks.

"It's complicated," Indranie says. She tosses the melting ice pack into the sink and turns on the coffee machine. I watch her put a little plastic cup into the machine, then place a mug into a slot. "It's not that Rey would rather die, not really—it's that she doesn't want to lose her grief."

I imagine unlocking the place where Pablo still lives in my heart and letting all that grief out. I can't. It would kill me. But if I could give it to someone else? Not feel it or only a little? I don't know what I would do.

"What happened to her?" Gabi asks. I feel a little foolish that it didn't occur to me to ask the same question.

Indranie hesitates. "She—it was an explosion. She was at a concert. Many people died. Rey survived. But her brother did not."

My face becomes numb as the blood leaves it, racing to my heart.

Gabi faces me. "She had a brother like us." Under the table, she squeezes my hand hard.

"Yes," I say.

"And he died too," she says.

"Yes," I repeat, wishing she would stop talking. Stop telling our secrets.

"I know," Indranie says. "I'm so sorry."

"Marisol and Pablo were best friends," Gabi says.

Indranie looks carefully at me, judging something. She's

already drunk the coffee in her mug and begins the process of making more. "Marisol, we thought maybe you could talk to Rey. You understand the pain she's going through. You can relate to her. If you could convince her to wear the cuff, she has a chance of getting better."

I want to laugh. She was wild, beautiful, and destructive. How could I relate to her in any way?

"What happens if I can't get her to agree?"

Indranie gulps her coffee like it's air. She scoops up our empty glasses of juice and takes them to the sink. She doesn't turn back to face us.

"Then the experiment is over."

Indranie won't say it because she doesn't want to scare Gabi. Or maybe because she feels pity for me, for both of us. But I can read it in her voice. If the experiment fails, there is no reason for us to stay. We will be sent home.

Chapter 10

The water is as warm as a bath. I hold myself under, surrounded by silence, as long as I can before coming up for air. The first sound I hear is Gabi's laughter.

"Sol! Watch me!"

I swim over to where she's practicing underwater hand-stands.

"Very good, pececito," I say when she comes up for air. She's always been good in the water. Pablo and I used to marvel at how things were easy for Gabi, her personality more sunshine than darkness.

Gabi laughs at me, and the sound echoes through the enclosed pool. When I try to shush her, she scowls.

"There's no one else to hear us, silly."

"I know. But still."

The pool is inside a building with glass walls and tile floors separate from the carriage house. "The pool house," Olga said when I asked where the pool was. There are so many houses here, houses for objects.

"You girls really should have suits of your own," Indranie says when we come back from our swim. Now that Gabi's suit is wet, it is nearly falling off her. "How about I take you shopping?"

"Aren't you busy? Working or doing things at home?" Gabi asks. I bump her with my hip. She shouldn't be asking personal questions.

"You two are my number one priority, my DIY project, and my homework assignment all rolled into one," she says.

We look at her, not understanding.

"I mean, there's nowhere I'd rather be. Come on, let's go hit the mall."

The mall looks exactly like the ones on *Cedar Hollow*, with lots of American stores lined up on both sides like boxes of jewels.

"Pretty great, right, Gabi?" I nudge her when she doesn't respond. She must be tired. She was excited to get a new blue-and-white bathing suit. Thrilled when Indranie took us to Starbucks. But now she is dragging her feet.

"It's not as big as Galerías." Gabi shrugs.

We stop at several more stores, following Indranie closely so we don't get lost. Gabi stops suddenly at a store with shoes and boots in the window.

"What?" Indranie asks, peering in the window too.

"Those boots," Gabi says dreamily. "Perfect for una moto."

I tsk, sounding like Mamá. "Which you don't have. You don't need boots." I pull her by the arm to the next store.

"What's a moto?" Indranie asks.

"Una motocicleta. A motorcycle," Gabi answers. "My favorite is a Ducati Panigale V4. It's the fastest, and Ducati are the best— they're Italian."

"I had no idea you were such a speed demon, Gabi!" Indranie says, pretending shock. "How do you know so much about motorcycles? Did your brother have one?"

The excited light in Gabi's eyes dims, then goes out.

"No, of course not. Who could afford such a thing?" I say. "We had a friend in Colonia Escalón who liked cars and motos. He showed Gabi all his favorites."

"That's pretty cool."

"I like to go fast," my sister says, not meeting Indranie's gaze. "I like when the wind is so strong that tears sting your eyes."

Next to the boot shop is a stationery store, and Indranie stops to look inside. Gabi walks back to the motorcycle boots, putting her face as close to the glass as she can without touching it. I begin to wonder. What if we walked away? How could they find us? I know where we are now is so much better than where we were, but the impulse, the push to run is still in me. I wonder if it's in Gabi too.

Indranie is looking at cards at the back of the stationery store.

"Let's go see what's over there," I tell Gabi. We cross the wide black-and-gold floor of the mall to a larger store. There are lots of racks of clothes and bedding and even perfume and makeup. I look behind me, where I can still see the stationery store. We could leave, just disappear. A hundred-dollar bill and nothing else. We could *go*. But where?

A lady sprays Gabi with a cloud of perfume, making me sneeze three times in a row.

"Bless you, sweetie," the perfume lady says at the same time that Gabi says, "Salud, dinero, y amor." *Health, money, and love.* All the blessings anyone could ask for.

How long have we been away from Indranie? Fifteen minutes? I have her cell phone number in the phone she gave me. If we are gone too long, I can call her. Or we could keep going.

"Trying on makeup, girls?" Indranie's voice is cheery and light, but I jump like a guilty cat anyway.

"Ni-ni! Look, I mean, smell me!" Gabi says, extending her wrist to Indranie.

"It's, um, pretty strong." Indranie laughs.

We thank the lady spraying perfume and walk past the stationery store, the computer store. Indranie buys us each a pretzel, which is one of the most delicious things I've ever eaten. I realize that the smell that is everywhere in the mall is from this pretzel, or the pretzel store. I eat and Gabi chatters and I think. How did Indranie know where to find us? And why does it bother me?

Back in the carriage house, as I help her set the table for dinner, Indranie reminds me that I have agreed to talk to Rey the next day.

"Yes. But what if she doesn't agree?"

"Let's just stay positive, okay? Her dad is talking to her now. We can afford to wait a little. Maybe we just stay in a holding pattern until we can change Rey's mind." I don't know what a holding pattern is, exactly, but I am good at waiting.

I was always waiting. Waiting for Papá to come home. Waiting for Pablo to remember that I existed and that we used to be friends.

"I could be the head of the family just as much as you could," I tell Pablo as we wait in the locker room for Gabi's swimming lesson to be over. His friends haven't arrived yet, so he's lowered his standards to hang out with me.

"¿En que mundo?" He laughs. "Who is going to take you seriously?"

"You're not even two years older than me. And I'm almost as tall as you," I say.

"No, you aren't, chaparrita. And you're definitely not as smart as me."

"Ha."

It isn't safe for Gabi to walk home from el Club on her own. Mamá sends me to get Gabi, but Pablo is usually already there. We don't know where he sleeps most nights. At eighteen, he's a man, he says. He doesn't need to come home like a child. I will never admit it, but I look forward to seeing him these few minutes a day. Once his friends arrive, I become invisible to him.

But it isn't Tato or El Flaco who came to meet Pablo today—it's Liliana. His sometimes girlfriend.

Every time I see her—no matter how much I tell myself to be calm—my heart stutters like a child reciting homework.

"Hola, Marisol. ¿Qué onda?"

I smile at her, but no words come out.

"Dame un beso, hermanita," she says. Give me a kiss, little sister. My chest hurts, but I walk over to her, let her put her arms around me and kiss me on the cheek. She smells like limes, I think. And like sunshine and dish soap.

"I told you she likes you, Lilí. She's just too serious," Pablo says. "She wants to be the one in charge. My little sister hates to wait. She wants to be una mamacita ya." He plucks a dirty towel *from the floor and flings it at me. It sticks for a moment to my hair before falling back to the ground. I'm so angry, my whole body stiffens.*

"Tranquila, amor," Liliana says, her arms still around me. She puts her lips to my hair and kisses my head. The anger drains out of me. I think, for sure, she must know. How my heart beats faster, how I dream about the way her skin looks under the neon bar lights. I think we are in this secret together. All I have to do is wait.

Olga and Manny are out tonight, eating dinner with their American daughter who works in Virginia. Olga has left us a beef stew with carrots and potatoes, and macaroni and cheese for Gabi.

As we eat dinner in the kitchen, I ask Indranie if there are any side effects of wearing the cuff. She considers this for a moment.

"Only the ones we spoke about. The effects of grief on the body. You have the printouts Dr. Deng gave you?"

I have them, but I have not read them. It's harder for me to read in English than it is for me to speak in English, and the words he uses are too medical and unfamiliar. But I don't want Indranie to know.

"Yes, but I meant anything else? Something I should look for?" I don't know why these memories of Pablo and Liliana and the weeks before we left are bubbling back into my mind. I expected dreams, bad dreams even, but not waking dreams, where I watch my own memories.

"I don't think so. But if—no, *when*—Rey's cuff begins transmitting, you'll keep notes, right?" Dr. Deng told me to do that too. He even gave me a little black-and-silver book that says DIARY on the front so I could write about my experiences.

"I will keep notes every day. Is there anything special I should write? Should I weigh myself?"

Gabi laughs next to me. I elbow her and tell her to keep eating.

"I don't think you have to go that scientific," Indranie says. She looks at the kitchen door, then stands abruptly, her chair scraping loudly on the floor.

A man in a gray suit stands in the doorway. For a moment, no one speaks. I have a wild thought that he is a burglar. But no burglar could be dressed that well. He looks sick, his skin as gray as his hair and suit.

"Scott." Indranie takes a half step toward him. "How's Rey?"

The man reaches a hesitant hand out to Indranie, before stopping himself.

"Please," he says, looking at me and Gabi. "Don't let me disturb you."

But he is the one who is disturbed. Fantasma. Ghost. I know this must be Rey's father.

"Have you eaten?" Indranie says.

"Um. No. I don't think I have." He seems more like a child than a man. Then I remember that his son has died and his daughter has tried to fly off a balcony. I look down at my food, not wanting to be noticed. For once, Gabi doesn't speak.

Indranie goes to the stove to serve Mr. Warner a plate of food.

"No, thank you, Indranie. I'm fine." He straightens his

shoulders in what I think must be a painful way. He stands like his whole body hurts.

"I just wanted a word with you before I leave in the morning." He catches me watching him. I look down at my food again, my face hot with embarrassment.

Indranie walks with Mr. Warner into the living room. She is careful to close the door to the kitchen.

Gabi raises her eyebrows at me, but I shake my head. Even if I wanted to listen, I wouldn't. It is always better to keep our heads down.

On Gabi's bed is a set of beautiful school clothes: a sky blue blouse with a dark blue vest and skirt. There are even matching blue socks and black shoes with a mirror shine. Gabi wants to put them on immediately, sleep in them.

"It will save time in the morning. I'll already be dressed," she says, only half kidding.

"You'll be as wrinkled as a date if you do that," I say.

"I've got one more surprise for you, Gabi." Indranie pulls a pair of boots out from a large shopping bag. The black motorcycle boots from the mall. Gabi's face erupts with happiness. She tries them on, stomping around the room. Her smile is contagious—both Indranie and I share it.

"Come on. Get into bed," I say, holding up the covers for her. I give her a stern look when she tries to get into bed with her boots. She takes them off and puts them right next to her bed.

"Good night, goose," Indranie says as Gabi sits up in bed with the book-light Olga gave her, a little lamp that clips onto her book. She's determined to finish reading the Harry Potter book because every kid in America has read it. She reminds me that Hermione wears a uniform too.

"Okay, Hermione," I say. "Good night."

I walk Indranie to the front door. I feel small in this big house with just me and Gabi. I am about to ask her if she could sleep here, just for tonight, so we aren't completely alone, but then Olga and Manny come through the door and I feel better.

"I'll see you tomorrow morning, all right? I'll take Gabi to school, then come back so I can bring you to see Rey. It doesn't have to be a big conversation. You can just tell her why you're here. See how it goes. We have time."

From the anxious way Indranie looks at me, then passes her hand over her eyes to hide her tiredness, I know we don't have time.

I say good night to Olga and Manny and go up to our room. I take my time brushing my teeth and my hair. The bathroom smells of the perfume the lady in the store sprayed on Gabi. A sample sits on the bathroom counter. I spray a little on my hair, hoping it will help me sleep.

I used to do the same at home. I couldn't find a perfume that smelled exactly like Liliana—maybe it wasn't the limes she cut in the bar, maybe it was a perfume that she wore—I never had the nerve to ask her. But my father's cologne that smelled of bay rum and lime was close enough. I would splash some on my hands, then on the back of my neck, where the alcohol would sting a little. I would go to sleep hoping to dream of Liliana. But I never did, or at least I don't remember if I did. I wore the scent of limes whenever we walked together, Pablo holding Liliana's hand—they were novios within a week—and me on her other side. She held Pablo's hand, but she whispered and laughed with me.

It is all for nothing because I can't sleep, let alone dream. Gabi has fallen asleep reading, the Harry Potter book tumbling out of her hand. I put the book away, careful to mark the page she was reading and turn off the book-light. I tell myself I can't sleep because I'm nervous about Gabi starting school tomorrow, but it's really about the girl. I will have to face her tomorrow and convince her to give me her grief.

It's chilly in the bedroom next to ours, but at least my restlessness won't wake Gabi.

There is a bookcase full of classics—just like in Mr. Rosen's library. I run my fingers past *Frankenstein, Jane Eyre, Fahrenheit 451*—I've read them all. I even read *Love in the Time of Cholera* in English, though I didn't understand it all. That could be the English translation, or it could be Márquez. It seemed to be about two people falling in love with each other but not staying with each other. I don't get the point of that.

I'm too ansiosa and unsettled to read. I sit in a chair next to high, wide windows, trying to calm my mind so I can fall asleep.

I think of all the windows in this house, not to mention the windows in the big house and in the pool house. So much glass, such a desire to see out. It's not that San Salvador doesn't have beautiful buildings with glass and balconies and gardens. It does, though many are old and falling apart. It's just that those buildings belong to everyone in one way or another. I've never seen so much space for just a handful of people. Except on TV, of course.

Tomorrow I will risk sounding silly and ask Indranie if she

can find out when *Cedar Hollow* is on. It's been more than a year since I've seen it, the last time with Mrs. Rosen as her belongings were packed up, moving her life back to America. We sat in her kitchen dunking pan dulce into cups of tea and talking about our favorite characters. Mrs. Rosen said that Amber was a moron, but I think she was trying to tease me.

I don't know how long I've been watching the person walking in the garden without realizing what I was looking at, but suddenly I really see him. A man with short hair and a cap moves through the bushes near the big house and out to the long rectangle of water. My first thought is—again—that it is a burglar. My second thought is that it's not a man, but a boy. Then I know who he must be. Rey's boyfriend.

I slip downstairs and put my jacket on over my piyamas, then slide the back door open silently. It's not too cold, but the grass outside is wet and I forgot to put on my shoes. I have also forgotten to ask myself, *Why do I want to spy on them? Why do I want to watch?*

I think a good argument would be that by watching Rey and her boyfriend, maybe I can get to know her a little, maybe I can figure out how to talk to her tomorrow. If they start kissing, I will absolutely leave them alone.

Past the door in the garden wall, I press against the bushes, moving closer until I can see and even hear clearly. I have not convinced myself that I am doing this for a good reason. I know that it's only curiosity that's brought me here.

Minutes go by. Insects hum in the darkness. The boy sits quietly, hunched over in a too-large black leather jacket, his cap turned backward on his head. He throws stones and grass into the pool. I wonder how long he will wait for Rey to come.

It's colder in the garden than it should be for April. But, of course, we are so much farther north than home. Or maybe I'm shivering because I have no business being in this garden. I am about to go back when I hear the boy speak.

"Where are you?" I hear the whispered words clearly. I'm close enough that I know it is a *she* who speaks.

"Where have you gone that I can't reach you?" Her voice is a broken thing. "If I knew where you were, if I knew you were okay, I could be okay."

The girl takes off her cap, and I see that it's Rey. Her long hair is gone, cut so short, like los militares, like army men. It's blond and thin like a baby's hair. The cap and the jacket do not belong to a boyfriend. They belong to her brother.

The moment I realize that I must leave, that I cannot hear this girl's prayer to her dead brother, is the same moment that I sneeze, three times in a row.

# Chapter 11

My eyes close and my head bobs down with each sneeze. I cross myself because there isn't anyone else to say salud, dinero, y amor.

"Who are you?" Rey stands next to the water, facing me. I wish that I could push farther into the bushes, to become invisible. But there's no chance of that. I struggle out of my hiding place, using my sleeve to wipe my nose like a child.

"My name is Marisol. I'm staying in the carriage house."

Rey's body relaxes, but her expression is confused.

"Where are you from?"

"Excuse me?" I say in perfect English. Why can't I be from here? Why do I have to be from somewhere else?

"Where are you visiting from? Cuba?" she asks.

"No!" I don't know why I sound so upset.

Rey shrugs. "You sound like Olga and Manny. That's why I asked."

"I speak English perfectly."

"Fine. Whatever." She turns away from me and starts to walk back toward the big house.

"Who were you talking to?" I ask, even though I know.

"No one," she calls over her shoulder.

"Were you talking to God?" I keep asking questions I know the answers to. But at least we're talking.

Rey turns back to me, her voice angry and cold. "What would be the fucking point of that?"

"I don't know," I say. "It makes me feel better to pray to God." This is a lie. I know I cannot be forgiven. But I pray anyway and tell myself I feel better.

"Fuck. Don't tell me you're a Bible-thumper."

I cross my arms. "A thump—what?"

"Jesus. Are you from Olga's church? Did she send you?"

She's confusing me. I know what her words mean on their own, but all together—and she's talking so fast, and crying too. I don't know exactly what she's saying.

I take a step closer to her. "I'm here to take your grief away." I don't think I'm supposed to say it like that, like I'm here to take her laundry to be cleaned. But I have to convince her to put on the cuff. She *has* to do the experiment. Gabi's safety depends on it.

She only stares at me blankly before turning away again.

"Wait," I call, hopping after her because my cold feet have gone numb.

"Don't follow me."

"I don't understand," I plead. At least she stops again.

"It's not your fault." Her voice is uncertain and high. I cannot judge how tall she is, she is so hunched over in her leather jacket. "You're probably doing this for Jesus or something. Helping the less fortunate. Ha." A tremor runs through her whole body, of laughter or maybe of pain. "I'm telling you, don't bother."

"Why not?"

"Because I don't want to give you my grief, or whatever this shitty lava in my chest is. I want to keep it all for my greedy self. Okay?"

Lava? Shit? I hate not understanding.

"You could share it with me." I step closer. "You can feel better."

"I don't want to feel better!" she yells. Her words linger in the night air, silencing all other sounds for a second, two. Then the insects begin to hum again.

"I'm sorry. I used to be polite. I was the good twin—can you believe that shit?" She makes a noise that might have been meant as a laugh but never becomes one. "But now I'm the only twin, so I can be pretty much as shitty as I want. Enjoy your visit. *Buena suerte.*" She salutes and turns away a final time to disappear into the house.

I sit on the floor of Rey's room waiting for her to speak.

"Rey, this is Marisol." Dr. Vizzachero shifts uncomfortably on a puffy chair made of beans. Indranie stands in the corner of the room by the door. Rey sits on her bed.

"We've had some, let's just say, interesting times these past two days, Dr. V," Indranie says with a grim laugh. "Rey and Marisol have already met."

Rey gives her a disdainful look before turning to face me.

"Sorry I thought you were a Bible-thumper," she mutters.

I try to keep my eyes on the rug, light pink and prickly like grass. Then, as if they are acting on their own, my eyes go back to Rey. She is in the same pretty white nightgown from yesterday, but it's torn and the edge is dirty. Her short hair makes her look like un diente de león blown too hard by the wind.

We've been here for a while, waiting for Rey to be ready. First, she lay on her bed, Indranie trying to wake her with promises of chocolate and coffee. When Dr. Vizzachero arrived, Rey hid in the bathroom. As Dr. Vizzachero, Indranie, and I sat without talking, we listened to Rey turn on the water, turn off the water. Flush the toilet. Flush it again. I check the time on the phone that Indranie gave me. Gabi has been in her new school for three hours, and we have been trying to talk to Rey for over an hour.

"I don't want to talk to you, Dr. V."

If the doctor is insulted, her face doesn't show it. "You don't have to talk, Reyanne. You can just listen."

"No, sorry, wasn't clear. I mean, I don't want you here *at all*. I know you say *honesty is best*. So, I hope you don't mind." Rey opens her mouth wide, showing all her teeth.

Dr. Vizzachero gets up from the bag of beans and gathers her things. "All right. Come and take your medicine before I leave, Reyanne."

Rey doesn't move from her bed.

"I can't leave until I see you take it," Dr. Vizzachero says, holding out her hand. In her palm is a collection of small pills.

Slowly, as if she is moving through water, Rey slides off the bed to stand in front of the doctor. She looks so defenseless with her bare head and enormous nightgown. But I also feel her violence and anger, and I think she will slap the doctor's hand away, scream at her until someone makes her stop.

Instead, Rey takes the pills and puts them into her mouth. Then we watch, Dr. Vizzachero, Indranie, and I, as Rey swallows the pills. We watch her as if we could see through her skin, into her body, and watch the little pills make their way into her stomach.

"Let me see," Dr. Vizzachero says. Rey doesn't say a word, but her body tightens, her eyes narrow.

"Open your mouth, Reyanne," Dr. Vizzachero says, as if it's a normal thing to ask of someone.

Rey's face becomes a mask of anger, but she opens her mouth and lifts her tongue, showing Dr. Vizzachero that it's empty. When the doctor is satisfied, Rey closes her mouth with a snap.

"I'll leave you to it, Agent Patel," the doctor says on her way out.

"Thanks, Dr. V. Thank you for all your work."

I feel embarrassed by Rey, as if her rudeness is somehow my fault. I want this part of the day to be over so I can be ready when Gabi comes back from school and tells me all about her day.

"Can I go back to sleep? Please?" Rey complains like a child.

"Not yet, Rey. Your father says no more sleep until you talk to Marisol."

"Just talk, right?" Rey asks Indranie. She doesn't look at me. I sit on the floor of her bedroom as if I am an invisible thing.

"Just talk. Just give it a chance." Indranie stretches out a hand to Rey, but Rey turns away from her.

"Okay. Then can you leave too?"

A flash of hurt crosses Indranie's face before it smooths back into its usual calm. She looks at me hesitantly.

"I'm not going to murder her," Rey says testily.

Indranie considers me for many moments. "All right, Marisol. Do your best, okay?"

I nod, even though I don't know how I will get Rey to look at me, never mind agree to put on the cuff.

"I'll send Olga for you after lunch." When the door closes behind Indranie, Rey's dark eyes finally find mine. I wait for her to speak, to move or do something. But she is slumped against the wall like a rag doll thrown by an angry child.

"I stink," she says. "And I'm fucking sick of it." In a quick motion—so quick I don't have time to shut my eyes—Rey pulls the nightgown over her head and throws it at me.

"Burn that," she says.

Because my eyes aren't closed, I catch it. I also see her completely naked. That is the image I see behind my closed eyes as I sit, holding her discarded nightgown, listening to her start the shower.

When Rey comes out of the shower wrapped in a too-big white bathrobe, I'm afraid she will get naked again and I won't be able to look away fast enough. But she is dressed underneath. She wears a big gray T-shirt and black jeans. Her feet are bare. I look at my sneakers and wonder if I was supposed to take them off.

"You didn't burn it," she says, nodding toward the pile of dirty clothes where I put her nightgown. Her room is so messy, it's an explosion of things—clothes and books and empty bottles of soda.

"I don't have any matches," I say, surprising myself.

"Ha!" she laughs, rubbing a towel in her short hair. "All right. At least you're not a zombie."

"Should I take off my shoes?" I ask.

"I don't care what you do. I only agreed to the damn implant so Dad wouldn't commit me. We just have to talk for a few minutes and then you leave. You tell Indranie you couldn't convince me to be a lab rat—no offense—and you go save someone else."

It takes me a moment to figure out what she means by *lab rat*—not an actual rat at all, but *me*. I'm the rat. It would be easier not to take offense if Rey didn't try so hard to be offensive.

"What do you like to do?" I ask. She is balanced on the edge of her bed, looking for something on a shelf.

"What?" Rey mumbles.

"What do you do when you are not . . ." What is it that this girl does when her life isn't falling apart? "When you're not studying?"

Rey takes a book from her shelf then jumps to the floor. In a moment, she's sitting in front of me, legs crossed like me, her knees touching mine. She leans forward. "Why are you really doing this? What's in it for you?"

"I'm helping my sister."

Rey pulls her head back a little. "What's wrong with her?"

"Nothing is wrong with her!"

Rey sighs. "I mean, does she need a kidney? Does she have cancer? How did they rope you into this mess?" She leans closer. I can smell her shampoo, a mix of honey and mint.

"We are from another country," I begin.

Rey snorts. "No shit."

"Why do you say that? *No shit?*"

"Because, duh, we already established that. You are so not from around here."

My mouth opens, ready to spill angry words, just as soon as I can make sure they're the right ones. I don't want to say something stupid. But I don't get a chance to reply.

"I'm sorry, but you, your face is just—" She hiccups with laughter. I don't understand what is so funny, but I know she's laughing at me.

"Are you going to kill yourself?" I blurt out. She pulls back, moving her knees away from mine, and leans against her bed.

"Not now." She looks away. "Maybe later."

Now I move in close. "What if this could make you feel a bit better?"

"It can't."

"But you don't know."

"I know wishful fucking thinking when I see it."

"But what if—"

"Stop! Just stop." Rey's shoulders are pushed up to her ears and there are tears in her eyes. I didn't realize. I was listening to her words instead of watching her body.

I look around her room, hoping to find something to inspire my words. Her room is so different from the one Gabi and I shared. But some things are the same. There are dolls, not played with in years. Books—so many more than we had. Drawings, like the ones we made, hung up as reminders of how we used to be. But this is different: she has a wall of movies. A whole wall of just discos, big movies that I saw years ago at the Cinépolis and movies I've never heard of. And there, on the bottom shelf, is a box of discos all in different colors like thin books. *Cedar Hollow: The Complete Collection.*

"You watch *Cedar Hollow*?" I can't keep the excitement out of my voice.

Rey passes a hand under each eye, clearing away tears. "Yeah. I loved that stupid show."

"It isn't stupid! It's amazing."

"Yeah, that's what I'm saying." She rolls her eyes. "It's amazing and stupid."

"Are these all the shows? I thought it would be on TV, but I couldn't find it."

"That show is ancient. You can't even find it streaming anywhere. That's the only reason I still have the DVDs."

I know I'm supposed to be convincing Rey to agree to put on the cuff. I know that the longer I take to do that, the less chance we'll have of succeeding. But talking is not working, and I feel so homesick. Watching *Cedar Hollow* would almost be like being home.

"Can we watch? Just a little?"

"You are weird, you know that?" Rey says, but she says it with a smile—a real one, not a nasty one.

She takes the disco out of the box and taps it against her lips.

"I guess it might play on the Xbox?" She cleans the disco on her sleeve and puts it into the machine.

"What are you waiting for?" Rey asks, patting the bed next to her.

I sit on the bed, but not too near. The familiar music from *Cedar Hollow* begins, Amber's and Aimee's smiling faces flashing on the screen during the opening credits. I know it's strange, but I haven't felt this happy in a long time.

Chapter 12

The lunch Olga brought us—sándwiches calientes with cheese, ham, and pickles, and a bowl of popcorn—sits half eaten on Rey's bed. Half eaten by me. Rey hasn't eaten anything. We have watched three episodes of *Cedar Hollow*, only I have spent some of the time watching Rey. I look at her to see if she finds the same things funny or exciting as I do. We're watching the episode where Aimee keeps her boyfriend from getting into a car with drunk friends—and then the friends in that car die in a crash—including Amber's boyfriend. I bury my face into Rey's pillow, afraid to look, even though I have seen this episode many times before. But Rey watches with glassy eyes. I nudge her at the beginning of each episode to see if she has fallen asleep.

"I'm still here," she responds wearily.

As much as I love seeing *Cedar Hollow* again, I find myself more preocupada with Rey—sitting next to me, seeing but not watching—than I am about Amber and Duke and their fighting.

When the third episode ends, I get up. Rey startles as if from a sleep.

"You're leaving?" she asks dazedly.

"Yes. Gabi will be home from school soon. I want to hear how her day was."

"What time is it?"

I look at the alarm clock on Rey's shelf. "It is almost two."

"In the morning?"

"In the afternoon."

She looks around her bed, then her room, searching for something. "No one else is here, right?"

I look at her with a question in my eyes.

"Sometimes they sneak back in," she says.

If someone were to sneak into my room, I would lock the door. "No one else came in. So, it is just me."

"Good. That's good. Oh. There's food," she says, noticing the tray for the first time. I feel bad that I ate all of the popcorn.

"Do you want me to ask Olga to heat it?"

"No." She sniffs the cold sandwich, then puts it down uneaten.

"You can take it," she says, pushing the tray away, as if I am a servant.

I don't take the tray at first, I just watch her, trying to think of a way to speak about the cuff, to convince her to try it, since that's what I'm supposed to do. But I don't know how.

"Okay," I say. "Goodbye." I balance the tray in one hand and open her door with the other.

"See you later, Aimee," Rey says.

For a moment, I wonder if she has forgotten who I am, but then I see her smile, funny and sly.

I say, "See you later, Amber," and close the door behind me.

Gabi is eating like she has never seen food before.

"Slow down, or you'll choke." I put the tray from Rey's room into the sink. Olga pours a glass of juice for me and gives me a plate of cookies to go with it. I don't like the way chocolate and orange juice taste together, though I feel bad asking for something else. When I would tell Mrs. Rosen about it, how I didn't like that Gabi's school served juice with cookies, she said, "That's because you're a proper American. You like your cookies with milk." Pablo called me creída—stuck up—and worse, but I was secretly happy to have American tastes.

"Olga, can I have a glass of milk, please?"

Olga looks at me from above her glasses. "You don't like jugo?" she asks.

"It's fine," I say, sitting next to Gabi. "I just like the way milk and chocolate go together."

"It's no problem to me," Olga says, pouring a glass of milk and putting it next to my glass of orange juice.

Gabi laughs and whispers, "Two drinks! Just like I hop." I return her smile and dunk the cookie into the milk.

"So? How was it?" I ask nervously.

"How was what?" she says, looking innocent.

"Ha ha. School, babosa," I say.

"Oh," Gabi says. "Was that today?"

"I'm going to hit you with a cookie."

"Okay! It was uh-mazing. It was maaaaa-gical." She draws the word out and rolls her eyes at me.

"How was it really?"

"It was incredible, obviously." She speaks fast, too excited to slow down. "I had computer classes, and there was this amazing cafeteria with all the kinds of food you could want, and, do you know what 4-H is?"

"You don't mean the number and the letter, right?"

"No! It's a club for animals."

"A club for animals?" I sound doubtful, but I guess such a thing could be true in America.

"It's for students who want to raise animals, you know, like animals from a farm?"

I wrinkle my nose. "So, we come to America so you can learn to be una granjera? You could have been a farmer at home."

"I get to hold bunnies and guinea pigs and chickens."

"Again, all things you could have done at Abuela's, but you never wanted to."

Gabi tries to look dignified while shoving another cookie into her mouth. It's a miracle she can talk at all. "This is different. There's a lot of science too."

"All right. That's good, then. Do you need to pay to join the club?"

I'm thinking of the hundred-dollar bill I still wear on the belt around my waist. Paying for a club to take care of animals seems like a dumb idea, though I wouldn't tell Gabi that. Especially if we don't get to stay the whole month.

Gabi's mouth is full. She takes a big gulp of jugo and swallows. "The teacher said it's all taken care of." There's barely a pause for breath. "Can I go swimming? I don't have any homework."

I look at Olga, but she shrugs.

"Okay. Go put your school clothes away. And don't swim for too long. You always lose track of time."

"You aren't coming?"

"No. I have my own stuff to do."

"Please, Sol?"

"Why? You love swimming." I'm distracted, thinking of Rey, of what I can do to get her to put on the cuff. I don't think watching TV with her will convince her of anything. But I can't think of anything else to do.

Gabi touches my arm, pulling my attention back to her.

"I don't feel good in the pool house by myself," she whispers, looking over her shoulder to make sure Olga can't hear. "What if someone comes in?"

Of course I go with her. Gabi can ask me to do anything. But I don't swim, just sit watching Gabi cut through the water like a dolphin, smooth and elegant. And anyway, when I'm in the water, I can't have my cuff on. I cannot let anyone think I am lazy and not doing my job.

I think about how I wasted a day watching TV with Rey. It's too easy here, in this house. Everything happens without having to work for it. After Gabi finishes swimming, she asks me to paint her nails, because everyone in her class has manicures every week.

"Everyone?" I say. "Even the boys?"

Olga has lent us her collection of nail polish. We sit on our bed, and I paint Gabi's nails a pale pink color—the least crazy color I could find.

"Now who is being silly?" She scowls.

"Vos, babosa," I say with a smirk. *Smirk* is another really good word in English. It sounds like what it is, as if saying the word turns your mouth into a smirk. When she reaches for a pillow to throw at me, I remind her that her nails are still wet and my smirk gets bigger.

"What's she like?"

"Who?" I dip the brush back into the nail polish bottle.

"La loca. Who else?" Gabi says.

I stop, the brush frozen in my hand. "Don't call her that. It's not nice." I finish painting Gabi's pinky and put away the polish.

"That's what they call her at school," Gabi says defensively.

"They do?" I shouldn't sound interested. I should tell her not to listen to what they say in her school. "How do they even know who Rey is?"

Gabi settles herself against the pillows, fanning her hands so her nails dry. She's enjoying this. "Well, it's a very small school. And it's exclusive—did you know that?" I shake my head. "It's only for rich people. And the Warner family is the richest. That's what Juliette says."

"Who's Juliette?"

"My friend." Gabi shrugs.

"What does Juliette say about Rey?"

Gabi sits up, eyes wide with excitement. "That she went crazy after her brother died. That she's been to the hospital, and they even had to tie her up and make her do drugs."

"Take drugs," I say.

"Yes, take drugs," Gabi says. "They only gave her—how do you say it, la dieron de alta?"

I search my mind for the English words. "Release, no, discharge. They discharged her from the hospital."

"Yes, that's it. They only discharged her a few days ago. Amazing, right?"

I'm silent. I don't know how to let Gabi know that seeing Rey glassy-eyed and staring into space was not amazing. It was sad and terrible.

"You didn't tell anyone at school about what I'm doing? About the experiment?" It would be like Gabi, wanting to fit in, to tell a good story.

"What? No, por supuesto que no. I'm not stupid."

"I know you're not."

She sighs dramatically. "I did tell them I saw her try to kill herself."

"What?" I groan.

"Cálmate. I didn't say anything to do with the experiment."

"Just don't say anything about Rey to your friends, okay?"

Gabi lies back again. "Okay. But you didn't answer my question. What's Rey like?"

I think about what she's like and try to put it into a single picture. All I come up with is what she isn't. She's not nice. She's not shy or happy. She's not easy to be with.

"She's difficult," I finally say. I lie down next to Gabi, careful of her still-drying nails.

"Is she mean to you?"

"No, not like that. It's only that one minute she's angry, and the next she's making a joke. A lot of the time, she's like a blank—not there."

"Pero, she didn't act like a crazy?"

"No, she just seemed very sad."

"I thought you said she was angry."

"You can be angry because you're sad."

Gabi turns onto her side to look at me. "And when she puts on the cuff? Will you be sad and angry and difficult? Will you feel all the things she's feeling?"

"I think so. But that's okay because it's only for a little bit. And anyway, it's her grief for her brother that I'll be getting. It has nothing to do with me."

"How will you be able to tell the difference?"

"What difference?"

"Between your grief and hers?"

I wish I could tell Gabi that I don't feel any grief over Pablo. It would be a relief to admit it. But she suffered so much after his death. She had to grieve on the journey, silently if she could, and in front of strangers when it couldn't be helped. She wouldn't understand that by the time Pablo died, he was already a stranger to me.

"It's not the same," I say. "That's all over with. We have a chance for a future. I know everything is going to be all right."

Gabi checks to make sure her nails are dry, then reaches for the TV remote. "I think it's like when Señora Flores wanted to send her son to America but didn't have enough money."

"I don't know this story."

"Yes, he didn't want to join Barrio, and they were pressuring him, you know." She flips through channels so fast, I can't figure out what's on the TV. "So, the coyotes told her that if he carried a package with him, they would charge him less."

I grimace. That can only mean drugs. Señora Flores must have known that.

"What happened to him?"

"I don't know." She frowns. "I saw her in the beauty salon, crying to Mamá."

"That's how you know about it. Orejaste."

"I didn't mean to listen. She was very loud."

"So, how am I like Señora Flores's son?"

"It's obvious. You have to carry something for someone else so you can be in America."

I take the remote out of Gabi's hand, annoyed with all the channel flipping. We decide on a show about a family with lots of kids and lots of pets. When the kids or the pets break things or get dirty, no one seems to mind.

Between watching Gabi swim, painting her nails, and watching TV, I have wasted the afternoon. We eat dinner, and then it's time for bed. Indranie comes in to say good night, and I tell her that I am worried.

"I didn't accomplish anything today. I need to do better."

"It's okay, Marisol," she says, keeping her voice down. Gabi has fallen asleep. The blue light from the TV flickers on her face. "Rey is stubborn, and she's been through so much."

She's been through the same thing that millions of other people have been through, I think. *What makes her pain more unbearable than anyone else's?*

"Try not to worry," Indranie says on her way out the door. "You're doing great."

I know I'm not doing great. I have to convince Rey to do the experiment. Tomorrow. No *Cedar Hollow,* no nail-painting, no distractions until Rey wears the cuff too. Or else there's no point to any of this.

Chapter 13

The next morning, after Gabi leaves for school, I ask Olga what Rey's favorite food is. When I want to convince Gabi of something, food is usually how I do it. And I could never convince Pablo of anything, even that the sky is blue, without the promise of something attached to it.

As she wipes the already clean kitchen counter and puts away the breakfast dishes, Olga gives me a long list of homemade meals that makes my mouth water.

"She is being difficult right now," she says with arms spread wide, annoyed. "She sent the beautiful breakfast I made her back sin tocar." Olga's face darkens. "All she eats is that orange soda and the pills from the doctor. What kind of thing is that for a young girl?"

"There must be something else."

Olga taps her front teeth with her finger. Her nail polish is as purple as her T-shirt.

"Well, when she is really bad, we get this, this garbage food from one of those fast-food places. Disgusting." She makes a face to match her words.

"Could we get that for her? Since she hasn't eaten?"

"The place is an hour away. I don't drive, mijita. And Manny is too busy."

I hadn't thought this would be so hard.

"Why don't I make some ropa vieja? She loves my stew," Olga says.

"No, thank you, Señora Borges. I'll find a way."

"I can't believe I'm spending my afternoon hand-delivering drive-through," Traci says as she gives me a plain brown bag. I had to wait almost two hours for Traci to arrive with the food from Rey's favorite restaurant.

"That's it?" I'm skeptical. It doesn't look like much.

"That's it," Traci says, shaking her head. "Extra pickles and a peach milkshake, which I drank, since it would have melted anyway." She hands me a magazine with a yellow race car on the cover. *Dream Cars Monthly.*

"That's for Gabi, not Rey."

"Yes, I figured." I smile. "Thank you."

"No problem. Tell your sister I'll take her out in my GTO next time I'm down."

"I will."

Olga heats everything up in the microwave, shaking her head the whole time. I run to the main house, because I don't want the food to get cold again. I have to admit, though I am not hungry, it smells delicious. When I get to Rey's door, I wave the bag into the room, hoping the smell will wake her up.

"Are you hungry?" I ask.

There's no answer. I open the door wider and walk in. It's only a little after noon—it won't be dark for hours. But in Rey's room, it's very dark—oscuro como la boca de lobo—dark as a wolf's mouth. A single candle burns weakly on the shelf above Rey's bed, a prayer candle like the one Mamá lights to San Simón.

Rey is curled into a ball under her bedcover. I can tell she is not sleeping.

"I have your favorite chicken fillet sandwich," I say, trying to sound as cheerful as I can. She doesn't move. Next to her on the bed is the white box with the metal cuff in it. It looks exactly the same as mine.

I move closer to the bed. "Rey?"

"It's so heavy."

I look at the cuff, thinking that's what she means. Maybe she tried it on and it was too heavy on her. Or maybe it's the blanket she's under.

"Want me to help you sit up?"

"There's no air."

I can hear it, her breath harsh as if the blanket over her chest is crushing her lungs. I don't know how to help her. I don't know if I should call Olga or Indranie or Traci. I turn toward the door.

"Don't leave." The desperation in her voice makes me stop.

"Okay. I won't leave."

This girl must be made of a different material than I am. Her brother died, and that is terrible. My brother died, and it is terrible. But I am not melting. No soy mantequita.

I edge toward the bed and put on the sweet voice I use with Gabi when she is being difficult.

"Come on! I have delicious chicken for you. You know you want to eat it. Yum, yum." I drop the bag of food onto the bed.

"Fuck you and your chicken."

Well. Gabi has never said that to me.

"I'm not going to stay if you curse at me like that."

She doesn't apologize, but she does drag herself up, her face emerging completely from the blanket. I'm shocked by her face, and how much it's changed since yesterday. It has become a mask. It reminds me of the sad face carved in stone in front of the Teatro Nacional, the mask for tragedia, with slashes for eyes and a mouth pulled down in sorrow.

I didn't notice how bad the room smelled yesterday—like dirty clothes and sour sweat—or maybe it smells worse today. Rey doesn't seem to notice. I try to open the doors to her balcony, but they are stuck.

"Dad had them seal the door yesterday. No death by balcony for me," she croaks.

"Are you okay?" I ask. Of course she's not okay. I want to kick myself for being so stupid.

"My brother left me. He fucking left me. Why didn't he take me with him?"

How I wish I'd had the luxury of self-pity. Maybe if I hadn't needed to take care of Gabi, I would have felt like Rey. But after Pablo died, there was no room and no time for anything but escape.

"Is it time for you to take more medicine?" I remember yesterday, Dr. V telling Rey to take her medicine. Who is making her take her medicine today?

"Dr. V wants me to be a good zombie. I want to be a good zombie too, but those pills don't do it." She smacks her head with her hand. "I need a lobotomy." *Smack.* "I need to forget." *Smack.* "Stop. Feeling. Anything." *Smack, smack, smack.*

I make myself move closer to her, though it's the last thing I want to do. If it is dark like a wolf's mouth in this room, then Rey is the wolf. She can bite with her words.

Indranie said to show Rey that I have lost a brother, show her that I understand. "When my brother, Pablo, died, I felt like that too."

But I didn't feel that way. From the moments after I saw him die, I refused to think about Pablo. Every secret we shared, every smile and silent understanding—I locked away. I fit Gabi in the space in my heart where Pablo used to be. She is the most important thing.

"It does get better. You will get better too." Even to myself, I sound unconvincing.

"That's what Dr. V says. She doesn't want me to put on the cuff. She says I have to get better on my own."

Dr. V doesn't want Rey to put on the cuff?

I put this new information aside to tell Indranie.

"After the funeral, they left me alone. I could stay in here and cry all I wanted. But when I started breaking things, they—" Rey presses her hands into her chest. "They wanted me to stop. Move on."

I nod like I understand. Like I sympathize. But I don't. What else is there to do except move on? Breaking things will not make anything better. Rey is not strong enough to accept reality. The light from the candle casts deep shadows on her face, making her look fragile. Es un pajarito, I think. A bird with broken wings.

"I don't know if I can stand it, you know? The weight of not having Riley, it's pushing on me all the time." She tilts her head back, eyes on the ceiling. "We were twins, did you know?"

"You told me. When I saw you in the garden."

"We didn't look alike, but I fit into his clothes. He thought he was too short, too slight, for a guy, but he was perfect. He was perfect," she repeats. "And when I put on his leather jacket, I can still smell him. I don't want any of it to go away." Tears spill down her cheeks. I feel frozen.

"If you take my grief away, I'll have nothing."

I have Gabi. As long as I have Gabi, I can *withstand* anything. Maybe the only reason I am not falling to pieces like this girl is because I have an anchor. I push the cuff on the bed closer to her so I can sit down.

"I don't think that anything can take someone away from you, not when you love them."

"That's bullshit," she says. But she doesn't sound angry.

"Okay, but bulls' shit can be true, can't it?"

She finally looks at me instead of the ceiling.

"No, Marisol. That's what *bullshit* means. It's not true."

I shrug. "All right. I don't know what *bulls' shit* means, then."

A ghost of a smile forms on her lips. The light brightens a little in the wolf's mouth. It makes me bold.

"What if you put the cuff on now, then you can eat and we can watch more *Cedar Hollow*?"

She hesitates, her fingers twitching toward the brown paper bag. She must be hungry.

"You'll do anything to watch that dumb-ass show, won't you?"

"Yes," I say, trying not to sound too eager. "Amber is very important to me."

"I'll eat," she says grudgingly. At least that's something.

Rey unwraps her sandwich, then takes it apart, making a pile for the bread, a pile for the breaded chicken, and a pile for the six pickles. She picks up one pickle and puts it into her mouth. I've never seen someone eat so strangely before. Rey catches me watching her, and my cheeks burn.

As we watch the fourth episode of *Cedar Hollow*, then the fifth, Rey eats all the pickles one by one before eating all the bread. Finally, she tears the chicken into pieces, eating it in the same strange way.

"What is the point of having a sandwich when you're just going to take it apart?"

"I call it deconstructionism. Tastes better if you eat all the parts separately."

"But then why get a sandwich?" I insist.

Rey tips her head to one side to look at me. "You got me there." She snorts, a sound that's almost a laugh. Suddenly, I want to make her really laugh, to hear what it sounds like. But I don't know how.

We watch episodes six and seven. I have never, not even in Mrs. Rosen's house, watched so much TV before. I feel like I've been sick, because I haven't moved around, haven't done anything. I stretch, not liking the stiffness in my neck.

"What should we do now?" I say, accidentally eating the last fry.

"Why can't we just keep watching? There's like five more seasons."

Because I'm no closer to convincing you to wear the cuff. Because I want to get lost in Amber and Aimee's world and I know I can't. I try to sound casual. "I'm tired of sitting. Do you want to go for a walk?"

"Outside?" She sounds disbelieving.

"Yes. Outside." I wonder if Americans walk *inside* their houses sometimes. You could walk a lot of kilometers inside this house.

She'll say no. She'll think and think and then finally choose not to move because that hurts less. Where yesterday I felt happy in this room, watching *Cedar Hollow* and forgetting that Gabi and I have no sure future beyond the next month, now it makes me feel itchy. I have been still for too long.

"Aimee and Amber would go for a walk," I say.

Rey looks unconvinced.

"They'd go for a walk in the creepy woods, all right. And then they'd get attacked," Rey says.

"Yes, but then they'd be rescued by attractive boys who would also take them to a cool coffee shop after. And buy them lattes."

Rey lets out a laugh, a real one this time, even though I don't think what I said was that funny. Sometimes things are funnier when they're unexpected.

"Fine. We'll walk." Rey gets out of bed, walking without shoes to the door. I follow her down a long hallway, but instead of turning the way I know, she keeps going, past closed doors, her bare feet making no noise on the thick carpets. Finally, she opens a door that I think will be a closet, but there is a staircase instead. We walk down to the first floor, to a silent, spotless kitchen much bigger than Olga's kitchen in the carriage house. At a sliding back door, Rey slips on a pair of rubber shoes.

I hurry to catch up with her long strides. From the outside, I recognize where we are more clearly. I look up and see the underside of her bedroom balcony. Directly in front of us is the rectangular pool where I listened to her talking to Riley.

When I do catch up with her, she's staring into the pool, all trace of her previous laughter gone.

I sit next to her.

"What is this pool for?" I ask, breaking the silence.

"What?"

"Gabi thought it was a pool for birds," I say, "but I told her that was ridiculous."

Rey's small smile returns. "It's a reflecting pool."

I look at the surface of the water as it reflects a sky that is brighter than the grass, the trees. The pool looks like it has light inside it.

I wonder if we are going to take a walk. Or if this is as far as we go. I wonder how I can get back to talking about the cuff.

"Tell me something true," Rey says. "Something that doesn't change."

"The sun? The moon?"

"No. Something important."

Am I supposed to say love? Or money? What can money mean to a girl with two houses and a pool for reflecting?

"My sister," I say. That's not quite right because Gabi has changed a lot in the last six weeks. When I thought she'd be too scared to move, she ran, sometimes pulling me with her. And when I thought she would be too young to notice the coyotes favoring some of us, and robbing and beating others, she saw everything and said nothing. I saw her change from a little girl into a survivor, right in front of me. But Gabi is *my sister*. That doesn't change.

Rey sits up. "Your sister does change."

"No, I mean—"

"Yeah. I know what you mean. You mean that how you feel about your sister doesn't change." She passes her hands over her head, forgetting that her hair is gone. Her face creases into a frown. "But what about when she is gone? That's a change, right?"

I understand her perfectly, but I don't understand the words *beneath* her words. "She's not gone."

"But Riley is."

For a moment, I imagine the reflecting pool dropping away from us, creating a hole with no bottom, darker than any wolf or night or evil thing. That is the hole Rey is in. If I don't help her out of it, we will be sent back. No amount of cuidado will save Gabi from the trouble waiting for us at home.

"It will get better. I can help it get better faster," I say.

"Were you sad when your brother died?"

"Of course."

"But you don't miss him anymore."

I don't want to lie to Rey. Not when she is showing me so much of her hurt. I have lied, happily, to get what I want for Gabi and me. But it feels like an insult to lie about this.

"I try not to think of him very much." This is true. I make sure it is true.

She turns to me, and her face is full of so much anger that it stops my breath. "Then you must not have loved him that much, if you can get over it that easily."

She doesn't know what Pablo was to me or what he did. She doesn't know anything about the choices I had. Or didn't have. There are so many words I could say to show her how I feel and who I am. But I'm afraid. If I show even a little bit, it will lead to more and more. Then I won't be able to keep it inside.

I stand to leave, knowing I have failed. Hoping I can try again tomorrow.

She puts a hand on my leg, just above where the cuff sits on my ankle.

When her eyes meet mine, they are full of pain—bewildered and lost. I reach my hand out, as if I could help her out of her hole, as if I could reach down that far.

"You aren't alone. Not anymore," I say, even though I'm embarrassed. Of course I don't mean me. She has her father, Indranie, and Dr. V.

Rey lets my foolish gesture, my reaching hand, hover in the air so long that I feel a spark of anger.

"Okay," she says, finally taking hold of me, letting me pull her up. "I'll put the cuff on."

Chapter 14

Rey's prayer candle went out, making the wolf's mouth darker. I turn on her desk lamp so I can help her with the cuff. She lies back on her bed, unmoving, as if the short walk has exhausted her. She's wearing loose pants, which is good because Dr. Deng said that the cuff has to touch skin for the transmission to work. I put the cuff on Rey's ankle, then sit back and wait.

"Now what happens?" Rey asks, keeping her eyes closed.

"I don't know," I say. How long does it take for the cuff to work? "Do you feel like you want to die?"

"Yeah," she says. "But not right this second." She pushes herself up, and the motion seems painful. She moves like my abuelita in the year before she died, when every movement was a compromise between determination and pain.

Rey eats the remains of her sandwich, the cold chicken she tore into pieces. *She cannot feel that much like dying if she is hungry,* I think. Maybe, somehow, the cuff is working.

"I have to go," I say, seeing the clock on her shelf. "It's really stinky in here." Rey sniffs at her shirt and coughs. I don't know why, but it makes me laugh.

"I'll leave the door open so there is some fresher air," I say.

Rey's smile vanishes. "I don't want the door open. I don't like being looked at like I'm a freak show."

Freak show? "I don't know what that means."

"Like I'm an object of curiosity. The resident crazy."

"Maybe I can ask Olga for a fan? And maybe we can clean up tomorrow?"

"A fan would be okay, I guess. But you don't have to clean up. The maids will do it. I mean, they would if I let them in." She settles herself back on her bed. I imagine she has spent so much time in her bed that there is a dip in the mattress, exactly her size.

"Do you want me to come back after dinner? You could meet Gabi."

As soon as I say it, I want to unsay it. I don't want Gabi to meet her. Rey would probably curse at her or maybe even throw something if she gets mad. I don't want Gabi to see that.

Rey shakes her head. "No. I'm not ready for other people. I don't even think I'm ready for you." She shakes her head again, as if her own words have surprised her. I pick up the scraps of her meal, the wrapper, and the bag.

"You don't have to do that," Rey says, flopping her head back on her pillow.

"If you leave food out," I say, "you'll get hormigas." When she doesn't respond, I translate. "Ants. You know. Bugs." Her eyes are glassy and I wonder how much of this she'll remember tomorrow.

I turn to leave.

"I'll see you tomorrow, right, Aimee?" she whispers.

"I'll see you tomorrow, Amber."

The next morning, I sit in the kitchen watching Indranie drink coffee relentlessly.

"Why isn't it working?" Indranie arrived before breakfast. She has looked more and more worried as the day has gone on.

"I don't know," I say, even though I know she isn't really asking me. My plan was to go straight to Rey's room with lunch, since food worked so well last time, and see how she was feeling. But now that she has the cuff on, Indranie says I don't have to see her anymore.

"Why?" I ask. It can't have been that easy. It must be a trick. Like dreaming you've done something difficult, only to wake up and find that you haven't done it at all.

"You did well, Marisol. I don't mind telling you, I was worried. I didn't think you or anyone else could get that girl to change her mind. Her father and I had talked to her half a dozen times, and nothing. You stroll in with your chicken sandwich and get it done." She laughs. For some reason, instead of being mad that I asked Traci to get the chicken sandwich, Indranie thinks it's funny.

"I could still see her," I say. "Check on her, see how she is."

"I don't think that's necessary," Indranie says as she slips her phone from her pocket. "When the treatment happens out in the real world, the donor and the receiver would probably never meet. They'd be in the same place for the treatments, but in different rooms. Which reminds me, I have to ask Dr. Deng about transmitting distance. Does distance affect efficacy . . . ?" She trails off, tapping quickly on her phone.

I slump in my chair. I shouldn't feel so unbalanced. I did what I was supposed to do, and I did it well. But instead of feeling satisfied, I feel lost. I hate the idea of not seeing Rey again. Of not sitting next to her and hearing her voice. I'll miss her.

"What's worrying me now is that nothing seems to have

changed." Indranie sighs heavily. "She's had the cuff on for over twelve hours."

"Maybe Rey is feeling better now. I can go and check on her if you want."

Indranie opens the refrigerator and looks inside. She's done this three times already, and each time she closes the door again, taking nothing out.

"The important question is, how are *you* feeling?"

"I'm fine." I shrug. "Maybe we are both fine today."

Indranie sits down, crossing and uncrossing her legs. The tray of Rey's uneaten breakfast sits on the table next to my empty breakfast plate. I was going to wash the dishes, since Olga is away at her sister's house for the day, but Indranie says it's not my job to clean up.

"If the cuff is working correctly . . ." Indranie pauses. "How do I explain this?" she whispers.

"I'm not stupid."

"I know you aren't stupid, Marisol." She reaches across the table to squeeze my hand.

"You know that energy can't be created or destroyed. It doesn't matter what kind of energy, it doesn't cease to exist, it just becomes something else. Sunlight becomes trees, trees become firewood, firewood burns and becomes heat." Her hands wave in the air as she moves through trees, wood, and fire. I don't understand what that has to do with me, but I think it's probably because she's not doing a good job of explaining it.

"Grief, or trauma, is like a kind of energy—a bad kind, a kind you don't want—but it cannot be destroyed, smothered, or stopped. It has to *go* somewhere."

I nod. "It goes to me. I understand, Indranie."

"But it's not *going* to you. That's the problem. And earlier today, when I saw Rey, she was worse than I've ever seen her." She puts her head in her hands, her fingers digging into her thick black hair. "Her father is becoming frantic. I almost called Dr. V." She looks exhausted. Agotada. The calm face I am used to seeing is gone.

"Dr. V doesn't want Rey to wear the cuff," I say, remembering.

Indranie drinks from her mug, but it is already empty. She shakes her shoulders, as if to shake off the tiredness. "Dr. V is paranoid. If this technology works, it could save Rey's life." Indranie clears her throat, and her intensity lessens a bit. "It could save a lot of lives."

I nod. "But first it has to work."

"I'm calling Dr. Derg."

Chapter 15

Later, Gabi and I sit on the lawn in front of the carriage house where Manny is cutting the bushes. We're pretending to help him, but mostly we're enjoying the sunshine.

"Did you see Rey today?" Gabi asks.

"No."

"Are you going to?"

"I don't know. Indranie says it's not a good time. Why?" I ask, putting the shiny cut leaves into a brown bag.

Gabi holds her braids up in one hand. "I want to ask her if she thinks I should cut my hair."

"Why would you ask a stranger that? And anyway, you shouldn't cut your hair," I say firmly.

"I wanted to ask *Rey*. She'll know all about American hairstyles," Gabi says, dropping her braids and putting on work gloves to help me with the leaves. I'm not sure if I feel offended that Gabi doesn't want my advice on her hair, or if this unsettled feeling in my stomach is because I'm jealous that she wants advice from Rey. I shake my head. It's probably indigestion.

"Do you have any homework?" I ask Gabi to change the subject.

"No! There is no homework on weekends."

"Really? At home, we had homework all the time."

"Yes! And you know what else is good about American school?" She punches her fist into the sky like she's at a fútbol match. I have to give her a look so she holds the bag still.

"What?"

"I get a homework pass for being good."

"What does that mean?" Manny has told us, many times, to stop fooling around and let the other gardeners do the work. But it's not good for Gabi to see me sitting down doing nothing.

"It means if I am good in school, I collect points. If I get fifty points, I get a homework pass. That means I don't have to do homework that day." She rubs her nose, and it reminds me of when she was little. "We also get a homework pass when the Oreos win a game."

I fold the bag closed and wipe off my hands. "Now you are being ridiculous," I say, pushing her into a pile of leaves Manny has left behind.

She sits up. "It's true! That's what my teacher said."

"An Oreo is a cookie. It can't win a game. It can't play a game. Your teacher was making fun of you."

Gabi's face becomes stormy. "She was not. She likes me." I see, immediately, that I made a mistake. I didn't mean to say it that way. Before I can explain, a silver car drives through the open gates and parks behind Indranie's car.

Dr. Deng gets out of the car and slowly walks over to us. He's not wearing his lab coat today but has on yet another colorful sweater.

"Hello, Marisol," he says tiredly.

"Hello, Dr. Deng."

He glances at my leg, and the cuff feels a little heavier on my ankle.

"I'm here to look at your cuff. Is there somewhere more private we can go?" His eyes flick to where Manny stands watching us with huge clippers in his hands.

"Gabi, find Indranie. She's probably talking to Mr. Warner in the big house. Tell her that Dr. Deng and I are in our room, okay?"

She nods before running off to main house. She goes around to the back, because no one uses the front door unless they are strangers.

I walk with Dr. Deng to the carriage house. He doesn't try to talk to me, even to ask how the experiment is going. He's making me nervous. I'm not sure if that's because he's so quiet or because I feel like the experiment is failing and he blames me. He follows me upstairs until I open the door to our room and sit on the bed.

Dr. Deng takes the chair from the desk and sits down in front of me. He snaps on a pair of gloves before rolling up my pant leg to show the cuff. Fear spreads through my body like pain. What if I have damaged the cuff somehow? What if I have not been careful enough?

Dr. Deng pushes his thumb against the outside of the cuff, and a light I have never seen turns on.

"I didn't know it did that," I say.

He looks up at me as if to say *There's a lot you don't know.* "It's only an indicator that it is rebooting."

Indranie comes in as Dr. Deng slips the cuff off my leg.

"Dr. Deng, thanks for coming." She moves a purple monkey out of the way to sit down next to me on the bed. I made Gabi leave home without any peluches—not even Oso, the red bear she's slept with since she was born. There just wasn't room.

The purple monkey showed up on our bed the first day. Then a faded yellow teddy bear followed by a glittery pink turtle. I haven't asked, but I think Olga is leaving them for Gabi.

"How's it going?" Indranie asks Dr. Deng.

"The connection is active. And I've been getting signals from this cuff without interruption since I installed it. I've reset it just now, in case it's a glitch, but I can't find anything wrong with this cuff." Dr. Deng pours powder onto my ankle, smoothing it onto my skin until my ankle is pale and white, like it belongs to someone else.

"Make sure you put powder on at least twice a day. You don't want to damage the skin under the cuff," he tells me, clicking the cuff back into place.

Dr. Deng turns to Indranie. "You said the sister cuff was activated yesterday?"

Indranie nods.

"Was it done correctly?" He looks at me, and my face gets hot. Maybe I did something wrong when I put the cuff on Rey. I followed the directions Indranie gave me. And anyway, it wasn't hard. Press the button, put on the cuff. Idiotproof, Indranie said.

"Yes, it was perfect," Indranie says, smiling at me, as if to make up for Dr. Deng's rudeness.

He stands up. "I'll go check on the other one," he says, peeling off the blue gloves and putting them into the little trash can.

"Rey," I say. "Her name is Rey."

Dr. Deng nods absently.

"I'll take you over," Indranie says. She walks Dr. Deng out, then turns back to me. "Don't worry, okay? Try to have fun. It's Friday."

"Thunder! Thunder!" Gabi dances around the living room singing a song I've never heard. All I know is that it's about thunder.

"Please stop, Gabriela," I say. I pull one of the many white pillows on the sofa onto my lap. My stomach hurts, my head hurts, and I'm worried. I don't want to sit here and watch TV with people dancing, or worse, some of the weirder kid shows Gabi loves, like the one with a snake that eats hot sauce and rides una motocicleta.

"Niñas," Manny calls from the door. Manny and Olga are going out to dinner. They invited us to go with them, but I said no, even though I know Gabi would like to go out somewhere. I'm bored and Gabi is bored, and nothing is working the way I'd hoped, so I'm in a bad mood.

They aren't dressed up for dinner: Manny is wearing the same shirt he cut the bushes in and Olga is wearing a yellow T-shirt with a bear on it, and the bear is driving a bus. I have never seen a grown-up, especially una anciana, wear clothes like this.

"Pórtense bien," Manny begins before Olga hits him with her elbow and he switches to English. "Be good. We will be back at ten p.m. Are you sure you don't want to come with us?"

Gabi jumps up and runs toward the entryway, but I scramble after her. "No, gracias," I say. "Have a good time!"

I don't even get the chance to close the door behind them before Gabi smacks me on the shoulder.

"Why did you say we didn't want to go?"

"Because I don't want to go." I know I'm being unfair. There's no reason Gabi can't go with Olga and Manny, except that I want her here with *me*. I move to get past her, but she blocks me.

"But I do! I'm bored, Sol."

I try to sneak under her arm, but she pushes me away. "Watch TV."

"I don't want to."

"Read a book," I say between clenched teeth.

"I want to have fun!" She stomps her foot.

I try not to lose my temper with Gabi. I remember what it felt like when Papá would lose his temper after a bad night of playing cards. He'd prowl around the room like a tiger, looking for someone to yell at or someone to hit. I'd look at Pablo, to make sure he was okay. He would be looking back at me. *We're okay,* the look would say.

"¡Púchica, Gabi! Look at where you are! This whole place is made for having fun. You're becoming a spoiled brat."

Gabi's face is shocked, and mine must look the same, because I didn't mean to yell at her.

"Is this a family thing I shouldn't be hearing? I can cover my ears."

Gabi and I turn around. Rey stands at the door wearing a pair of loose pants that hang low on her hips and a gray shirt that says WORLD'S OKAYEST SISTER.

I'm so surprised, I'm speechless.

"If you're bored, why don't you come hang out with me?" She looks different, almost unrecognizable. Her face is luminous, like the reflecting pool when it captures the sky. *She looks happy,* I think.

My head hurts, and I don't want to go anywhere.

But I don't know how to say no to that happy face.

Rey leads us to the main house through the gardens. Gabi chats with her, using her arms to act out the robot vacuum commercial again. I hang back a little, trying to think. Rey seems so different tonight. Her smile is alive and when Gabi zooms in circles around her, Rey's laugh is pure sunshine. Maybe the cuff is starting to work.

Rey looks back at me, eyebrows raised, and winks. Luckily, it's starting to get dark, because I don't want her to see my reddening face.

"First, we raid the kitchen," she says once we're in the main house. "Put out your arms, Gabi. No, bigger, like a big basket." Rey pulls bags of potato chips and pretzels out of the cabinets and puts them into Gabi's arms until there's no more she can carry.

"Next!"

I hold out my arms and she gently bends them at the elbow, like I'm a doll. "Like *una canasta*," she says.

"You speak Spanish?" I ask, surprised.

Rey grabs bags of snacks from a drawer and piles them into my arms. "Nah. I took German. Mostly to piss off my dad, who wanted me to take Mandarin."

"So how did you know how to say *basket*?"

"I've been googling some things," she says mysteriously.

This Rey is *so* different. She isn't the hurt animal I saw yesterday, and she isn't the "zombie" I saw the day before.

"Did Dr. V give you another medicine?" I ask.

"Nope. High on life." She grins. She grabs the soda and some plastic cups, then we follow her through the house until I'm a little lost.

"This is the TV room," she says.

It's not a TV room; it's a room full of TVs. There are screens on a desk in the corner and a gigantic TV on the wall, the same size as the screen in our local movie theater. On either side of the enormous white couch are tables with more screens.

"Why do you need so many TVs?" I ask as I drop the snacks onto the side table. Rey snatches up a bag of Doritos, squeezing it until it pops open.

"We don't need them. No one even uses this room anymore. My dad used to have business meetings here sometimes. Whenever they were working on a new drug that seemed like it might be a moneymaker, Dad would bring backers here to impress them."

"TVs impress them?" Gabi says.

"Some people, right?" Rey points to a door at the back of the room. "There's an honest-to-Christ projection room in there for 35mm film. When we were little, Dad would get Disney to send him movies before they hit the theaters. Then we got a digital projector." She sits in the corner of the couch and pats the place next to her, an invitation to sit. Gabi's waiting for me to sit first. And my legs are glued to the floor.

"Then Mom split and family movie night died a gruesome death. Now we have Netflix." Rey places the bag of Doritos on her lap before looking at us with raised eyebrows. "Guys, those snacks won't eat themselves."

Gabi takes a bag of popcorn and sits next to Rey. I pour everyone a cup of orange soda, like I am the host, and sit next to Gabi. I don't know why I'm so nervous. I spent hours alone with Rey watching TV. Now that Gabi is here, I should be more comfortable. Still, I look anywhere else but at Rey.

"What should we watch?" Rey asks.

"*Cedar Hollow*?" I say.

"Ugh, not again with that show!" Gabi moans.

"Not a fan of Amber and Aimee? I'm insulted," Rey says.

"It's only that Sol watches that over and over and over, and it's so boring sometimes."

Rey looks over Gabi's head to me. "Aimee, I thought you said your sister was cool."

"I thought so, Amber." I shake my head sadly. "I guess she's not."

Gabi rolls her eyes. "Son bayuncas, you know?"

Rey's eyes are full of laughter. I thought they were brown, but now I think they might be a very dark blue. I can't look away fast enough.

"Is your sister calling me a vegetable?"

"She's calling you silly."

"I'm calling both of you silly. And weirdos."

Rey settles back into the couch. It's such a bright, clean white, and Rey is leaving orange dust from the Doritos on the armrest. I cringe, thinking of Olga's face when she sees it.

"Well, despite your lack of taste, Gabi, we won't subject you to the masterpiece that is *Cedar Hollow*. No DVD player on this TV. And since it's Canadian, you can't legally stream it in the States."

I sit up very straight, stunned. "It's Canadian?"

"Yeah, of course. You couldn't tell from the accents and the goofy clothes?"

Rey doesn't wait for my answer, which is good because I don't know how to answer. *Cedar Hollow* was how I learned about America. And it wasn't even American.

Rey clicks the remote, jumping from image to image until she lands on a picture of three men in front of an exploding car.

"WAIT!" Gabi shrieks. "That's the car guys!"

I don't know what that means, but Gabi is nearly jumping off the sofa, she's so excited. Rey selects the TV show, and we are soon watching three old men race in cars and sometimes crash them.

I'm happy Gabi is having a great time, but I'm so aware of Rey's every move and every smile that I barely notice when the show is over. The next episode starts a few seconds later. Gabi leans against me, like she used to, and I am calm.

"Do we wake her up? She's way too heavy to carry, right?" Rey says.

Gabi is asleep, her head tilted back on the couch and her mouth open.

"She probably weighs as much as you do. I can't carry her anymore."

"Are you calling me fat?"

"I'm not calling you anything. Don't say things for me."

Rey bounces her head softly against the back of the sofa. "You mean, don't put words in your mouth?"

"Yes, that's what I mean."

"You're right. I'd much rather hear your own words." She smiles.

Está jugando, I think. She's playing. "You are so different now that you have the cuff on."

"I'm not different," Rey says sharply. "This is what I'm always like."

"Oh. Good. And you feel okay?"

"Yeah. Feel fine. Awesome."

Her eyes close, and the half smile on her lips relaxes. Maybe she'll fall asleep too, and I'll have to leave them both here, or I'll get some blankets and sleep here too. It's a nice idea, the three of us sleeping on this soft, wide sofa. But I know Manny and Olga would be worried if they couldn't find us.

"We should go." I reach over to Gabi to shake her awake. Rey grabs my hand, startling me.

"Wait. Not yet. Um. I had a question." She lets my hand drop. I sit back, waiting. But she doesn't speak.

"What's your question?"

She licks her lips. It makes me nervous, thinking that her question might be one I don't want to answer.

"Um. What does *que onda* mean?"

I frown. "It's like 'what's up.' "

"Yeah, that's what Google said. I wasn't sure, though. It also said that *onda* means *wave*. Google is sometimes shit at translations."

"No, that is correct—it means both things. It's an . . ." I search for the English word, but I don't find it. "It's like a saying, like when you say you are on your high horse, but you aren't on a horse at all." I close my mouth, feeling like I'm saying nonsense.

The shine in Rey's eyes becomes glassy, like she was the first day, staring off at I don't know what. Maybe it just takes time for the cuff to work properly.

"I'm glad the cuff is working," I say to fill the awkward silence.

"Oh, yeah," she drawls. "It's for sure working. I just, I'm just really tired now." She leans back into the sofa, staring at the frozen image of the three men and the exploding car.

I wake Gabi up, and just like when she'd fall asleep in the

back of a coyote's truck, she wakes up completely knowing where she is, as if she were only resting her eyes.

"Did the BMW win?"

"I think so," Rey says dreamily. "The BMW is the one with the four wheels, right?"

Gabi starts to explain, in exhausting detail, what kind of car she's talking about. Before she can put Rey totally to sleep, I tell her to help me clean up.

"Leave it," Rey says. "The maids will do it."

Gabi and I exchange a look. It's not my business, but I can't help asking, "Who are these maids?"

Rey's face creases into a look of total confusion. "I don't know their names. They usually come when I'm not here." She closes her eyes, slipping into sleep. Gabi helps me pick up the snacks and cups and take them to the kitchen.

Gabi and I walk across the garden back to the carriage house.

"I *like* Rey." Gabi says it like it's a challenge.

"Okay."

"Don't you like her?"

"Sometimes."

Not now. I'm angrier than I should be. If Rey doesn't remember the maids who invisibly work for her, why should that bother me? I *will* be happy—I will *make* myself be happy. The experiment is finally starting to work, and that means we are only a month away from being safe. Nothing is more important.

Chapter 16

Indranie pulls up the leg of my piyamas. "It's on right. And Dr. Deng says it's transmitting fine. I don't understand." She frowns at me. I woke up with the same headache I had last night. Other than that, I feel fine. And that is what's making Indranie frown. I'm not having any of the symptoms I am supposed to have.

"But Rey is feeling better," I say. "That proves the cuff is working."

"How do you know how Rey is feeling?"

I lower my gaze. "I saw her last night. She came over to meet Gabi."

Indranie sighs heavily. It's Saturday, but she's still wearing a suit. Either she's been wearing the same suit every day I've seen her, or she has lots of suits in the same gray color.

"I don't think it's a good idea to see her anymore, Marisol."

"That's fine." I'm still angry at Rey, but for no good reason. If I'm honest, I'm upset that she didn't know the names of the maids who clean her house. When all this is over, she'll forget my name too, barely remembering the girl who cleaned up her sorrow.

"Have you and Gabi got any plans today?"

"Gabi's going over to a friend's house. A girl from school."

"That's great! What about you?"

I haven't thought about it. "Maybe I'll swim. Or read."

"That sounds like a perfect day to me." She stands, straightening her suit jacket. "I have to run over to Dr. Deng's lab for some data, but I'll be back tonight."

"Won't your boss be upset that you're spending so much time with us?" Now I'm like Gabi, asking questions that are not my business. But it's strange how Indranie is always here.

She gives me a slightly embarrassed smile. "I'm helping Scott—Mr. Warner. I need to be where you and Rey are."

"But it's personal, right, not work?" I remember Rey saying, *That woman tries too damn hard.* Even though Indranie doesn't seem to sleep here, she's here early and stays late. That sounds personal to me.

"I should go. No rest for the wicked," she says, but she doesn't leave.

Idiom. That's the word I was trying to think of last night. "No rest for the wicked" es un dicho—it doesn't mean that Indranie is not resting or wicked. I wish I'd remembered *idiom* before I told Rey about a person on a high horse.

"You look deep in thought. You okay?" Indranie asks.

"Why does Dr. V call you *Agent* Patel?" If I'm asking questions, I might as well keep going.

"Oh. Well, that was my unofficial title when I was with USCIS. Dr. V uses it as kind of a joke. I'm not at Homeland Security anymore."

"What's U-S-C-I-S?" I ask, saying the letters carefully.

"United States Citizenship and Immigration Services. We processed asylum cases."

"You gave people asylum? Like what Gabi and I want? That's what you used to do?"

"No, actually, I was an analyst. I helped the asylum officers with research."

"But you don't work there anymore?"

"No."

"If you don't work there anymore, how can you help us?"

Indranie sits back down on the bed. "I don't want you to worry about that. I have a lot of friends at USCIS, and I know how the system works. I can get you and Gabi asylum status." She sounds convincing, one hundred percent sure of herself.

Sometimes, coyotes would tell people that the trip to the United States would take two or three days. That it would be like a pleasant bus ride. That they would stop at hotels and sleep in clean, warm beds. But this was only a story to convince people to pay the money, to take the chance. Tía Rosa told us the truth. She didn't want us to be fooled. She'd talked to the people who had been on the journey before, the ones who had made it all the way to Mexico, or maybe even just miles from the US border, before getting caught and sent back. But the ones who hadn't heard the stories, or didn't want to believe them, got a nasty surprise on the seventh, eighth day on the road. On the ten-mile walk through the selva to avoid checkpoints. Those people were crédulos. They let their hope get the best of their judgment. If they were very unlucky, their misguided belief would lead to death. Too much belief is a dangerous thing. I don't know if Indranie is una crédula, or if I am, for trusting her. I only know that whatever I am told, my path is the same.

Finally, after drinking a strong cafecito that Olga makes for me, my headache eases.

I'm lazy today but also uncomfortable, like there is an itch I can't reach. Manny drove Gabi to Juliette's house and I miss her.

I sit at the desk in our bedroom with a copy of *Frankenstein* and a sheet of paper. In Mr. Rosen's library, I would take five or more books at a time, laying them on the floor. I liked to open the same books in English and in Spanish and work out how they were translated differently, making notes when I found something funny or unusual. Mr. Rosen would ask me if I was done ransacking the place, but he was only teasing me.

I push away the thought of the Rosens, of how much we owe them and how we won't ever see them again. I try to compare *Frankenstein* in English to how I remember it in Spanish. But I can't concentrate.

"Hey."

I turn to see Rey in the doorway. That's the second time she's appeared unexpectedly, the second time that I have to wonder which Rey is standing in front of me. She's wearing a puffy pink dress, like for a quinceañera, but it hangs on her, a little too large. Her legs are white as chalk beneath her dress, and her slouchy boots are wide enough to cover the cuff on her ankle. On her head is a sparkly flower headband, like una corona.

"Hello," I answer coolly.

"Where's Gabi?"

"She's out with a friend."

"She asked me about haircuts. I downloaded some cute pics from *Short Hair Style Guide*." Rey holds out her phone to show me the images, but I turn back to my book.

"Gabi will be home in a few hours. You can show her then."

She hovers at the door. "Are you pissed at me?"

"No. Of course not. Why should I be?" I don't see any advantage to being honest.

"I don't really remember too much about last night. I was so tired. I sort of zonked out, you know?"

"I saw."

"Did I say something rude? I do that sometimes. I'm sorry if I did." She sounds genuinely sorry.

I hesitate. It's not even something I should care about. It's only that she was thoughtless, and why should that matter to me? "No, you were fine. Everything is fine."

She smiles hugely and holds up a set of keys. "Does that mean you'll go for a drive with me?"

"Now?"

"Yes, now, of course now—I'm all dressed up for a reason."

"Are you going somewhere fancy?"

"You mean, 'Are *we* going somewhere fancy?' Well, you could say that," she says, pretending to pat her hair into place. "But I wouldn't."

"You are confusing," I say, this time choosing to be honest. Still, I get up and put on my shoes and a light jacket. "Are you allowed to drive?" I don't know what Rey is allowed to do, but I know that if I had tried to fly off a balcony, Mamá would have locked me in her bedroom.

"I am legally allowed to drive, and no one has told me, explicitly, not to go anywhere."

"Sounds like excuses."

"Well, if you come with me, you can make sure I'm safe and sound." She smiles widely, all her teeth perfect pearls.

"I don't need to change clothes? You're sure?"

"You look amazing," Rey says.

I don't bother looking in the mirror for confirmation. I know my plain face will stare back at me like it always does. I follow Rey to the driveway. Indranie's car is gone.

"Where's your father?" I ask. Rey unlocks the car doors, and I get in the passenger seat.

"Probably joined at the hip with Indranie."

"They work together?"

"They do everything together."

We sit in the car for a moment, the keys on Rey's lap of pink fluffy lace. She's gripping the steering wheel hard. I wait.

"Sorry. Just waiting for all the lights to come on." I don't understand what this means, but I'm guessing it's an idiom. Unless she's waiting for real lights to come on? I look out the window for lights. It's pringando, raining a little, but not dark enough yet for streetlights.

With a deep breath, Rey turns on the car.

"Do you know how to drive?" she asks.

I don't even know what I'm doing here. I shake my head.

"Okay. I'm just asking. I know how to drive."

I cringe as Rey moves the car through the house gates, coming too close to the brick on my side. I feel the scrape of metal and brick in my back teeth.

"Dr. V only gives me shit to make me numb. Pixie sent me something better. Makes all the lights come on in my brain, you know?"

I don't know. "Who is Pixie?"

"She's amazing. You'll meet her later."

I don't know where she's taking me, who her friends are, and even if Rey is as okay as she says she is. But there's a clearness in her that I've not seen before, like something dirty has been washed off her face. If I am honest, at least to myself, I'm in this car because I want to see more of this Rey.

"Where are we going?" I ask.

"Where aren't we going? *That's* the question." Rey bites her lip as she pulls the car onto the main road.

"All right. Where aren't we going?"

"No, stupid, it's a rhetorical question."

"I'm not stupid," I say. When people hear an accent, or when you pick a slightly wrong word, suddenly they think you're stupid. It happened so much, in Texas and then in Pennsylvania, that I get defensive.

"Sorry. My tongue has a mind of its own." She laughs nervously.

I don't respond.

"I mean, obviously you aren't stupid. You're reading Riley's books, so you can read at least two languages. That's smart." She sounds suddenly exhausted. "I don't know why I say stupid things."

"I say the wrong things all the time. Welcome to the club."

She turns her brilliant smile on me, and it lingers until I look away. The farther we get from Rey's house, the happier she becomes. I can understand it. The place that is un refugio for Gabi and me, a place where we can sleep without worry of being attacked, that same place has been a golden cage for Rey. Today, she is escaping her prison.

Rey touches a button on her phone, and the car radio lights up. Music starts to play and the words *Perfume Genius* and *Slip Away* show on the screen.

"Do you like this song?" Rey asks.

"I don't know." I shrug. "It's okay?" Sometimes, we would

hear popular music from the United States, but mostly we'd listen to our own music, local bandas who play music that everyone can dance to. Música alegre, happy music.

Rey sings along. "Don't look back, I want to break free. If you'll never see 'em coming, you'll never have to hide."

That seems backward to me. Like when you're little and think closing your eyes will keep others from seeing you. But the music bursts with hopefulness, starting slow, the beat building into an explosion of sound. It makes me want to dance. It makes me wish the words were true.

She drives carefully, not speeding and not hitting anything. As she sings along to the radio, I feel like I'm in a dream, waiting to see what vision my mind comes up with next. Rey said we'd go to one place, then come right back, before Manny picks Gabi up from her friend's house, before anyone notices we're gone. I'm sure we're doing something that someone will be upset about. And yet, here I sit, next to her, inviting La Mala Suerte to come and visit.

We drive to a city. Not a huge city, like Washington, but not a little town either. Something in between. We pull into a parking lot where a low building sits in the middle like an island. There is no sign outside that I can see, and no windows.

"Is it open?" I ask.

"Archetype is always open," Rey says. She pulls on a leather jacket—the one she wore in the garden, when I mistook her for a boy. The one that belonged to her brother.

"Arquetipo," I mutter as Rey opens a glass door, then pulls back a thick velvet curtain the color of café con leche.

"*Ar-que-tipo,*" Rey repeats. "So that's *archetype* in Spanish?"
I nod.

"What does *archetype* mean?" she asks.

"You're kidding! You don't know?"

"Are you calling me stupid?" I can't tell if she's serious or not. Her lips twitch. She's not serious.

"I would never do such a thing."

"So, Professor Morales, tell me what *archetype* means. And do it now, before someone asks me to define it."

"It means *the thing*. You know, like, *the thing itself.*"

"So, you're the archetypal Marisol Morales—is that right?"

"I guess I am."

"There couldn't be another." She walks through the entrance, leaving me on my own to wonder at her words. Between the cold of the glass door and the warmth I feel coming from inside, I have the urge to run, like I did in the mall. Because something's changing, I can tell that much, even if I don't know what it is or if it's para bien o para mal. I walk through the curtain. There's nothing to run from. I'm being ridiculous.

# Chapter 17

I could never have expected what is inside the short, rectangular building. Because inside is an alien world. Tables rise out of the earth-colored floor, surrounded by cave-like seating carved out of the walls, as if shaped by a giant hand from tierra. In some little spaces, no more than huecos, couples sit close around flickering candles. A few tables are set high up, as high as mango trees, and must be reached by steps set into the walls. Vines and shapes like snakes come out of the floor and ceiling.

No one looks our way as a woman in a red dress leads us to a table. "Watch your step," she says. "The floor is a little uneven."

"Can we have the one under the skylight?" Rey asks.

The woman nods and leads us further into a maze of rooms, all warm and curved and the color of crema.

When we get to our table, it's in the center of a room directly under a glowing glass light that, if it wasn't raining, I might think really did reflect the sun's light. We climb up two steps to reach a little ledge where we can stand while moving ourselves into our seats. The woman in the red dress stretches to hand us menus.

"Your server will be right with you. Enjoy!" I cannot imagine how the waiters will even reach us with our drinks.

"It looks like the inside of an egg," I say, sliding into the booth, which has the smooth rounded shape of an eggshell. Rey sits next to me, close in the small space. There are soft white pillows to sit on.

"Pixie says I like this place because it's like going back to the womb. That's just Pixie being gross," Rey says.

"Who is Pixie?" I ask.

"She's my friend. She works here." Rey cranes her head to look around the restaurant. "She'll appear eventually. In the meantime, you should tell me everything about yourself."

I laugh. "Everything?"

"Well, I already know you have an awesome little sister. That you're obsessed with *Cedar Hollow* and that you had to leave your home in El Salvador."

"Yes. We had to leave."

"Will you ever go back?"

I'm confused by the way she asks. As if I have a choice in staying or going. "I want to stay here. If they'll let me."

"What do you mean, if they let you?" Rey leans close to me, her expression intense.

"Indranie says she'll be able to get green cards for us. And for my mamá. Just as soon as the experiment is over."

"If anyone can do it, it's Indranie," Rey says firmly. "She's got governmental superpowers, or at least that's what Dad thinks."

A pretty blond girl with very pale green eyes jumps up to our table.

"Speak of the devil and the devil appears," Rey says lightly. But the blond girl's face looks so angry that I don't think she likes the joke.

She leaps at Rey, hugging her so hard she almost pulls her out of the booth. Then the pretty blond, who must be Pixie, bursts into tears.

"I'm so sorry," she cries.

"Okay," Rey says, putting her arms around the girl, holding on as if her life depended on it. "Don't, please don't cry. I am barely keeping it together as it is." Rey pushes her hip against mine, and I move farther down the half-circle.

Pixie sits next to Rey and wipes her tears with her hands.

"I'm so sorry, Rey. We miss you. At school. Everyone is so—"

"Sorry. I know. Everyone is so sorry," Rey says wearily. Some of the spark in her face has faded. I blame Pixie, though I know that is wrong.

The girl shakes her head as if to clear it. She takes a deep breath. "Okay, so . . ." She gives me an empty smile. "Who's your little friend?"

Archetype is full of small spaces where you can whisper, laugh, and gossip. The three people at the table in front of us, also high up, are taking photos of themselves with their phones. Except for the many candles on every table and the flash from the autofotos, the room is dark. Only our table, higher up and under the "skylight," has light enough to read the menus.

Pixie and Rey ignore the menus and me. As soon as Pixie asked "Who's your little friend?" she went on to describe something funny that Rey's friends did, without waiting to hear who I am.

Little friend. Pixie's words sting. I sit up as tall as I can and focus on the menu. I'm convinced some of these words are not in English. Cocodemon? Zelorella? Are these people's names? But the descriptions are pretty clear. Everything is ice cream and dessert. And everything is ten dollars or more.

"Then Dave sent it to me thinking he was sending it to you, and I did not hesitate to screenshot that crap and blanket the fucking planet with it. He deserves it for being so smugly Dave-ish all the time."

I watch Pixie and Rey and I wish I could've made Rey laugh like that. It would mean that I was doing my job well, that I was helping her get past her grief.

"You are a cruel taskmistress," Rey says.

"Deserves. It." Pixie looks down at Rey's puffy pink dress. "What in the holy hell are you wearing?"

Rey's smile falls and her hand goes to the flower band in her hair.

"I wanted to get dressed up." She glances at me, then away. "I've been slacking off. Got to keep up appearances." She says it like it's a joke, but I don't think it is.

"Well, you look like a zombie prom queen, and not in a good way," Pixie says. "You know I say that with love, right?"

"What?" Rey says, looking away. "I stopped listening to you, like, five minutes ago."

Pixie leans into Rey, giving her a hug I don't think Rey really wants. "Love you like the sister I never had," Pixie says. Her eyes turn to me, and the look she gives goes from confusion to disdain.

Rey puts her hand on my shoulder. "Pixie, this is Marisol, the girl I told you about. She's helping me be sane."

"That's really not possible," Pixie says. "Hello, Marisol."

"Hi," I say. We are silent for a minute more than is comfortable before Pixie takes out her phone and slides her thumb along it, the light from the phone bright blue on her face.

"In my official capacity as underpaid wench in this establishment, let me offer to get you some cloudy tap water to start—and ask if you have any questions about the menu." Pixie tilts her head toward me.

"What's butterscotch?" I ask. "Is it like caramel?"

Rey answers. "Yeah, a little. It's sort of better. Hey, did I tell you this is Pixie?" she says, looping her arm through her friend's arm. "Pixie, this is Marisol, the one I told you about."

I glance at Rey to see if she's kidding around, or if something is wrong. But she looks fine, happy and relaxed.

"Yeah, I heard. She's keeping you sane," Pixie says. "Any friend of Reyanne's is a friend of mine." She looks bored, insincera when she says it.

"Thanks." The more Pixie talks, the less I talk. I'm afraid I'll say the wrong thing, use the wrong English words.

"So. What can I get you?" Pixie asks.

I hesitate. I have Mrs. Rosen's hundred-dollar bill in my wallet, but it seems too wasteful to spend even a tenth of it on ice cream. I hesitate so long that I feel my face getting warm.

"I'll have my usual with extra fudge and extra peanut butter sauce and extra—"

"Shut up already—I know all your extras," Pixie says to Rey. She makes a note on her phone, then looks at me expectantly.

"I, uh."

"What do you like?" Rey asks, looking over my shoulder at my menu when she already has her own menu open in front of her.

"She likes vanilla," Pixie says. "Bet you anything."

"I hate vanilla," I say, because I want to prove Pixie wrong. "I'll have the chocolate one with butterscotch. Extra butterscotch."

"See?" Rey grins. "She's extra just like me."

"Got it. Two extra queens." Pixie jumps down to the floor, graceful as a dancer, and walks away.

"She's great, isn't she?" Rey murmurs.

"I like the little bows in her hair." At least I found something positive to say.

"She was Riley's girlfriend," Rey says, keeping her eyes closed. I wonder what she is trying not to see in this room. Or if it is the opposite, that she is seeing something behind her closed eyes that she wants to hold on to.

"Oh," I say awkwardly.

Rey opens her eyes and smiles sadly. "It was years ago. But we became friends even though he broke her heart. It wasn't her fault. Riley wasn't good at being with one person, you know?"

"What was your brother like?" I ask. Then I'm horrified to have asked about Riley when Rey was feeling so much better. "I'm sorry. Never mind. I was being stupid," I say.

"You're the smart one, remember? Professor Marisol Morales?" Rey smiles. "It's okay. The only thing I'm sick of hearing is 'I'm sorry.' I'm not sick of talking about Riley."

Rey leans into the curved back of our cuevita with a sigh.

"My brother was wild. He was born a whole eight minutes before me, and I have been trying to catch up with him ever since. That's what my mom always said."

Rey keeps her gaze on the skylight, seeing images there that I can't guess at.

"Mom came for Riley's funeral and left the same afternoon. She said she couldn't bear the pain. Ha. Right? Ha fucking ha." She closes her eyes again, the same soft smile on her face. I feel foolish for thinking this was the real Rey. She is only a new kind of zombie.

"What happened to your brother?" she asks, taking me out of my self-pitying thoughts.

"Pablo?"

"Indranie only said you had a brother who died. Is that him?"

"Yes."

Rey shifts her body toward me. "Yeah. I'm not going to say 'I'm sorry.' Fucking hate when people say it to me. But you know."

I nod.

"What was he like? Was he older?"

"He was." In my mind, I review the long story of Pablo and me—turning over every memory like stones in the ground. Some memories are sweet—swimming in the lake by Abuela's house, letting the hot air dry us in the summer. Running to the store to get milk for the baby—when Gabi was that baby—so we wouldn't have to listen to her wail. Some memories are sharp enough to make me bleed.

"He was my best friend for a while. But we grew far away from each other."

I press my hands together under the table, waiting for her to ask the details of Pablo's death—like everyone does. Como buitres. Vultures. But she doesn't.

"When Riley was being a total dick—which, believe me, happened more than I liked—I'd remember what it was like when we were little. And then," she lowers her voice like she's going to tell me a secret, "I'd imagine us as adults, like me with an incredible job somewhere and an apartment filled with sunlight and a cute dog—finally, because Dad's allergic—and I'd imagine Riley with, like, more facial hair." She giggles. "And I gave him a briefcase too, which is so dumb, but whatever. And we'd be all right. All the bad shit would be in the past, and we'd be best friends again."

A tear leaks out of her eye, though her face is curiously blank.

I touch my hand softly to hers, under the table, to tell her it's okay. She grabs on to me. I think, *I am pulling her out of a deep well.*

Rey wipes the tear away when a tall man in a skirt comes by with a tray of drinks and desserts. It's much more than we ordered, a drink for each of us and heaping bowls of ice cream, crema, butterscotch, and chocolate sauce.

"Pixie does it again," Rey says with a grin. "She never lets me pay for anything and always overcompensates."

"You like?" Pixie says, stepping up to the table to check on us.

"Yes. It's too much. Thank you," I say.

"You're fine." She waves my thanks away. "That is all I've got time for today, Rey-Rey. Got to serve the unwashed masses."

"You love unwashed. And masses."

Pixie salutes with her middle finger as she jumps down from the step and disappears into the cavernous restaurant.

"She's great, isn't she?" Rey says again.

I sip at my cold coffee-and-cinnamon drink instead of answering.

Rey takes a tiny bite from her bowl heaped with ice cream and peanut butter sauce, and frowns.

"Why don't we go home now?" I say.

"We have to finish all these desserts. It would be rude not to," Rey says, stabbing her spoon repeatedly into her dessert.

"Okay. But you aren't even eating." She holds her spoon over her bowl of ice cream and a strange expression crosses her face.

"My stomach is full of butterflies," she says.

I think about that idiom. "Because you are nervous?"

"Because I ate butterflies," she says, and bursts into laughter.

Her laugh turns into a cough. She takes a sip of water, her hand shaking as she puts the glass down.

"I think the butterflies want me to go to the bathroom." Her expression turns sharp and uncomfortable.

"Are you okay?"

Rey tries to climb down from our table without falling.

I help her down from the booth, then hurry to follow, as she weaves between waiters and customers.

The bathroom is at the very back of the restaurant. Behind a swinging gray door, just like the one at the detention center, I hear the sound of plates and voices from the kitchen. Rey stumbles to the door at the end of a dark hallway. She hunches over, hands out to keep from falling.

"Rey?"

She shakes her head as she goes through the door with a question mark on it. Nowhere on the door does it say Damas or Caballeros or men or women or anything. I trust Rey knows where she is going and follow her in.

The bathroom is large with every surface—sinks, walls, and doors—painted baby pink. At the end of a long counter of sinks, against a wall covered with mirrors, two girls kiss.

I can see my own face, full of shock and disbelief, reflected in the mirror. One girl is a little on the short side, like me, wearing jeans and a sweater the same pink as the tiles. She pulls the girl she's kissing impossibly close. The other girl is tall with long black hair swinging in a braid. I cannot stop staring at them. They will yell at me when they catch me, when they see me looking at them like a spy, como una mirona. But I can't stop.

From a stall, I hear the sound of vomiting. The girls stop kissing, and the one in the pink sweater peeks around the taller girl and catches my eye. If I could disappear, I would. I almost run out. But a small choking sound from Rey draws me to her. I kneel down next to her in the tiny space. Her whole body trembles. I pull papel from the dispenser and help her wipe her mouth.

"Are you okay?" I ask. *Always, always with the stupid questions, Marisol.* That is Pablo's voice in my head, I realize.

"I threw up the butterflies," she cries.

I help Rey stand and walk to the sink. The tall girl with the braid wets a paper towel and hands it to me.

"Is she okay?" she asks, though clearly Rey is not okay. Rey leans heavily against the sink, against me. I can feel her shake as if with terrible cold.

"Want me to call someone?" the girl in the pink sweater asks.

"No, uh, I don't think her father would like that." The girls exchange looks in the mirror.

Rey's pale skin looks gray. She's sweating even though she's cold to the touch.

"Do you know the girl who works here? With the little bows in her hair?" I swallow my pride. "Her name is Pixie. Can you ask her to come and help?"

Chapter 18

Though I don't like her—for giving Rey poison, for calling me a "little friend," for knowing more about Rey than I do, and, oh yes, for giving us free ice cream—I am happy Pixie can drive. Otherwise, I don't know how we would get home.

I sit in the back of Pixie's car, Rey's sweaty head in my lap, wiping away her tears with my sleeve. I should have brought papel from the bathroom, but I didn't think of it.

"How you doing back there, Rey-Rey?" Pixie calls. Rey doesn't speak, making a thumbs-up sign instead. But she hasn't stopped crying since the bathroom.

Indranie's car is still gone. I don't know if that means she came back and left again, or if she hasn't come back yet. It felt like an eternity in Archetype, as if it had to be the middle of the night. But it's barely seven o'clock and not yet dark. I check the phone Indranie gave me. If she had found us missing, she would have called. There is no message, no missed calls.

Pixie follows me as I help Rey into the main house and upstairs into her room. Everything has been cleaned up. The floor is clear and all the clothes have been put away. I suppose that she finally let "the maids" do their job.

I help Rey take off her brother's jacket, then I put it on the chair and lay her on her bed. Pixie stands by the door, arms crossed and face worried but useless because either she can't or won't help.

Rey's eyes open a little. "At least I didn't get puke in my hair," she says weakly.

"Yes, very smart. We should all cut our hair so short to avoid puke." My smile dims. "Do you want me to call Indranie? Or your dad?"

She shakes her head slowly. "Fuck no. I've had enough of her, and my dad." She turns onto her side. "Just let me sleep."

I get a washcloth from the bathroom with a little soap and water on it. I wipe traces of vomit and tears from Rey's face.

Pixie watches, making me uncomfortable. I wring out the towel in the bathroom, and wet it again with cold water. When I come back into the room, Pixie has put Riley's leather jacket on.

"Please take that off," I say, unable to hide the anger in my voice.

"What?" She's startled, as if a piece of furniture has started to talk.

"Take that off. Please. It's Rey's."

"I know whose it is. I used to wear it." Her voice is unfriendly. But so is mine.

"In any case, it doesn't belong to you now. She'll wake up and wonder where it is. She'll be upset."

I want Pixie to take it off, now. Before the jacket smells more of her than Riley. Before she makes the jacket hers again.

Pixie slips it off slowly, then drops it onto the floor, where it lands in a stiff heap. I want to pick it up, to drape it over the chair again. I hate that it is so, so *disrespected*.

I look over at Rey. Her eyes are closed. Maybe I don't have to call anyone. Maybe it will be all right.

"I know what you are," Pixie says. She walks up to me, her angry face close to mine. "Rey told me everything." She sweeps her foot against my ankle, tapping the cuff under my jeans.

"You're nothing more than an indentured servant." She points her finger at me, and I fight to keep looking into her eyes when all I want to do is look away. "A glorified maid. A service *dog*."

It has been a long time since someone made me so angry that I forget who I am, who I am protecting. But this girl is digging up all my hidden anger.

I take a step back. "You should go before Mr. Warner gets home. He always checks to make sure his *dogs* are in the house." I shouldn't let myself get so angry. I can't help it.

Pixie leaves without another word. Maybe because she knows I'm right, that if Mr. Warner or Indranie found her here, they'd have a lot of questions for her. Or maybe she leaves because she's already done enough damage.

I find myself in the carriage house kitchen without a memory of walking through the gardens to get here.

"¿Qué te pasa?" Olga asks.

"Nada." I sit in the chair, exhausted. Olga plays merengue on an old-fashioned radio, like my tía used to have, the kind that plays cassettes. She lowers the volume and puts her hand on my forehead.

"You're not getting sick, are you?"

"No. I'm fine."

She smooths back my hair the way Mamá would if I were home. I am sick. Homesick. Sick with worry over Rey.

"You're so quiet. You miss your hermanita, right?"

I forgot about Gabi. How could I have forgotten about Gabi?

"When is she coming home?"

"Manolo went to get her, just now. They'll be home any minute." She turns away. "¿Tienes hambre? I made arroz con pollo, but I also have sopa, si estás mal del estómago."

I find words to say to Olga so she doesn't worry. I even eat the soup she gives me because she thinks I'm unwell. When Gabi gets home, we sit on the couch in the living room, and I let her tell me all the things she's done and seen. Her happiness falls over me like music.

"Juliette goes to parties all the time. She's going to a party at Jake O'Brien's house, and he's a *freshman in high school*."

"What?"

"It's true. She can go to parties even on school nights. She says her mother trusts her completely and doesn't want to be a helicopter parent."

"What's a helicopter parent?"

"You know, when you are always flying around your kid. Watching all the time. Being annoying." She turns on the TV. "I had to ask too. I told her we don't have helicopters, I mean, helicopter parents in Ilopango."

"We don't have helicopters either," I say.

"Maybe someone does."

"Like who?"

Gabi thinks for a minute. "Señor De León."

Señor De León is the owner of a bus company. We took one of his buses from San Salvador to Guatemala City, at the very beginning of our journey here. Even he doesn't have enough money for a helicopter.

"Did you eat?"

"Yes. With Juliette. She's a vegetarian. She says she won't eat anything with a soul, so we had steamed broccoli and rice."

"Comida de conejos," Olga mutters, coming in with a bowl of popcorn for us to share. "I have real food in the kitchen, Gabriela. You come and eat something else, anything you want, okay?"

"Okay, Señora Borges. Thank you."

When Indranie comes in and asks Gabi about her day, the Juliette stories start again. Indranie encourages Gabi, laughing in the right places. It's so comfortable, it almost feels like home. That's as far as I let myself think. I don't let myself imagine living somewhere nearby with Gabi and Mamá, or going to school, making friends. *Seeing Rey.* I keep my attention on today and tomorrow only.

"Did you see Rey today?" Gabi asks me.

"No," I lie. "Why would I?"

She shrugs. "She said she'd help me find a cool American hairstyle."

Indranie laughs bitterly. "I'm not sure she's the best person to ask. She cut all her beautiful hair off, just to spite me."

"Why would she do that?" Gabi asks, though I think I know. *That woman tries too damn hard.* Indranie wants to be Rey's mamá, that much is clear.

"Because," Indranie says, pulling at the end of Gabi's braid, "she was mad at me. I don't know why."

I doubt that's true. I bet Indranie knows exactly why Rey was mad at her.

"Anyway," Indranie continues, "I checked in on Rey when I got home. She's sound asleep. Which, by the way, is where we should all be. It's getting late."

We say good night to Indranie and Olga and go upstairs to our bedroom.

"So," Gabi says, bouncing once on her bed. "How is Rey?"

"I told you, I have no idea."

"Mentirosa."

"Gabi, come on."

"I can always tell when you're lying."

"I'm not lying."

"Asi que, you didn't see Rey today?"

She's like one of those annoying dogs—she never stops yapping until she gets what she wants.

"I did. A little," I admit.

"I knew it!" she crows. "You like her now? A little?"

I don't know what she means by "like her," but I'm already shaking my head. Gabi flops down on the bed.

"You know, you are ridiculous," she says.

"Thanks a lot."

"Juliette says that—"

I put my hands up to stop the flow of *Juliette this* and *Juliette that*. "I don't want to hear any more about what Juliette says."

Gabi's eyebrows draw down, and I think she's going to really start a fight, but I don't think I can take it. I feel so hollowed out.

"You are too crabby to talk to," she says, jumping up from the bed and going into the bathroom.

"I'm going to check on something. Don't wait up for me."

"Something. Sure, uh-huh."

"Gabriela, sos una peste, ¿sabes?"

She leans out of the bathroom. "Yeah, it's my job to be a pain, remember?"

Rey's sleeping peacefully, her chest moving up and down. But she's still got her boots on, and that can't be comfortable. Gently, so I don't wake her, I pull off one of her boots to reveal a sock with a picture of a girl on a bike and the words *Hell on Wheels.*

It's so funny and odd and perfect. It's a very Rey kind of sock. I pull the other boot off, careful not to disturb the cuff. Rey's cuff is on her left leg; mine is on my right. Dr. Deng didn't tell us which leg to put it on—or exactly how close we had to be to each other for the cuffs to work. I feel so defeated that the experiment isn't working, like there has to be something I can do to make it work.

My headache pounds behind my eyes. I decide that after a day like today, I need a good night's sleep. I don't know what tomorrow will bring, and I'll sleep better if I stay here and make sure Rey is okay. That's what I tell myself.

I grab a blanket from Rey's closet, take off my shoes and socks, and lie down on top of the bedcover the way Rey does. I spread the blanket on top of both of us; with her bare shoulders and arms, she must be cold. The bed is big enough that we can lie down, side by side, without touching. This will be fine. I relax my shoulders, letting my body sink down into the bed.

Rey shifts toward me, her eyes opening to slits.

"Are you okay?" I whisper.

"No." A tear runs down her face.

"Do you still want to die?"

"I do." Her voice is faint, sleepy. "But I'm too tired to do anything about it." I wonder if the drugs that Pixie gave her will make her feel worse tomorrow, erasing the few hours tonight that she felt good.

I have that same hot/cold feeling in my bones that comes before a sore throat and a day in bed. Maybe I am getting sick.

When I'm almost asleep, I feel Rey's long fingers wrapping around mine.

Chapter 19

I wake up just before dawn feeling awful. My eyes are stuck shut and my head is groggy, aching. I unlace my fingers from Rey's and wrap the blanket around her. I don't want Indranie to find me in Rey's room.

Gabi is still asleep when I get to our room. I crawl into bed, shivering so much that I'm afraid it will wake my sister. I fall asleep thinking that I have to ask Olga for some remedios. *Gripe,* I think. That's what I have.

The next time I wake, the sun is up and I can't remember where I am. I wonder if this is a safe house or the detention center. But then I see Gabi in the bathroom and I remember that we're safe. I watch her, reflected in the mirror, as she tries to curl her beautiful hair.

I sit up and start coughing so hard it takes me a minute to control myself.

"Sol, are you okay?" Gabi asks from the bathroom door.

"Tengo gripe, amor," I say, my voice cracking.

"Pobrecita. Do you want me to make you té con limón?"

I smile, though my head is aching. Gabi has never made me lemon tea when I was sick. I have made it for her one hundred times or more. "You know how to make tea in this house?"

"Yes, Olga showed me. There is una tetera eléctrica. And I know where she keeps the honey."

"Yes, please." I sink back into the pillows, suddenly weak.

Gabi untangles the curling iron from her hair and for a moment there is a big, fat curl. But the weight of her long hair—almost to her waist—unravels the curl soon enough, until it's only a little wave. Gabi groans in frustration, pulling the cord of the curler out of the outlet hard.

"Careful," I croak. "That belongs to Señora Borges. You don't want to break it."

She gives me a look that is *I know* and *Leave me alone* and *Ugh* all rolled together.

I watch her, in the fog of my aching head, as she gets ready. I am sure she has grown since coming to America. Her skirt looks too short already, her legs stretched long.

I get out of bed to go to the bathroom and almost fall over.

"¿Qué pasó?" Gabi rushes over to me, but I wave her away, grabbing the nightstand to steady myself.

"Nada, I'm fine. It's a cold. You have to go to school. Ask Olga to make me tea." She leans in for a kiss, but I turn away. "I don't want to give you my germs."

"I don't want your yucky germs. And there's no school today. Did you forget? It's Sunday. Juliette is coming over to do a 4-H project."

I didn't remember. "Juliette again?"

"Sol, she's my first friend here. I don't want to screw it up. Please be nice."

"I won't even see her. I'll keep my germs here until I'm better. Won't infect your friend, promise." I smile weakly. "Weren't you going to make me tea?"

She looks me over, hesitant. "Go, peste," I say.

When she finally leaves, I slowly make my way to the bathroom. My bones feel hollow and full of stones at the same time. I swear I can hear them rattling inside me. There is so much saliva in my mouth that when I swallow a mouthful, there is only more waiting. In the bathroom I see my reflection and I know why Gabi was worried. My skin is more yellow than café, and my eyes seem too big for my face.

My brain is making fantasias. I put my hands on the sink. I tell my hands to turn on the faucet so I can wash my face, brush my teeth, and begin my day. But they won't listen to me.

So slowly that I have time to observe it but not stop it, my knees unlock and I slip to the floor. The three light bulbs above the bathroom mirror grow bigger, expanding like suns. I hear my name, but I couldn't answer if I wanted to. I close my eyes and hope they go away.

"Marisol. Marisol, wake up now."

Desagradable, I think. What a disagreeable voice. I wish it would be quiet.

"Marisol, honey. Can you hear me?" That voice is better. I open my eyes. I am back on my bed. Indranie is next to me, holding my hand. Behind her, Dr. Deng watches.

"What happened?"

"You fell down. Are you feeling better now?"

"Yes. I have gripe. A cold. No, not a cold. A big cold. What is the word in English? I can't remember." I push the sweaty strands of hair from my face.

"Did you hit your head?" Dr. Deng steps in front of Indranie.

He puts a cold hand on my head, then lifts my chin to look into my eyes.

"Gripe," I murmur. What is the word in English? I know un resfrío is a cold and gripe is . . . a bigger cold. What is the word? And why can't I remember?

"She's fine," Dr. Deng says.

"She's clearly not fine," Indranie responds with a frown.

Gripe, gripe, gripe, gripe, I say in my head.

"I see that she is exhibiting signs of distress, but there is no fever, no sign of viral infection, seizure, or concussion. Her BP is normal, and I tested her blood sugar just to be sure. She's not diabetic. Anything else will have to be tested at a hospital. Which, as you know, would end the experiment."

"I know," Indranie says.

Gripe. La influenza. "Flu!" I nearly shout. "I have flu. That's what gripe is. It's flu." I look at Gabi. But it's not Gabi sitting on my bed, it's Indranie. And Dr. Deng. Why are they here? I swallow, afraid the saliva filling my mouth will dribble out.

"Marisol," Indranie says. "How are you feeling?"

"I have flu," I repeat.

"Does your head hurt?"

"A little. And I have to swallow a lot. Can I have some water?"

I drink from the cup that Dr. Deng hands me, and the cold water washes away the thick, salty saliva in my mouth.

"Do you feel dizzy?" Indranie asks.

I put the cup on the nightstand. "Not now."

"It's not likely to be flu," Dr. Deng says. "I swabbed her for influenza A and B, just to be sure."

"What can we do to make her feel better?" Indranie asks.

"I can give her an antihistamine. The worst it will do is

make her sleepy. It may give her a bit of relief if she really does have a cold."

Indranie turns back to Dr. Deng. "Could it be working? Could this be part of the transference?"

Dr. Deng frowns deeply. He looks like a cartoon dog. I would laugh if I didn't feel so awful. "It could be. It's hard to say. We have no other point of reference—no subjects have tested this long."

"Dr. Deng—" Indranie starts to say.

"I have flu," I interrupt firmly, so they remember I'm still here and actually listen to me. "Or something like it. I'll be fine in a few days. Can I have some more water, please? I'm thirsty." Dr. Deng's eyes find mine. I'm surprised to see he's smiling.

"Exactly. You'll be fine in a few days. Very smart." He hands me the cup of water again, and I empty it.

"Let's talk downstairs so Marisol can rest," Dr. Deng says.

Indranie takes my hand again. I can't tell if my hand is cold or if her hand is very warm.

"You rest up. But if you need anything, Olga says to ring this, okay?" She places a crystal bell, nearly see-through, on the nightstand. Only in America do they have glass bells you cannot ring too hard in case they break. I close my heavy eyes. The only thing I need is sleep.

"Sol, Sol! Wake up!"

I'm very far down in sleep but Gabi's voice pulls me awake.

"¿Qué pasó?" When I open my eyes, Gabi is excitedly dancing around the room.

"Juliette invited me to a party next weekend. For her birthday."

"What?"

"She says we're besties. BFFs. You know, like your show, the *Hollow* one."

"You never liked that show," I say. I sit up against the pillows, then move over to make room for her.

"Okay, but you talk about it all the time. It was like I was watching."

The pain in my head is gone, but I still feel very tired, as if I've had the flu for days, but my body doesn't ache and my head is clear.

"Anyway, back to Juliette's party. I need to ask Rey what I should get her. I mean, we can borrow a little money from Indranie, right? I won't buy anything expensive, but I want to get her something *good*."

"You haven't even asked permission to go to this party," I say.

Her face darkens, but she controls her anger with effort.

"I know you don't feel well," she says finally. "So, we can talk about it later."

"You can't just go to some stranger's house. I don't know anything about this friend of yours."

"What's the big deal? Juliette's family is nice. Her mom drives a Lexus."

"Gabriela, are you serious? What does it matter what kind of car she drives? And I'm not worried about her mother. What about these other kids? And Juliette? How come she is your best friend in two days?"

"You think I can't make friends?"

"I'm not saying that. You're twisting my words."

"What was the point of coming here, Sol? So we could

continue to be miserable? I don't want to be miserable any-more. I'm tired of misery."

"The point of coming here was to keep you safe. It's not to have some fantasy life. We've been here less than a week, and you think you have a best friend?" I don't want to say it's a waste of time, becoming friends with this girl, with these kids, because that's cruel. But if we are lucky—lucky like we have not been in years—Gabi and I won't be living here in a month.

"I know that! I live in the real fucking world," Gabi shouts at me, and I feel like she's hit me. A moment ago, she was happy, dancing around and excited. Now we're fighting again. I don't know how to get out of it.

She pulls her hair into a ponytail.

"If Mom were here, she'd say yes—you know she would."

"If Mamá were here, she would be ignoring both of us and crying for Pablo!"

Gabi scrambles off the bed. "I cry for Pablo too, you know. You aren't the only one."

I don't know what to say. I haven't seen Gabi cry, not since the night Pablo died. Not once. And I have never let her see me cry.

"What does that have to do with anything, Gabriela? And I didn't say you couldn't go. I only said you had to ask!"

"You aren't my mother," Gabi says coldly. "And I don't need your permission."

She's looking at me like I'm an inconvenience. I'm so sick of this stupid argument.

"I might as well be tu mamá. I have to do everything for you except wipe your nose!"

Gabi stomps back to the bed. If we don't stop arguing soon, Olga will hear us. I don't want to have to explain.

"I want to go to Mrs. Rosen's house. Now. I don't want to wait until this experiment is over. We had a plan, and we should just do that plan," Gabi says, crossing her arms.

My anger deflates, seeing the tears in her eyes. "Gabi, I explained this to you. It's not that simple. New York is far away. If we were there, you wouldn't be able to go to this party anyway. It would be too far."

Gabi lifts her chin defiantly. "Mrs. Rosen would let me go. She would be reasonable."

I push myself out of bed with more energy than I knew I had. "You are being ridiculous!"

"I want to call her. She should be the one taking care of us right now. You said she'd be our guardian until Mamá came. So, let her decide."

"Gabi—"

"I don't want you telling me how to paint my nails and making me eat things I don't want to eat. And I don't want you making fun of my friends."

I grab my hair because I don't know what to do with my hands. I want to grab Gabi. Make her understand. "Gabi, I don't make fun of your friends—"

She picks up the cell phone Indranie gave me and throws it onto the bed. "Call Mrs. Rosen." Her face is a mask of anger.

"I can't call her, Gabi."

"Because you're afraid she's going to agree with me. Because you don't want me to do anything. You just sit on me and try to make me small. You don't want me to grow up, and you want to control me—"

"She's dead, Gabi!"

It's like turning off a light. She just stares at me, empty. In the space between my last words and my next, I wish too many things. I wish Pablo had never met Antonio. I wish I had never seen Liliana at the bar. I wish Gabi had stayed home the night Pablo died. Or even if all that couldn't be different, I wish we could have made it to Mrs. Rosen's house, seen her once more, or that we had never been caught. At every place where we could have had a chance, La Mala Suerte has pulled us into disaster.

Chapter 20

Olga makes me stay in bed the rest of the day, even though I feel all right, just weak. There is no television in this room and my eyes are too tired to read much—though Gabi has borrowed all the Harry Potter books from someone. I read a little of *The Goblet of Fire*, which is my favorite, but I don't get far. Gabi doesn't come back into the room, but I hear her and her friend Juliette laughing and moving around downstairs. I think she will forgive me, later in the day, but I don't know. Mostly, I sit and doze, remembering things that I've been trying to forget, as if I've let my mind get weak as well as my body.

Like, I remember what Liliana was wearing on the last day of Pablo's life. I remember it more clearly than I remember what I was wearing or what Pablo was wearing. That's not completely true. I remember watching his blue shirt turn purple with his blood. I push that thought away, my brain a stubborn horse refusing to be led. Instead, I let myself remember Liliana and her feather earrings.

We stood outside el Club Atlético. "Mira, hermanita, what Pablo bought me," Liliana said, lifting her long hair to show me her tiny ears. The earrings were long, almost touching her shoulders, shaped like feathers the colors of sunset. First dark orange, then gold, then light blue turning darker to azul marino. She laughed and twirled, letting her feathery earrings fan out with her golden hair.

"Can I come in?"

I open my eyes. I didn't realize that I'd closed them. Rey stands at the door to my bedroom. I sit up.

"I brought you some tea and snacks," she says, coming into the room holding a tray. "It's about time I return the favor, right?"

I don't want to nod because that would sound like I'm agreeing with her. "Thank you."

"Want me to put it on the bed? Or the nightstand?"

"Bed is good."

She looks healthy, if not happy. I hope it isn't something else that Pixie gave her. I hope this is the real Rey. I search her eyes for the wildness of last night, check her hands to see if they are restless. Her eyes are clear, her hands steady. She wears a white T-shirt and jeans that fit her better than the other clothes I've seen her in.

"How are you feeling?" I ask. "After the butterflies, I mean."

She laughs. "Oh, yeah. That was one of the stupider things I've done, and I've done some monumentally stupid things, so, yeah," she sighs, sitting at the end of my bed. "One of Pixie's fixes."

"She means well," I say. It's the kind of thing Aimee would say about Amber, after she did something stupid. It's a very useful frase.

"Pixie always means well, but she's good at making things worse. When she and Riley were together, they were like a gorgeous train wreck. After they broke up, I sort of inherited her."

She hands me a cup of tea. It smells wonderful and flowery. Olga knows how to make good tea.

"She's sad he's gone. Maybe that makes her do stupid things too," I say after a sip of hot tea.

"She's sad. Everyone is sad. But no one else is missing part of their body." Rey eats a cookie off the tray. "Maybe Dad feels like that. Maybe I don't give him enough credit. But he never talks about Riley. No one does. That's worse than anything else in a way. It's like they want to erase him."

I don't think that's the worst thing. I think remembering would be worse. So I stay silent for a moment.

"What happened to Riley?" I ask. I sound awful, like Dr. Vizzachero or the woman at the detention center who told me to call her Mary. Like I am going to write down Rey's answers and look for their meaning later. "I'm sorry, I shouldn't have asked that."

"No, it's okay. I feel better today than I have in weeks. I feel like I can breathe." She takes a deep breath as if to prove her words. "It hurts. Fuck, it hurts, but it doesn't seem impossible today. And talking about Riley feels right. At least you understand."

She looks down at her hands, and I'm glad. I don't want her to see my face getting hot.

"Riley and I were at a concert. The Sounds at the 9:30 Club. Some Swedish indie rock band that Riley loves." She scratches her head. "Loved.

"I went with him because Pixie wouldn't go. She was pissed at him. Oh, I can't remember why.

"We went, and it was fun. I didn't get to go out just with my brother anymore, you know? He was always with a girlfriend, or just a girl, or with the other indie kids he hung out with. I think his indie friends were always surprised that Riley had a twin and that she was so—underwhelming."

"I don't think you're underwhelming. You're—" I hesitate, searching for a word that is enough and not too much. *Wonderful* sounds foolish and *great* sounds like something you'd say about a pizza. What word can I use to describe Rey? *Luminous. Fierce.*

"You're great," I finish lamely.

"You say that because you never met Riley," she says, smiling. Have I ever seen her smile like that? "He was a fucking star. I mean, that's how brightly he burned. Everyone turned toward him, and everyone adored him. My mother adored him."

I don't say anything. I can't imagine someone burning brighter than Rey.

She laughs. "Well, at least *Dad* adored me. I was his girl. I'm the good twin, the least-likely-to-cause-trouble twin. Well, I *was*."

I don't know if I should tell her to stop, that it's okay not to say any more, or if I should wish for her to continue.

"I was so *happy* that night, it seems weird to think about it now. I was finally over a bad break-up and I liked my new therapist—not Dr. V, obviously. I felt invincible, like it was me and Riley against the world . . ." Her voice wobbles suddenly, as if it will fall away into silence. Her smile is gone. I feel like I am next to her, in her memory, watching a performance with a brother who shines so brightly. And I know a terrible thing is about to happen.

There's a knock at the door, and Gabi comes in with a girl. They are laughing and nudging each other. When Gabi sees Rey, she becomes serious.

"I'm sorry. I didn't know you were busy." From the tone of her voice, I know she is still mad at me.

Rey stands, making room for Gabi. "That's okay." I see the effort it takes to pull herself away from her memories of Riley. I can admit that I want to know what happened to him, but I'm so relieved not to have to hear it. Once the image is out in the world between us, I don't know what will happen.

Gabi sits on my bed, but her friend stands behind her, arms crossed. I remember that I haven't brushed my teeth today.

"Sol, I wanted you to meet Juliette Guinto. From school," Gabi says. The girl gives me a polite smile. She has shoulder-length dark hair, dark eyes, and little crooked teeth.

"Nice to meet you, Juliette," I say. "It's almost your birthday, right?"

"Yeah," she says, "on Tuesday."

"And the party is next Saturday?"

"Yes. My mom says it's okay to invite Gabi, but I had to ask her family."

"Well, that's me," I say lightly.

I was the one who made a big deal of not knowing enough about Gabi's new friend. Now I have no idea what I'm supposed to ask her.

"Will your parents be at your house during the party?" I ask.

"Um, yeah. And my mom said Gabi could sleep over too—if that's okay with you."

I feel Gabi watching me, her face stubborn and hopeful at the same time. I think about everything she's seen and lived through. More than any child should have to in a lifetime.

"I think that will be all right," I say slowly. When they jump and squeal loud enough to wake up ten generations of the dead, I tell them, nicely, to go somewhere else.

Rey, who has been quiet, gives a half snort, half laugh. "Have fun, Gabs. Don't do anything that requires stitches!"

When Rey turns back to me, she's holding up the *Cedar Hollow* DVDs. "Okay, so season three, right?"

I smile. "Yes, but first I need a shower," I say, climbing out of bed. I remember when wearing the same clothes for weeks was so normal that I didn't even notice. Now I feel dirty after just one day. I hope I don't smell.

"It's cute the way we're reversing our roles here, you know?"

I look at her blankly.

"I'm bringing you tea, and you're sick in bed and probably stinky." She takes another cookie off the tray. The cookies are disappearing fast. "Try not to flash me, okay?"

"Flash?"

"You know," she says, pretending to open her shirt. I blush hard and almost run to the bathroom.

After a long shower with the water as hot as I can withstand, I come out wrapped in towels. Rey is on her phone but glances up at me long enough to say, "No flashing," I think because she knows it embarrasses me. I grab clothes out of the closet and run back to the bathroom. I dress and put powder on my ankle before putting the cuff back on. I am mostly myself and calm when I come back out. My tea is cold on the tray, and there is half a cookie left for me.

"Sorry," Rey says, looking at the nearly empty plate. I laugh. Rey opens her computer and puts the first disco into the machine. "I had to find my dad's old laptop with the disc drive—that's how old this shit is." The little tray disappears into the computer, and it slowly comes to life, the image from the beginning of *Cedar Hollow* filling the screen.

"Dad told me why you left El Salvador."

I look at her. "I told you that. Because of Gabi."

"Yeah, but I didn't know it was because people killed your brother and want to kill you. It's crazy. Like something out of a movie."

"I don't want to talk about it."

Rey puts her hand on my arm. Through the fabric of my T-shirt, her hand feels as hot as una plancha. "I'm glad you got here safe."

I can't explain how we aren't safe—how I don't know if we'll ever be safe. How I don't know, right now, if Mamá is safe with Tía Rosa, or if she is someone else I should be worrying about. Because of all that, I stay silent. We watch the third season of *Cedar Hollow* on the bed, shoulders touching so we can both see the small screen of the computer that Rey balances on her knees, then on a stack of pillows. It isn't a very comfortable thing, but I realize that I'd rather be uncomfortable and close to Rey.

We watch as Amber finds her mother sitting at their kitchen table and confronts her for drinking too much after losing her job.

"You can't just sit there and wallow in self-pity, Mom!"

I think about Mamá in her *bata* sitting at our kitchen table, worrying about Pablo as if it were another one of her jobs. Pablo, who was almost never home, would sometimes appear late at night or early in the morning. He was the head of the family now, and he was taking care of us. Money would appear on the table to prove his words. Then he'd leave, and Mamá would still sit, crying as silently as she could.

"Hey. You okay?" Rey says gently. A tear rolls down my face. I didn't even know I was crying. I am so close to Rey that I can see the veins behind her ears, the soft, blonder-than-blond hair on her head. She smells of cotton and warmth. She brushes her fingers over my face to wipe away the tear. I feel fragile and light, a soap bubble in the air.

"I'm happy," I say, which is not the right answer. I should have said "I'm fine" or "I'm okay." But it was the true answer.

"Making a mental note: Cries when happy. Okay, got it," she says, turning back to watch Amber and her mom declare that they'll always be there for each other.

Indranie comes in and, seeing us scrunched up on the bed, frowns. Rey pauses the show so Amber's laughing face is frozen on the screen.

"Gabi told me you guys were hanging out together."

"What's wrong with two lab rats hanging out, in the name of science? It's not against the rules, is it?" Rey says.

"Not exactly against the rules, no," Indranie says. She puts a tray of Olga's food on the nightstand. She feels my forehead and smiles that there is no fever. "How are you feeling, kid?"

"I'm better. Just tired. Rey is taking care of me," I say.

"I can see that," she says, raising an eyebrow. "This is from Dr. Deng. He says you just need rest and this will help you sleep." She puts a tiny white pill next to my bowl of stew. "But you have to take it after you eat. Olga says you haven't eaten much today."

I shrug. It doesn't matter. I want Indranie to leave so we can watch more *Cedar Hollow* in peace.

She walks over to Rey's side of the bed and kisses her on the cheek. "You're looking better too. That's good news. Your dad is out of town, but he's back tomorrow. He says he texted you."

Rey nods toward her phone. "Yeah, it was about a thousand emojis long. Did you teach him how to do that?"

Indranie smiles. "I may have mentioned that emojis have some credibility among today's youth."

"You set him up. I admire that about you."

Indranie laughs and says she'll check in on us later. We eat stew and fresh bread and watch disaster after disaster hit the people in *Cedar Hollow*. It never occurred to me that maybe they were even unluckier than our family. But, so far, no one has tried to kill Amber and Aimee.

Right before the last episode of season three, Gabi comes in, brushes her teeth, and puts on piyamas. I hadn't realized how late it was. Gabi climbs into the bed between us.

"Can I watch too?"

"You hate this show, remember?"

"Then can I get you to watch *Top Gear* again?"

"Sorry, Gabi. Hanging out with the lab rats means watching *Cedar Hollow*, right, Aimee?"

"That's correct, Amber."

"Why are you Amber," Gabi asks Rey, then turns to me, "and you're Aimee? They both look the same to me."

We both exclaim that this is completely false, that they are deeply complex characters.

"They do look a little the same from the back," I say, noticing how they both have the same hair color.

"We didn't decide who was who," Rey says. "It sort of just happened, right?"

I nod.

"Aimee's shorter. That's why you're Aimee, right?" Gabi says.

"I'm not short," I say.

"Chaparra," Gabi snorts.

"What does that mean?" Rey asks.

"Shorty," I say.

Rey and Gabi laugh over my insistence that I am not short, only average. I'm glad Gabi isn't so angry with me anymore.

"Rey is Amber because she's the leader," I say. *And she's the most beautiful.*

Rey groans. "Season three is Amber *leading* Aimee from one mistake to another, like she's the Pied Piper of terrible choices. No thanks."

Gabi asks a lot of questions about Amber and Aimee for the first five minutes of the episode, and Rey answers them patiently. I watch them together. It should amaze me that Gabi is so comfortable with Rey, but it doesn't. Gabi is made of something strong, flexible, and good. I am made of stone, at least that's what it has felt like. Now I feel my insides loosening, letting go of fear just a little bit. It feels danger-ous to be soft, como mantequita. What if I forget how to be hard when I have to be?

The disc ends and Gabi gets up, stretching. I go to the bathroom to brush my teeth and take the pill from Dr. Deng. When I come back, Gabi is asleep on her bed and Rey is waiting for me in mine.

"Hey, Aimee," Rey says.

Rey and I lie down on the bed facing each other. She takes my hand again, and a shiver stops my heart. She kisses my forehead, and I hold my breath.

"I don't feel like dying tonight," she says.

She's smiling, though her eyes are growing heavy, her body relaxing into sleep. I feel like an animal tracked by a hunter, not knowing if it is better to leap backward or jump forward. The answer isn't in Rey's eyes, as kind and soft as they are. The answer is in Liliana's eyes. Her voice.

You know I stay with Pablo so I can see you, right?

Liliana's voice repeats in my head like a curse.

So I can see you.

"Come shopping with me, hermanita. You know what your brother likes," Liliana says, her hip against our screen door. Before Liliana, I never cared what Pablo's girlfriends wore or did. But I let Liliana pull me down the street to the market stalls. I leave Gabi home with Mamá. I feel guilty for leaving her, but not enough to stop me. I buy her a rainbow-colored hair bow to make it up to her.

Liliana wants me to try on a thin top, the kind she likes to wear that shows her belly. It's yellow with little black stars and moons. She stands, half dressed, in the curtained part of the stall that sells ropa de fiesta. I won't take off my top, even behind a curtain, in the market stall. I won't buy shiny bracelets or lipstick, either. Those decoraciones aren't for me; they feel heavy, annoying. On Liliana, they make her look more beautiful still.

She doesn't believe me when I tell her how beautiful she looks. She laughs, threading her arm through mine, and leading me past the stalls selling cazuelas and mosquito coils, shawls and candy. In the coming weeks, Liliana will show up at our door often, ready to take me out. I never ask where Pablo is or why they aren't together. I'm just happy to have Lilí to myself.

I bribe Gabi not to tell anyone where I go. "It's our secret, Gabi. I'll bring you back a treat."

Gabi nods. "Our secret."

But Gabi has her own secret. One night, as we travel through Mexico in a coyote's truck, sleepless and sick with panic, waiting to see if they'll leave us behind or shoot us for making too much noise, Gabi tells me how Antonio would take her a pasear—to places she was not allowed to go without me or Mamá. And to places where you needed money, to Galerías, or all the way to La Gran Via. They'd go in Antonio's car, instead of having to take buses. She called Antonio her other big brother, and Antonio wouldn't let her get out of his car until she gave him a kiss. Often, Pablo would be there. He would let it all happen.

"I had to tell you. It's my fault Pablo died. I didn't know Antonio was tan malo. He was always nice to me. And he was Pablo's friend." My sister's eyes are dry yet swimming in fear. She confesses that night because she thinks we're going to die.

"It's my fault," she says again.

I hold her close, making us both as small and quiet as I can, and tell her she's wrong. It's Antonio's fault. Antonio killed Pablo, and Antonio is dead. That's the end of it. It's over and in the past.

But the past is here with me now. I can't get it out of my mind, no matter how hard I try. Despite being flooded with shameful memories, I don't pull away from Rey. I don't move. I wait for sleep because it has to come. It is the only mercy I can expect. But when sleep does come, it is a ball of fire.

Chapter 21

The music is too loud. A machine on stage pumps out clouds of smoke. Strobe lights turn the smoke colors—from pink to blue to orange. A boy is next to me, dancing to the music. Every few minutes, he looks back at me, to see if I'm all right. Once, he leans in close and yells in my ear, "Having fun?" I nod that I am, and my body dances too. I don't like the music much, but I like being with this boy. I like the feeling of people around me and everyone having a good time. A pretty girl with short black hair smiles and winks at me as she dances past. I grin because it's been a long time since a pretty girl—any girl—has flirted with me. The air tastes good, like electricity and sugar. I don't know what it is, but then I do know. It's happiness. I'm happy to be here, just here. There is no one missing and nowhere else I want to be.

An explosion splits the room, cutting off the music. There hangs a second of perfect silence before someone screams. An accident, I think, something wrong with the equipment or lighting. The boy's hand grips mine hard, and he pulls me forward. Behind me, smoke pours out of a hole in the wall. We are leaving because there is something wrong. The boy is looking back at me. "I'm okay," I shout. I'm okay. Then, in front of him, made just for him, another explosion splits the room into silence and chaos. I stumble to my knees. My hand is still outstretched, but it's empty.

Where is the boy? I cough and cough, my ears ringing. The band is gone from the stage, and someone pushes past me, knocking me to the ground.

I have to find the boy. But there are too many people running, too much screaming for me to think. Someone steps on my hand with their boot, crushing my finger. I pull my painful hand into my leather jacket. Not my jacket. My brother's jacket. I was cold, and he let me wear it. I hunch down in the jacket like a turtle in a shell, as if it can protect me. I cover my head with my arms.

I think I hear someone screaming my name, but it could be my mind playing tricks on me. I uncover my head long enough to see if I can find the boy. He always comes for me. He never leaves me behind. There are other people lying on the ground. Bodies, I think, but then recoil from the word. How much time has passed? An hour? Two minutes? Another boom vibrates through the world, shifts the ground under me, and I'm paralyzed again. Something lands hard across my legs. I raise my head to see that it's a girl. She wears a T-shirt with the name of the band we're seeing. She's covered in blood, and her eyes do not blink. This scares me more than the smoke or the explosion or the boy I can't find.

I use strength I didn't know I had to pull myself out from under the dead girl and roll toward the stage, where part of the black velvet lining has come apart, revealing a space. I crawl into it, under the stage, and scream his name, even though no one can hear me. Where is he?

"Her eyes are open."

"Yes. But she is completely unresponsive."

Indranie's and Dr. Deng's voices float in the dark.

"Can that happen with your eyes open?"

"Yes. Her optic nerves are not passing information to her brain. She is locked in."

"This isn't supposed to go this way," Indranie says nervously.

Are my eyes really open?

"She's breathing and her pulse is only a little slow. I'm giving her an NMB reversal agent. That will hopefully bring her out of this catatonic state."

I hear glass bottles tinkling, and I remember visiting Papá's work when I was little. The Pepsi bottle crates being stacked made a grinding sound, rough glass against rough glass. It made my teeth hurt.

"Did you take the cuff off?"

"No." Dr. Deng's voice is cold.

"Are you out of your mind? That's what's causing this!" There's panic in Indranie's voice. I have never heard her sound so distressed. I wonder if I am dreaming.

A large hand, damp and warm, touches my arm. I feel a needle pinch my skin.

"Calm down, Indranie." Dr. Deng's voice cuts through the fog of my mind. "We don't know anything other than you found her like this an hour ago."

"We can make a pretty good guess," Indranie says angrily.

"We won't get another chance like this. Think of all the people this will help. Think of Rey. Do you really want to stop the experiment now?"

Indranie is silent.

I tell myself to get *up*. But nothing moves except my heart, which beats like it wants to jump out of my body, leaving me behind. I wish I could cry, but I can't. I will stay like this forever. God will find me like this on my last day, unmoving. My eyes suddenly sting unbearably. Water leaks out of my eyes, and I can't even blink it away. Then, finally, the ceiling comes into focus, whiteness instead of blackness until I can see.

"Marisol. What happened?"

It takes me a long moment to move my mouth to answer Indranie.

"I—" My voice crumbles to dust. Indranie helps me sit up and take a sip of water. I am so tired of being in this bed.

"I saw Riley die."

Dr. Deng, for once, is looking at me with intense interest.

"Can you describe it?" he asks.

I describe it as if I had been there. In a way, I have.

"Did Rey tell you that's what happened?" Dr. Deng asks urgently.

"No. She never told me. She was going to, but we got interrupted."

They exchange glances instead of words.

"It's the cuff," I say. "It has to be. It's finally working."

"Working?" Indranie asks. "That's not working. That's malfunctioning."

Dr. Deng sits on the bed across from me. He avoids my eyes. "It is working. Better than we could have expected."

"Peter," Indranie says, "this was not what we discussed."

Peter? He doesn't look like a Peter. He looks like—well, like his first name is Doctor and his last name is Deng. Peter is such a friendly name, and Dr. Deng is definitely not friendly. I have lost the thread of their conversation, so I try to catch up, to push away my tiredness.

"It's because they were touching. You told me yourself. Last night, they sat close and watched a movie. This morning, when you found them sleeping, they were holding hands."

While Dr. Deng's face is excited and determined, Indranie's face churns with worry. She doesn't look like herself.

"But Rey was feeling better before last night. They weren't holding hands before then."

Dr. Deng laughs a sarcastic sound. "Is that what you think? I'm not so sure. I have an idea that these two have been getting close under your nose."

If Indranie is surprised, she hides it. "The protocol for phase one explicitly sets the distance between participants at a minimum of seventy-five feet. That's why Marisol stays in the carriage house. We haven't even completed the first week."

"Where's Rey?" My voice trembles, and my hands twitch on the blanket. I still feel half frozen.

"Don't talk to me about the protocol—I wrote it! I know what it is and isn't supposed to do. Besides, the test with the soldier proved that it would work at closer range. We have a responsibility to take advantage of whatever opportunity comes out of the trial."

"That's not how any of this is supposed to work!" Indranie shouts.

I have an overwhelming fear so strong that it is almost enough to get me out of bed. I see Rey flying off the balcony. I see her body smashing into the ground. See her eyes open and unblinking like the girl at the concert. I feel a boot crush my hand at a concert, smoke choking me. But that isn't real. At least it isn't real for me.

"Where's Rey? Where is she?" I thought I was shouting, but the sound that comes back to me is weak. At least it's enough to get their attention.

"She's fine, honey," Indranie says, patting my hand. Dr. Deng lets a smile cover his face. I think of the kids' song "La Víbora de la Mar," the sea snake. That's what he looks like.

I struggle to get up. It's so much harder than it should be.

"Shhh. It's okay. Lie back down, Marisol." Indranie pushes me gently into bed and pulls the covers around me.

My every heartbeat is fear, first for Rey, then for Gabi, and I don't have time to be ashamed that my sister is not first.

"Where's Gabi?"

"She's outside. She's fine."

"Where's Rey?" I ask again. "Is she really okay?" These two can be lying to me, and I would never know.

Their worried expressions mirror each other.

"Rey is doing great," Dr. Deng says.

"I want to see her. Them. I want to see them."

Indranie helps me stand, holding on to me because my legs tremble from the effort. She walks me across the room until, finally, I drop into a chair by the window. Indranie pulls a blanket off the bed to put around me. It doesn't matter. I can't stop shivering.

I watch my sister and Rey from the window as they play a made-up game—part chase, part dance, part cartwheels, all laughter. They are fine. Better than fine: they're *happy*. Rey's laugh is loudest, longest. Her joy rolls off her in waves. I should be able to feel it from where I sit. But I can't even lift the corners of my mouth to smile. A heaviness sits under my skin, above my bones—an invisible, smothering blanket. Pavor, angustia, pánico, a collection of heavy, gut-churning feelings. I am drowning.

Chapter 22

Aimee—"

"*Don't say anything. You lied to me, Amber. I'm supposed to be your best friend. And you lied.*"

"*You don't understand. He told me it was okay; he told me there wouldn't be any side effects.*"

"*That makes you stupid and a liar.*"

Aimee slams the door hard, and I startle. The timer on the shelf goes off, but I don't get up. I have finally found a position where almost no bones hurt. Rey stands to reach the timer, and the bed shifts under me. My shoulders and hips scream in protest. I bite my lip to keep from crying.

"Time for meds," Rey says. She dumps pills into her hand and picks out three different-colored ones.

"These are totally the pharmaceutical greatest hits." She holds one up, diamond-shaped and blue. "Classic SSRI. Helps with suicidal thoughts. Also, may cause suicidal thoughts. Aimee was right: side effects are a bitch."

I know Rey's joking should make me happy. But I don't feel it. I asked Dr. Deng why I can't feel happiness, even when everything is working out.

"That's what depression is," he said.

It has been three days since the cuff started working—Indranie says it's malfunctioning; Dr. Deng says it's working better than expected—and two days since I moved into Rey's room. Dr. Deng suggested Gabi was disturbed by my crying at night. He said, "Wouldn't you like your little sister to get as much rest as possible? After all, she needs her rest so she can learn. She's doing so well in school." I hated watching Dr. Deng form words about my sister. I hated that I knew, that everyone in the room knew, that the reason he wanted me and Rey in the same room was to increase the success of the experiment. With every touch between us, Rey's grief floods into me. Only, she doesn't know. And I won't tell her—not now that she's finally feeling happier.

I swallow the pills without water because my mouth is always filled with saliva. A side effect of grief, Dr. Deng says.

Indranie worries that getting Rey's memories from the night of Riley's death means the experiment is out of control. Dr. Deng tells her not to worry, that we're ahead of schedule, practically in phase two protocols, whatever that means. To make Indranie feel better, Dr. Deng gives me medicine for depression. He might as well give me candy. Nothing touches this suffocating blanket I live under.

"And now we do shots," Rey says, uncovering the two small plastic cups of a clear, bitter liquid we both drink every night.

"It's almost like a party," she says after we drink the medicine as quickly as we can so it doesn't linger in our mouths. "Saddest party in creation, but hey! We have Amber and Aimee."

Despite her grin, Rey watches me with worried eyes when she thinks I don't notice. I know I look bad. I have lost weight despite Señora Borges's best efforts. I cannot swallow much more than this palmful of pills.

"Another episode?" Rey asks.

"Sure," I say. And the process begins again. Amber spends the episode doing something stupid and Aimee rescues her, then tells her all the mistakes she's made. I don't think I realized before how much they yell at each other.

"Does Amber seem like a good friend to you?" I ask Rey. Since I don't usually say much during *Cedar Hollow*—or much at all—Rey pauses the DVD and looks at me.

"What do you mean?"

It's hard forming words that make sense, even in my mind, but I try. "Does it seem like Amber cares about Aimee? As a friend?"

Rey shakes her head with a smile. "Nope."

That is what I thought, but it still makes me sad. Sadder.

"Amber is on *fire* for Aimee." Rey laughs.

"What?"

"She's got the hots for her. Carries a torch, you know."

I don't know. My confused expression must tell Rey that.

"Come on, Marisol. You have to see it. Amber's in love with Aimee. That's why she's so mean to her."

I sit up, nearly banging my head on one of the bookshelves above Rey's bed.

"That's not true," I say. Then, "How do you know this?"

"Of course it's true. If you looked, you'd see. Total, unrequited love. It's obvious."

"Do they say this? Have I missed an episode?"

"No, not out in the open, but everyone ships them." I'm not sure what Rey is saying, if she is joking or if this is something real. She plays the video again, and I study Aimee's face. Is there any sign at all that she knows how Amber feels? I shake my head. It's ridiculous.

"Tell me you don't ship them," Rey says.

"I don't know what that means."

"You want them in a relationship, you know—you want them to be together. You're rooting for them."

"But they are not in a relationship, not in real life."

Rey rolls her eyes at me. "These are not actual people. They aren't real life at all. So, what's wrong with having a little fun with it?"

I can't organize my protests; I can't say what I'm feeling the right way. But I know that it can't be true. "But Amber is so pretty," I say. It's a stupid thing to say, meaningless. My face flushes at my words.

"So, lesbians are ugly?" She raises just one eyebrow—the way Gabi can. On the screen, Amber is having a talk with her father.

"I'm not saying anyone is ugly. But . . . I don't know what I'm saying. Amber has a boyfriend. They both do."

Rey turns her body toward me, ignoring the screen. "Is this a problem for you?"

"What do you mean?" She is so close to me, I am afraid to move.

"I mean, is this a Jesus thing?"

"I don't understand." I'm getting tired of saying those words.

"Is this, like, a homophobic Jesus thing? 'Thou shalt not fall in love with your own gender' or whatever the fuck? Do you even know any gay people in El Salvador?"

My body stiffens, turns to glass. If she looked closely, she'd see through me.

I clear my throat. "How would I know?"

"You'd know. Come on. In school? Dancing in clubs? Holding hands?"

"No. No, I don't know."

Rey pulls away, frowning. "Don't get upset about it. It's cool. Jesus is, um, he's fine. And I get it. Takes people some time to *evolve*. My dad took years to *evolve*. He's still *evolving* out of his primordial old white man amoeba."

I struggle to make sense of her words. One meaning is clear, though: she thinks badly of me. "You don't know anything about me. You think things about me because of where I'm from. That I'm a, a Bible-thumper, you called me."

Rey stops the DVD as Amber and her boyfriend are fighting in a car. Their frozen faces are full of fear and anger. It seems like it's everywhere.

"Are we seriously having this fight? I don't want to argue with you, Marisol. I'm sorry. Forget it, okay?"

I think the wave of grief I feel rising in me is my own. "You don't know anything about me. I don't even believe in God."

"You don't?"

It's not something I like to admit, even to myself. And I would never let Gabi know this, because I tell her that God holds her in his hand, and that nothing bad will happen to her because He loves her. I tell her this because she knows, deep in her soul, that I cannot keep her safe, not really and not forever. I've told her so many lies.

I shake my head. It is swimming with tears that I cannot release.

"I believe in luck. Bad luck. That's all I have." The effort to keep the tears inside makes me shake so hard that I can't hide it from Rey.

"Oh God, Marisol, I'm sorry." She hugs me and I receive two gifts at once, one I want more every day and another that I wish I could leave behind: the soft feel of Rey's skin on mine and the sound of a boy dying.

"You can't leave me," I say to the boy on the ground. I crawled from my space under the stage and found him nearby. I don't look at his legs—at where his legs should be—because if I see it, I will not be able to stop seeing it. They aren't there, my mind tells me. They are atoms and dust and shards of broken glass.

"Reyanne, Reyanne, Reyanne." The boy clutches my hands in spasms, like heartbeats.

"Riley George Warner, you cannot leave me here. We came into this world together, and we are going out together," I sob.

"Reyanne, Reyanne, remember me, okay? Don't forget me."

"You're not going anywhere, jackass." I am crying into his shirt; the smell of clean laundry and his own skin surrounds me. It's a scent I know as well as I know myself.

"Hold my hand," he says. I cry harder because I'm already holding his hand, and he can't feel it. Hands on my shoulders pull me away from Riley, and paramedics cut open his shirt and crowd me out. They're helping him, I think. They're taking him, I think.

Rey pulls away from me and stares into my blank face. I think she's repeating my name. I cry silently, unable to stop the tears. Worry marks her face, and I know she wants to help, but when she leans in to hug me harder, longer, I flinch. I know it is my job to take this grief away from her. I'm doing the best I can, but right now, it's too much.

"I, I, uh, need the bathroom." I stumble into her bathroom and close the door. I hate that I can only help Rey by hurting myself. But what did I expect? I knew. No one lied. Well, maybe they did lie, but so what if they did? It doesn't matter that they didn't tell me carrying someone else's grief would feel like being torn in two. Who says life is fair? Every vision I have of Rey's grief is followed by memories that live in me despite how hard I've tried to suppress them.

"¿Quién dice que la vida es justa?" Mamá says when I complain it's unfair that Pablo can be out all night when I have to be home by dusk. I want to visit Liliana at the bar, but Mamá looks at me wearily. "Es muy peligroso salir de noche para una niña," she says. I want to say, Sixteen is old enough that other girls go out, dancing and laughing, and I want to be with them. But I know my words won't make a difference.

When Gabi shows me her nail polish—big bottles of expensive colors, a whole box of them—I barely stop to wonder where they came from. My mind is full of Liliana and how I will sneak out to see her.

"Paint my nails, Sol? They come out nicer when you do it."

I watch my mother take her medicine, the one that guarantees her hip won't hurt and that she'll sleep through the night.

"I'll make you a deal," I whisper to Gabi. "If I paint your nails, you'll keep my secret."

She rolls her eyes. "¿Otro secreto?" she asks. I nod.

Gabi's expression turns sly. "You have a boyfriend, don't you?"

"¡No! Por supuesto que no," I say.

"Okay." Gabi shrugs. "But you could tell me, you know. I know all about boyfriends." She grins.

When Gabi's nails are done and she is parked in front of the TV, when Mamá's snores can be heard behind her closed door, I leave. I run straight to el Club, afraid I've taken too long, that she'll leave without me. At the back door of the bar, I bang, hard, knowing it will be difficult to hear over the sound system.

Finally, the door opens.

"Is Lilí still here?" I ask Belén, who works at the bar with Liliana.

Belén gives me a flat, uninterested look and shouts behind her, "¡Lilí, tu amiguita está aquí!"

In March I'll be seventeen—only two years younger than Lilí. Maybe then Belén will stop calling me "little friend." Liliana appears behind Belén. Seeing me, her face falls in disappointment.

"What?" she asks.

"Aren't you glad to see me?" My heart trips in my chest. Lilí's face takes too long to find a smile.

"Seguro que sí, hermanita. Give me a second, okay? I'm supposed to be working." She turns to talk to Belén, pulling her long hair off her neck into a ponytail. It's something I've seen her do a thousand times, imagining that someday I would dare to kiss the spot on her neck, just under her ponytail, where I know she'll be ticklish.

"Okay, ¿qué pasa?" she asks, closing the door behind her.

"I missed you," I say, determined to keep the smile on my face.

"Aren't you supposed to be home? Won't tu mamá be upset?"

"Do you want me to leave?" I can't keep the hurt from straining my voice. A moment ago I was bold, like a drunk singing in the rain. Now I'm the fool, crossing into traffic, laughing at disaster.

Lilí sighs heavily. Then, the smile I love to dream about lights her face. She takes my hand and opens my crossed arms.

"I guess what Mamá doesn't know won't hurt her," she says, pulling me close with the patience of a fisherman, reeling, reeling. My head fills with the scent of Liliana's perfume and I can't think. She pulls until her arms wrap around me. I'm close enough for kisses, something she's never allowed before.

I've wanted this for so long, this feeling that I should have had with boys and never did. But it's happening at a speed I can't understand. Something feels wrong.

I try to breathe, to catch my heart before it runs out of my chest. I need a second to think.

"¿No me quieres?" Liliana asks. I can't tell if she's joking or if she means it. She can't mean it. She can't think I don't want her.

Lilí's feather earrings tickle my nose. She lowers her head to me, and I think of the tacones altos she always wears, making her taller than me. Her lips move above mine, and I don't have a thought in my head other than the sound of her breathing, the warmth of it on my skin.

"It's true," she says with a cruel laugh, "sos tortillera."

A slap would not have been sharper. The words take a second to reach my brain, but they hit my stomach immediately, a sickness rising through my body in waves. Liliana pushes me away. Her face distorts into a sneer.

"Go home to Mamá, you twisted thing," she spits. "I'm a real woman, the way God intended. I wouldn't soil myself with one like you." She pushes me again, and I lose my balance, falling into the street. I am the fool, I think as my face burns hearing the laughter from a couple across the street. I run home, full of shame.

Chapter 23

Indranie takes my temperature the next morning.

"How are you feeling today?" she asks.

I want to say that I feel like dying, the way Rey used to say to me, but I don't. Feeling like this, it's my job.

"Okay. Sad." She gives me a strained smile and makes notes in her file. I guess it's my file. Everything they know about me is in that file. I wonder if I would recognize myself if I read it.

Indranie gives me my three pills for the morning. She'll leave tonight's pills with Rey, who will make sure I take them. All these people taking care of me, making things as easy for me as possible. These are the same people giving me all this pain.

Manny makes me walk around the reflecting pool with him once a day. We don't talk—thank God he doesn't make me talk. I don't know if I would vomit up a mass of bloody, broken words, or if I would be terrified by how little I could say. He only makes me move my body, to get some of the stiffness out of it. It is the one part of my day that I look forward to without any mixed feelings, because the only thing I have to do is walk. Manny occasionally tells me the names of plants. I listen or I don't—it makes no difference to him. Sometimes, he puts his hand on my shoulder and I flinch. I can't help it. My first thought is always that a touch is going to hurt. But his touch doesn't hurt the way Rey's does. I haven't told anyone about the touching. How being skin to skin with Rey transmits her grief and sadness right into my body as if they were my own. If Indranie knew, she'd stop the experiment.

An hour before school ends, I eat something, then take a shower and brush my teeth. Olga helps me because she and Indranie are afraid to leave me in the bathroom by myself too long. They do not trust me behind a closed door. Now I understand how Rey felt, being watched all the time.

When Olga leaves, I sit, my hair combed back, my thin face a mystery to me, practicing my smile in the mirror on Rey's desk. I smile until it seems almost natural, almost genuine. Performing for Gabi is the hardest part of my day. She knows I'm sad because of the experiment, and that it's my job to make Rey feel better. But I can't let her see how much I'm hurting.

There is a knock at the door, and I look at the clock. 3:00 p.m. Gabi is home. I put my smile on. "Come in!"

But instead of Gabi, Mr. Warner opens the door.

I stand up. "Rey isn't here," I say, keeping my voice even.

"I know. She's meeting with Dr. Vizzachero."

Mr. Warner motions for me to sit back down, and I do, turning the chair to face him as he sits on Rey's bed. I'm ashamed that it is unmade. That my piyamas have been thrown on the floor.

"I, ah. Wanted to see how you're doing." He was a gray ghost when I last saw him; now he has more color, and he doesn't move like he's in pain.

"Why?" I ask him. I can see from his expression that it's an unexpected question. But it's truly what I want to know. Why does he want to see how I am doing? Does he ask all the people who work for him how they are doing? Maybe he does. Maybe he asks Manny and Olga how they're doing. But still. I've only seen him once before. He hasn't shown much interest in me.

"Well, you are, of course, an, um . . ." I watch him struggle with the word, wondering if he'll call me illegal—or a service dog like Pixie did. I guess we are illegal. We shouldn't have to be here this way. But when you don't have a good choice, you make a bad choice.

"You and your sister have been through a lot, haven't you?"

I sigh heavily. "And even so, our asylum request was denied." Bitterness rises in my stomach.

"Indranie knows how to get you in front of an asylum judge, to get your case approved. Just a few more weeks and all this is over." He waves a hand at *this*, and I assume he means me, burdened with his daughter's grief.

"I'm grateful for the chance you gave to me and my sister." I'm careful with my words because I want him to believe me. But I don't feel very grateful right now.

"We were lucky to get you."

Get you. Detain you. Catch you. The only luck involved was the bad kind. Then it occurs to me, for the first time, that my bad luck is Mr. Warner's good luck. I don't know why I never saw it that way before, but it's so obvious. The only reason Gabi and I have this chance at asylum is because Riley died and Mr. Warner's company is involved in this experiment. La Suerte isn't only Mala. She is two-faced. How beautiful and balanced, how terrible and cruel La Suerte is.

"I just wanted to thank you, actually." He walks to the balcony door. "When Riley and Reyanne were little, we lived in a smaller home." I can see his smile reflected in the glass of the doors. "The trouble the two of them would get into, you wouldn't believe. One time, they saw searchlights in the sky . . ." He turns to me. "You know what that is?" I nod.

"They used them in war, oh, a long time ago, to look for enemy planes and that kind of thing. Now they use them in Hollywood too, you know, for movie premieres." He turns back to the window, and I wonder if he's seeing those searchlights in his memory. "Riley spun a tall tale about those lights—that there was a movie premiere with famous actors and actresses just down the street. He convinced Reyanne to sneak out of the house and follow those searchlights. They climbed out a bathroom window and down a trellis." I think of how easily Rey climbed the bushes to her balcony. It is something she's always done. With her brother.

"They followed the lights for three blocks until they found them." His smile grows wider. I feel like I am seeing a part of Rey come alive that I didn't know, but I recognize her, my image of her as a little girl, walking into the world unafraid, the way Gabi has always done. Younger sisters are never afraid. "You know what those lights were for?" He turns again to look at me, and there is real laughter on his face. "A supermarket opening! Ha! They'd escaped their nanny for a supermarket opening." He comes back to the bed but doesn't sit. "Reyanne would have been upset, but Riley was quick. My Lord, was that boy quick. He convinced her that a supermarket opening was even better than a movie premiere. He made her feel like it was the biggest adventure in the world. They walked up and down the aisles taking free samples of meatballs and I don't even remember what else. We found them an hour later, full of food, and being given soda and lots of attention by the check-out girls. No amount of scolding and punishments could get the smiles off their faces." He has a faraway look in his eyes.

"I always remember the meatballs for some reason." Suddenly, his eyes focus, and he looks at me as if it is the most important thing for me to understand. "I thought I was going to lose Reyanne. She's so bullheaded—I thought she'd made up her mind to follow Riley the way she used to when they were little."

"She almost did," I say, looking to the balcony doors.

"Yeah. But now that you are doing this . . ." He gestures to the cuff on my leg. "Well, it seems like she might be okay."

I wonder at Mr. Warner's grief. Why didn't he find an illegal who he could convince to take his grief for him? He is a powerful businessman—he must be able to do it. Instead, he wears his grief like a stain.

"Well, I wanted to thank you," he repeats, turning to leave, "and let you know that we'll do everything in our power to make sure your asylum request is approved."

"You mean, *our* asylum requests. Mine and Gabriela's."

He looks confused. Maybe he doesn't remember who Gabi is. "My sister. She's—" She's everything to me. "She's like Rey, like Riley is to you."

He nods. "Yes. Indranie will take care of it. Everything will be fine," he says with a grimace I think is supposed to be a smile, then he leaves with a small wave of his hand.

A week ago, Gabi and I were watching TV with Rey and it seemed like any moment, something was going to happen. I just had to wait.

Now everything is happening. I'm draining away Rey's grief and her father is thanking me. Dr. Deng says I'm good at this. I can *withstand* a lot of trauma. If Pablo were alive, he would call me un burro. A donkey, a stupid pack animal. After all, that's what Pixie meant when she called me a service dog. An animal that does the work no person wants to do.

But I know something that makes this grief bearable. It will end. In a few more weeks, I will take the cuff off, and Gabi and I will be safe. Indranie says we will go in front of an immigration judge, one who specializes in asylum. She knows him. He'll do this for her. After that, I don't yet know what safety looks like. I don't know how long it will be before we can bring Mamá here and find a place to live. And after that, how long will it be until we feel that safety deep in our bones?

When I ask Indranie these questions, she tells me not to worry.

Pixie is coming over today with Rey's other friends for a picnic in the garden. Gabi and her friend Juliette are invited. It's almost May and the weather is finally getting warmer. I can tell it's warm because Gabi goes outside in T-shirts without her chaqueta. And Manny sweats as he works in the sunshine. But I do not feel warmth—or cold—for myself. I wonder if I'm too busy feeling other things to feel the heat of the sun. I am invited to the picnic, but I won't go. The thought of being around Pixie and so many of Rey's friends makes my stomach churn.

The medicine Rey gives me every night—anti-sads, she calls them—helps with this in a way that surprises me. I still feel all the horrible feelings, the waves of anxiety and terror, the deep anguish. But I have almost no will. That's what the pills do. "Without them," Dr. Deng says, "you might do something stupid."

My routine also makes the grief bearable. Rey and I sleep in her bed. She says it's so she can take care of me the way I took care of her when she was sick. When she is asleep, I grit my teeth and hold her hand. Dr. Deng says to do it while Rey is asleep, as that could make the transference easier. Easier but not better. Some part of my night is filled with the memories of Riley's death. Sometimes, it is only the moment the paramedics pulled Rey away from her brother, slowed down, agonizing, every second seeming to take hours. Sometimes, it is the memory of Riley's funeral, of Rey crying so loudly that everyone in the church stares and her mother tells her to be quiet. In the hours before the sun comes up, I cry quietly on my side of the bed, afraid to wake Rey, afraid she will ask me what's wrong, afraid I'll tell her.

I wake in the morning exhausted, with a weight on my chest that I spend the rest of the day trying to lift. Rey is up and showered and dressed and, most important of all, happy. She gets my tray of breakfast from Olga—piled high with food despite how little I eat—and fixes pillows around me so I'm comfortable.

"It's going to get better soon," she says, patting my hand awkwardly. To Rey, it must seem like the cuff hasn't worked its magic on me yet, that it's only a matter of time. "It took me a few days too. Before you know it, we'll both be off the anti-sads and tearing it up."

"Cabal," I say, adding "exactly" when she looks confused.

"*Cabal,*" she repeats. "*¡Puchica!*" she adds for good measure. I stretch my lips into a smile.

"Gabi taught me that one. Means *damn*, right?"

"You'll be translating for the UN in no time."

"What?"

I rest my head on the pillow. "That's what someone used to tell me. Mr. Rosen used to say I'd be translating for the UN in no time."

"Was this some kind of punishment for war crimes, or did you actually want to translate for the UN?"

"Don't be so disrespectful, Reyanne," I say, in what I hope sounds a little like Indranie's voice. "I always wanted to be a translator. I love words."

"Then that's what you will be," she says, as if saying so will make it true. "Are you sure you won't come to the picnic?"

"Yes. I'm just too tired."

"You have to meet Dave and Stitch when you're up to it. They're two of the oddest and best. And I want them to meet you. I've been talking their damn ears off about you."

I'm scared to think of her talking to her friends about me, telling them—what?

"If I don't produce you soon, they'll think you're one of my many hallucinations."

"Why would they think that?"

"Oh, I used to swear I saw faces in the folds of clothes in my closet. Sometimes they were people. Sometimes they were fauns."

At my blank look, she says, "You know, like Narnia."

"Oh! Mr. Tumnus!"

"I love me some Tumnus." Rey laughs.

"But why would they think I was one of your hallucinations?"

She tips her head down, considering me. "It's been a really long time since I've been excited about meeting someone new, you know?" she says, gripping my hand.

It's difficult to explain what happens when Rey holds my hand. I want it to feel good so much that for the first few seconds, it does—warm and safe, shivery. Then, my fingertips feel like they're too hot, then too numb. A wave of nausea travels up my hand, my arm, all the way through my body. It's that feeling when you've heard a whisper, a rumor of terrible news, the moment it begins to sink in that the world just became a barren place. And all this happens in an instant, while Rey is telling me how excited she is to be back at school, how much she wants me to meet her friends.

"I just want you to like them," she finishes, thankfully letting go of my hand.

I take a moment before replying, closing my eyes, adjusting as the sick feeling dissipates.

"I hope they like me," I say.

"They will like you. They have to. Pixie already talks about you all the time."

I open my eyes. I wish I could raise a single eyebrow like Gabi. "All the time?"

"She says you're cute. That's a very high compliment for Pixie. She likes to pretend she's all surface."

"I think there's lots of deep stuff going on in Pixie," I say.

"Right?" Rey smiles. "I'll come back after the picnic. Tell you all the gossip." She stands and kisses my forehead, like I'm her little sister.

I hate it.

And I can't keep the disappointment from my face. Rey's smile slips. "What's wrong?"

I know I'm good with words. That's why I don't understand how they can fail me so completely now. *I'm not your little sister, Rey, I don't want to be kissed that way. You're the first thing I think of when I wake up, even before I think of Gabi. That terrifies and thrills me.*

But it isn't just words that I'm losing control of, it's my own feelings. Every time Rey looks at me, my heart and mind whisper together that maybe this is more than friendship. It's a tragedy that I can feel so many of her emotions and not know if any of them are for me.

"Nothing. I'm just tired." I close my eyes, pretending to fall asleep.

 # Chapter 24

I sit in the kitchen watching Olga pack a big basket with food while Gabi eats her after-school snack. I make myself smile and ask questions to show Gabi that I'm fine and that she can be happy.

"Juliette is trying to get her mom to let us see this movie . . ." Gabi says, talking faster and faster. Her English is improving every day now that she's in school. "Where the grandparents are zombies, I think? And she said they try to kill the grand-kids, but they aren't really their grandparents."

I try to follow. "So, the zombies dress like the grandparents? Like Caperucita Roja?" I can't imagine a zombie movie based on Red Riding Hood, but anything is possible.

Gabi shakes her head. "No, they aren't really grandparents. They're serial killers."

"What kind of thing is a cereal killer?" I ask. "Cereales that will kill you?"

Gabi laughs at me, and I notice that she is wearing her mo-torcycle boots. Again.

"No, *serial*, as in many. A serial killer is a person who kills a lot of people," she says simply, stomping around the kitchen looking for more chocolate chip cookies. I can't decide if I should be telling her to wear a different pair of shoes, or that Olga doesn't like us to wear shoes in the house. Or should I tell her that she can't see a movie about serial killers? I am so tired. I cannot be her mamá today. I can barely be her sister.

"I don't like you watching movies like this," I say feebly.

"Relax." She pouts at me, and I almost smile. "We probably won't see that movie anyway."

"Isn't she having a party?" I can't keep all of Gabi's things straight in my mind. She has 4-H—the club for animals—in the afternoons. She goes to the library with Juliette—I wave to Mrs. Guinto when she is dropped off. And Indranie has already taken Gabi to buy a birthday present for Juliette. I remember they showed me, but I don't remember what it was.

"That's tomorrow night. Remember? Saturday? You said it was okay. Mr. Guinto is going to—"

"Yes. Okay," I say, turning my grimace into a smile. I don't remember. And when I try to, my head hurts more.

Manny brings Juliette into the kitchen, and the two girls squeal and laugh so much that Olga scolds them to go outside if they have to be so loud.

I watch Gabi sweep Juliette out to the garden.

"You're not going to the picnic?" Olga asks.

"No. Not today."

"If not today, when will you go, nena?"

"I won't."

Olga turns her head to one side like a curious bird watching a worm. "Estás muy flaca."

"I'm not skinny," I say, putting my hand on my stomach. I

think of Mrs. Rosen and her "puppy fat." Even she would not find any puppy fat on me now.

"Yes, you are. Muy flaca. And you do not eat. I get one girl better, and I have one girl worse. What is happening to the world? I need all my nenitas to be good, healthy girls."

I smile. I like the thought of Gabi, Rey, and me being Olga's girls.

"Why don't you go to the picnic? A little. So you can watch out for Gabi," she says, shoving a roll of napkins into the basket.

"She doesn't need watching. Everyone loves Gabi."

"That is what I am saying. Everyone loves her. Good things and bad. You should watch over her."

I scowl. "You just want me to go to the picnic. That is why you're saying it."

"Maybe." She shrugs, closing the top of the basket. She lifts it off the table and hands it to me. "Go, take it to them. See for yourself."

I go to the bathroom to make sure my hair is combed before taking the basket out to the reflecting pool. I know why I'm doing this: plain, stupid curiosity. My plan is to give Rey the food and slip away before anyone really notices.

The basket isn't heavy, but soon I feel like dragging it instead of carrying it. Near the reflecting pool, a large blanket is spread out on the grass. A speaker plays music, and Juliette and Gabi sit close to each other near the pool. I see Pixie sitting next to Rey and two boys I don't know.

One of them, a tall white boy with red-gold hair, stands up and jogs over to me. "Need help?" he asks.

I shake my head.

"I'm Dave. You're Marisol, right? Rey told us about you. We've been wanting to meet you."

We reach the blanket, and I stand like a fool for too many seconds.

Rey comes over to me. I think she's going to take the basket from me, touch me. I panic, dropping it so that fruit and food containers spill out. Dave moves quickly to put everything back in the basket.

"I'm sorry," I say.

"I'm so glad you came," she whispers in my ear. She gives me a quick, scalding hug. "Come meet everyone." She takes my hand, pulling me forward.

"You met Dave—he's semi-normal." I feel Rey's emotions pouring into me, liquid, like bad medicine. I clench the hand that Rey isn't holding.

"Semi-human, you mean," the other boy says. He's morocho, black, with his hair in braids and the longest eyelashes I've ever seen on a boy. He waves. I force myself to smile. These are Rey's friends. And they were Riley's friends too. Being with them makes her happy but also brings her painful memories of Riley. Like la nata rising to the top of a mug of warm milk, her feelings separate. She keeps the cream and gives me the bitter.

"That's Stitch," Rey says, smacking his face gently as she passes. "He thinks he's funny."

"Just because I don't want a stupid nickname," the boy

named Dave says, "doesn't mean I'm semi-human." He examines the contents of the picnic basket with greedy interest.

"I have a long list of reasons," Stitch says. I try to concentrate on what the word *stitch* means. I say it under my breath. *Stit-cha*. I can't remember what it means. "I'll share my reasons with Marisol when she's ready for the truth." He winks at me.

"Because the truth is out there?" Pixie asks. She looks bored and, underneath that, unhappy to see me. I avoid her eyes. I cannot absorb any more feelings.

Mercifully, Rey lets go of my hand. The faucet slows to a trickle. Rey sits on the blanket, leaning back on her elbows, her long legs pale as mountain sunshine. She pats the space next to her for me to sit.

"No way. We're not going down an *X-Files* rabbit hole. We just binge-watched the new series," Dave says.

"Remember when Rey wore her THE TRUTH IS OUT THERE T-shirt for the sixth grade science presentation?" Stitch laughs.

Dave laughs with him. "Pretty sure she got an F on that project for the total lack of any actual science."

"I got a D. My illustrations were really good." Rey gestures again for me to sit next to her. As soon as I do, Stitch hands me an orange.

"Or do you want an apple?"

"This is good," I say.

"Told you she was practically mute," Pixie says. When Dave shoots her an angry look, she continues, through bites of an apple. "What I can't understand is your horrible, car-crash fascination with *Cedar Hollow*."

"*Cedar Hollow*, metaphor for repressed suburban life," Stitch says. "Discuss."

"I spent freshman year wishing those two would bone already," Dave says with a grin.

Rey points her toes at him, graceful as a dancer. I notice she has painted her nails yellow to match the flowers on her dress. "You're an idiot on so many levels, David—someone could write a book about it. A very long, boring book, bonus cyanide tablet included."

I can't understand them. I am listening to a conversation that has been going on for a long time. And I realize that is what this is. A friendship for many years.

"How long have you all been friends?" I ask. I don't want to prove that Pixie is right by not talking, though I'm scared of making a fool of myself.

Rey is busy putting food on plates. Slices of ham and salami, little crackers, and cheese and grapes. I peel my orange slowly. I want to have something to do.

"Since middle school," Pixie says. "We've been friends, frenemies, lovers for too many years to count."

"You're gross," Rey says.

"And it's not too many years to count," Dave says. "Six isn't too high to count for you, is it, *Peaches*?"

"It's *Pixie*, you troglodyte," says Pixie.

"So many name changes, I forget which one we're on now," Dave says. He's skinny and pale, like Rey, but covered with freckles. I watch his freckled fingers make a tower with crackers and salami. Do all Americans eat so strangely, or just Rey and her friends?

"You could always call her by her real name," Stitch says.

"I wouldn't," Pixie growls.

Suddenly, I very much want to know what her real name is.

"Can I guess?" I ask.

"Yes!" Rey says, squealing with delight. "Guess Pixie's real name and you get a prize."

"The prize is, Pixie kills you with her laser beam eyes," Stitch says, pointing his fingers like guns.

"No, the prize is a kiss from me, of course," Rey says with a small, secret smile.

"Ugh. You always have to be the damn princess," Dave complains.

"You didn't use to mind."

"No guessing," Pixie says.

But I want to guess. I want to make Pixie feel as uncomfortable as she makes me feel. If that means I'm mezquina, then fine. Or maybe I just don't want anyone else to win the prize.

I try to think of the most normal American name I can think of. Katie? Susan? What names have I heard on American TV?

"Amber?" I say.

"No! But that's a good guess," Rey says to me. "It's not Aimee either. You'll never guess. I think her parents lost their minds."

I listen to them tease each other in ways I cannot follow. Most of it, I think, is friendly. I feel Pixie watching me. I don't guess at her name anymore, and they drop the game for other games, other memories. They seem happy. Juliette and Gabi sit down to eat with us, and I am surprised by how much Rey and her friends like being with the younger girls. They don't make them feel unwanted, like they are pests. And when Gabi tells them she wants to cut her long hair to be more sophisticated, they say, with serious faces, that her long hair is very cool, very on trend.

The food doesn't taste like much, but watching Rey is enough for me. I'm fascinated by the headband of yellow flowers she wears. It's only silk and plastic, but she wears it like a crown. Stitch asks her if she's going to grow out her hair, and Rey answers that it depends.

"What does it depend on?"

"How long I feel like this."

Pixie looks confused. "What do you mean, *like this?*"

"Good. I mean, I feel good now, but I might not always, right, Marisol?"

I'm unprepared for her question. "What?"

"This is good, really good, right now. But it doesn't always work like that. This new treatment has ups and downs. Marisol had some tough days too, right?"

"Tough days," I repeat, hoping it sounds like an answer.

"So," Dave says, "you're doing these treatments too?"

"Oh, yeah, we're the Lab Rats—that's our official name. We might get Lab Rat T-shirts. Matching tattoos." Rey laughs. "It's our job to figure out if it's safe for you regular Joes."

That is my job, Rey. Only my job.

"Sounds shady as hell," Pixie mutters.

"Not shady," Rey says, sounding a little defensive. "Dad wouldn't test it on us if it wasn't safe."

Pixie snorts in disbelief.

"But how does it work?" Dave asks. I feel Gabi watching us. Half of me wants to stop them from talking about this, to disappear, and the other half wants to tell them *exactly* how it works. If Pablo were here, he'd say, *No te achiques*, don't make yourself small. I feel less than small. I feel invisible.

"Well," Rey admits, "I don't know how the science works."

"You don't know how it works, but you still wear that thing?" Pixie says.

"You don't know how combustion engine thingies work, but you still drive a car," Rey shoots back.

"You are both so bad at science," Stitch groans.

"Gabi! You like cars! I bet you know how they work," I blurt out, wanting to get them talking about anything other than the cuff. Gabi looks startled, then a little embarrassed at all the attention on her.

"I like cars," she says shyly, "but I don't know how they work, exactly." She shoots me an angry look, as if to ask, *What are you doing?* I don't know the answer to that. I wish I had never come out here.

"Anyway," Rey says, taking back the conversation. "I don't know how it works, and I don't care." She sits up, crossing her legs. The cuff circles her ankle like an ornament. It has never seemed this way to me when I see it on my own leg. It has always seemed to me like un eslabón de una cadena. "This little beauty takes our grief away." She smiles at me.

Our grief.

"I don't get it. I mean, I'm happy for you, believe me. But I don't get how that's physically possible," Dave says.

"It's probably placebo effect," Stitch says.

"Bullshit. You don't know anything," Pixie says.

"It might be!" Rey says brightly. "It might be all in our heads, but it doesn't matter, right? If it works?"

Rey reaches for my hand, and I am truly part of a chain. I cannot escape. "Marisol convinced me to try it. She said it would make me feel better, and it has. It helped her when her . . ." She stops, then finds her voice. "When her brother died. And now it's helping me." She looks to me. As if I can say anything to help her words.

"And when it wasn't working that great for me, Marisol helped me."

"That's her job, right?" Pixie says.

"Fuck off, Pixie," Stitch says.

"No, I mean, she's like an old-fashioned maid or something, right? A paid companion? You watch those shitty British shows, Dave, don't tell me you don't. Marisol's like a lady's maid."

I watch Gabi's face. She's confused, angry, her beautiful eyes watching as Rey's friends talk about me as if I'm not here, as if I don't matter.

"I watched *one* episode of *Downton Abbey* with my grandma years ago, and you can't let it go," Dave mumbles.

"Pixie. Don't be a bitch. I'm getting really sick of your jealous crap," Rey says, and it's enough to shut Pixie's mouth.

I see disaster coming. I see Gabi stand, her face a swirl of emotions. I see Juliette, confused, unhappy with how things have turned. I see it all, but I can't stop any of it.

"You have it wrong. The wrong way around." Her English is stilted. It happens sometimes—too much emotion clouds our thinking. When we're angry, words come to us in Spanish first and we stumble as we translate.

"My sister is *curing* Rey's grief." She knows the words aren't quite right, and I feel her frustration.

I stand up, facing my sister. "Gabi, it's okay. It's not a big deal," I say, hoping she understands the words I'm not saying. *Leave it alone.* But she won't look at me.

"She's helped me so much," Rey says.

Gabi gulps. "No, you don't understand. She's not helping. She's *taking* it."

Don't, Gabriela. Don't say any more.

Rey looks at me, a line of confusion creasing her forehead. I am helpless to respond. "You'll feel better soon." Rey sounds hesitant, unsure. "The treatment will start working for you too. I know it will."

Gabi doesn't give up. "It will never work for Marisol." Her voice trembles as her eyes move from the boys to Pixie, then finally to Rey.

"Sol takes your grief, Rey, and keeps it. That's how it works. She suffers for it. I've seen it."

In two steps, I am next to Gabi, grabbing her wrist, pulling hard. "Basta, ingrata," I spit at her, so nastily that it's like I've slapped her. Her eyes widen, and her mouth hangs open. I see tears start in her eyes.

"Don't hurt her," Rey says to me quietly. I see that Gabi is crying, and I'm surprised that it's possible for me to feel more shame. I let go of Gabi's wrist as if it is fire.

"I would never hurt Gabi," I rasp. But who am I talking to? I don't understand what's happening. Gabi stands by Juliette, who hugs her protectively. *That's my job,* I think. *I'm supposed to protect Gabi.*

I turn to run back to the carriage house. The sun shines and the sky is beautifully clear. But La Mala Suerte has found me, and I cannot escape.

Chapter 25

Nothing stops me. I see Manny talking to other gardeners in the stone-walled garden as I pass. I walk through the carriage house, hearing Olga moving around upstairs. Right through the front door. Indranie's car is gone, and I am surprised but not sorry.

The half-moon driveway is covered with fine red pebbles. My shoes kick up little clouds of dust. I don't walk too fast because that draws attention, but not too slow because that invites thinking. Just like on the carretera, I keep my head down. When I pass the open black gates, I wonder what they are for. Who do they keep in or out? Or are they all a show? A reminder that only the ones who are invited may pass?

The road is quiet. Neatly paved and deep black—no holes or defects in this road. On the other side of the road is a lake. It is difficult to see past the trees and bushes that line both sides of this road. I know that to go back to Washington, DC, I turn left. To go to the town with the Archetype ice cream place, I go right. To feel water cover me, destroy the cuff on my leg, wash away the weight of too many memories, I have to walk into that lake.

I stand at the side of the road, my chest rising and falling as if I've been running for hours, days. I can't get enough breath in my body for what I have to do. Every sound is explosive in my head. A car speeding past. A door opening and closing. I remember being underwater in the pool, surrounded by silence, weightless. I want that again.

I take a step toward the water, my feet heavy and plodding. I stop, my breath coming too quickly, like a dog. I take another step, as if I am already pushing into the water and it is already dragging me in. But when I move again, a hand grabs my arm and yanks, hard. For a moment, I am falling backward. Indranie catches me.

"Are you trying to get yourself killed?" she shouts, pulling me farther back from the road as a car blurs past, too fast almost to see. I stare at her, my mouth open. *Answer the question, Marisol. Are you trying to get yourself killed?* I don't know.

She points across the street accusingly. "There's nothing but Lake Carter on the other side of this road."

"I didn't know that."

"But you were crossing the road. Why?" Her eyes are suspicious, worried, frantic. Nothing like her usual wall of calm.

"I—I don't know." I shake my head. I was going to do something. I was walking toward something, or at least that's what it felt like. Now that feeling has disappeared. I don't know where I should go. A wave of emotions—I don't know who they belong to—breaks over me. I start to cry. I am inutil. Una desgracia.

Indranie pulls me into a hug. It is many minutes before I realize that it's her sobs I hear, her tears that fall hot on my cheek. I feel in my pocket for a brown napkin, the kind from a fast-food restaurant. I give it to her.

"Don't cry," I say. No llores. It must be the most useless

thing to say to someone when the world is falling apart. When there is more pain inside than can fit. I know what that feels like, what it looks and sounds like.

"I'm so sorry, Marisol."

"You didn't do anything."

"Oh God," she says, crumpling the napkin against her face, covering it. "I did everything I could to ruin your life. But I swear I didn't want you to suffer. I only wanted to keep Rey safe."

I shake my head, wordless sounds coming from my mouth. If Indranie hadn't found us, given us this chance, we'd already be back in Ilopango, desperate to find the money to try again before it was too late. None of this is Indranie's fault. She looks at me, tears making her brown eyes look like glass.

"Listen to me. I lied to you."

It is not cold in Indranie's car, but she has put the heat on. We drive down roads I don't recognize. If Indranie were driving me to the border, thousands of kilometers away, I don't think I could protest. I am so tired.

"I'm not a bad person." She starts to speak, then is silent again. I wait. I'm good at waiting.

With a heavy sigh, she tries again. "I went to the detention center looking for someone for the experiment," Indranie says. I push into the soft leather of the passenger seat. I am here again, in Indranie's car, like I was at the beginning.

"Dr. Deng's animal trials on the CTS device were successful. He told Scott he needed human participants to begin clinical trials." It takes me a moment to remember that Mr. Warner's name is Scott. "As CEO, Scott uses lobbyists to

get Congressional funding and fast-tracking from the FDA."
Indranie isn't talking to me, not really. She's confessing.

"But he couldn't get any of that without clinical trials. We
tried to get other test subjects. Homeless people. Psych pa-
tients. People who might try anything as a last resort. But no
one would agree. It was too dangerous." Her beautiful hands,
nails perfectly painted, grip the steering wheel, but she keeps
her eyes on the road. I know I must listen. But I'm afraid of
what she will say. Afraid to hear any more grief.

"When Riley died, Scott wanted to scrap the whole project. He just wanted to concentrate on helping Rey." Outside, I
watch the faces in other cars—blurred, white, and searching.
At this moment, I wish I could switch my life with theirs.

"But I convinced him that the CTS device could help Rey.
More than help her. If it worked, it would erase her grief. Like
magic."

I turn to look at Indranie. Can she really have been so
crédula? To believe it would be like magic? Magic is power
without consequences. That's why it isn't real. Everything has
consequences.

"We found an army vet who agreed to a one-time test as a
favor to Scott. Dr. Deng said we needed someone close to Rey's
age—that would work best for the monthlong trial. I remembered the Immigrant Family Center in Pennsylvania from
when I worked at USCIS." She shakes her head slowly. "Believe
me, I feel sick when I think about it."

I don't think I'll ever believe Indranie again.

"I told myself we'd be giving some kid a chance of a lifetime.
We'd be saving two people if it worked. I didn't want to think
about what would happen if it didn't work. And Dr. Deng told

me it couldn't fail." She bares her teeth, and I know it cannot be a smile.

"I told the director I wanted to talk to someone who spoke a little English. He said he knew the perfect candidate, a bright, polite girl with excellent English."

Her words strike me, I know they do, but I can't *feel* it. It's like watching a knife slip and cut your finger, before your brain tells you it hurts. I am stuck in that moment.

"I waited in the hallway. I looked into dormitories—all those terrified faces, mothers and children, little babies, all crammed into rooms, rows and rows of metal beds, piles of clothes. I wasn't sure I could do it."

Indranie pauses for so long that I think she has forgotten me. I search for my anger and my rage, but I can't find them. I can't feel anything but heaviness. The faces in other cars seem to turn toward us, as if they too can't help but listen to Indranie's words. When she speaks again, her voice is thick.

"It was nearly twenty minutes before the director told me they couldn't find you, or your sister. I knew it was time for me to leave. I couldn't get mixed up in a scandal of missing immigrant children," she says bitterly. "I told myself that was it. We needed to find another way for the experiment to work, another way to make Rey want to live."

Indranie turns her face to me, and I can't look away. Her words are like a hook in me. I think of everything that must have happened on the day Gabi and I escaped the detention center. Every small flick of La Suerte's hands, tightening around our future.

Indranie blinks, her attention back on the road. Tears escape down her face. "Then I drove past you and Gabi. Two brown girls walking on a dirt road less than a mile from the detention center? No bags, no coats? I circled around and stopped. My heart was racing in my chest, and I thought, *If they come with me, I can help them. If they come with me, it will be better than staying in that awful detention center.*" Her eyes find mine again. "I told myself it was safe. I told myself you were better off." She doesn't wait for me to answer. "Once you were in the car, I convinced myself that it was the right choice. It was going to work with you, I knew it."

"You were right," I say, because even if I'd known all this, known how dangerous the cuff could be, it wouldn't have changed a thing. "It does work."

I realize with surprise that we are stopped at the front gates of the Warner house. It's completely dark outside. Indranie cries, covering her face with her hands.

"I lied to you. Your asylum request wasn't denied. There's every chance it would have been approved. It would have taken time, but the chances were good. Luck was on your side. I'm so sorry."

I was numb when I walked out of the house. I stayed numb as Indranie drove around in circles, loosening her story, string by string. Now I want to feel something—anger, blistering rage, disgust—all the emotions that I have earned the right to feel. But the only emotion that seeps through me is sorrow.

"It's my fault. And my responsibility," she gasps, wiping at her eyes again. Her hand comes away with a streak of black makeup. "You have to take the cuff off, Marisol."

"I can't."

She turns to me angrily. I almost don't recognize her face—it's folded into itself, hateful. But the hate on her face isn't for me. "You were *this* close to killing yourself! You think I can live with that? I can't. I won't. You're going to take that cuff off."

"I can't," I say again. And although I know I can't take it off, I don't know why.

¿Por qué? I ask myself. Why can't I take the cuff off if I don't have to suffer to keep Gabi safe? Why do I dread taking it off instead of feeling relief at the thought?

Because of Rey.

Because she knows how it feels to lose a part of herself. Because despite her pain she paints her toenails sunshine yellow. Because I can't abandon her to her grief. I can't leave her there alone.

I don't have anything else to say. As I open the car door to get out, Indranie grabs my shoulder. "You can't absorb all her grief, Marisol. You can't withstand so much."

Withstand. I have been *withstanding* for a week, and it has been agony. Today, I was close to giving up. If Indranie hadn't stopped me from crossing the road, maybe a car would have hit me. That would have been an accident. Or if I had made it to the lake, how far would I have walked into the water? All the way to the bottom? I don't know. But I know I cannot stop.

I leave Indranie sobbing in her car. I walk past the gates, freely entering a world that wants to destroy me.

Chapter 26

What did you do?" Olga demands when I trudge into her kitchen, sitting gratefully at her table. There is no sign of Rey's friends, or of Gabi and Juliette.

"Nada."

"Mentira."

I am so tired, I don't know how I keep my eyes open. "I yelled at Gabi. Then I went for a walk to calm down. Where is she?"

"Who?"

"Gabi, of course."

"I thought you'd like to know where Rey is, since she has been looking for you in every place."

"No. I need to talk to Gabi."

"She went to sleep."

"So early?"

"She took a bag of those papitas and said she wanted to be by herself. I made her eat a supper first, por supuesto."

I know I should go to Gabi and apologize. But it's a relief not to have to talk to her right now.

Indranie rushes into the kitchen, stopping when she sees me. A look passes between her and Olga that I don't completely understand.

"Marisol, I need to talk to you."

"No. I'm too tired. I don't want to talk now."

Indranie walks toward me, but Olga gets between us.

"Can I get you something to eat, Indranie?"

"What? No, not now." She looks around Olga, practically over her head since Olga is so short.

"Marisol, please listen," Indranie begins. I turn away. She's said too much already. I won't listen to another word.

"No, no," Olga says pleasantly like she's commenting on the weather. "It's not good now. She's too tired, ¿no es así, amor?"

I nod.

"Talk tomorrow," Olga says with a smile that anyone can see is a challenge. "All things are better in the morning." Indranie, helpless in the face of Olga's protection, promises we'll talk in the morning.

When she leaves, Olga lets go of the back of my chair and levels a long look at me. I brace myself for a cascade of questions.

"Rey is still looking for you."

"All right. I'll go find her," I say, even though I have no intention of doing that.

"No, primero you eat."

I eat with Manny and Olga in the kitchen, the only sound the scrape of forks on plates. I force myself to eat because Olga is watching me, but shame sits next to grief in my stomach, fighting over which is the bigger monster until I am full. I excuse myself and thank Olga for the delicious dinner. They are going out again tonight, and I am glad I can be alone.

I hide in the big, comfortable room with the large TV and

soft cushions. I switch channels for a while, looking for *Cedar Hollow*, until I find an old movie—black and white, the kind that Mrs. Rosen would have liked. "Aren't they beautiful?" she'd say, drinking Martini & Rossi over ice. "They don't talk like that anymore, honey. It's all fast talk and gibberish now. It's a god-damn shame." The women and the men in those old movies were beautiful. They looked like they were lit with candles, and they moved like dancers. I watch the old movie without seeing it.

When Rey finds me, a different kind of movie is on the TV, one with a car chase and explosions. I rub away the dried salt of old tears. Sometimes I cry without realizing it.

"Hey," Rey says.

"Hi," I say.

"I've been looking for you."

There's nothing to say to that except what I'm thinking. *Please don't ask me to hold your hand tonight. Just not tonight.* But I can't say those things.

Rey sits next to me, turning off the TV. There's a thin hum, then silence. She's still wearing her sunshine yellow dress, but the flower headband is gone. There are tears dried on her face too.

"I'm going to sleep down here for tonight," I say quickly, desperately.

"Why?"

"Because I need—rest."

"What if you need me? What if something happens to you? No one will be there to help you. If you get bad." She curls her fingers over her ear, still not used to her hair being so short. I've seen her do that more times than I can count.

"I won't get bad tonight."

"Is what Gabi said true?" she asks.

"No."

Rey's expression is carefully blank. "No? So, you aren't absorbing all my grief? Is she just confused?"

I grab on to that explanation greedily. "Yes, she's just confused. She doesn't know anything. You know how kids are, saying stupid things sometimes." I just need her to leave. If I can rest for one night, I can be stronger tomorrow.

She looks at me, nodding slightly. "See, that's how I know you're lying."

"What?"

"You're lying. You'd never talk about Gabi like that. Like she didn't matter."

I'm shaking my head before she finishes her sentence. "That's not what I'm saying."

"I know what you're saying. And I'm calling bullshit. Remember *bullshit*? It's when what you're saying isn't true. *Bullshit*." She leans into me when she says it, like she is taunting me with her words.

Finally, I find my anger, so quickly that it turns into useless tears.

"You don't know anything about bulls' shit. You are surrounded by it. Your house. Do you know what your house is? It's a house for things, not people. And you. You are not even a real person. You are just—"

Do you like to kiss girls, hermanita? I have tried so hard, for so long, to keep Pablo's voice out of my head. *Are you one of those twisted girls? Tortillera?* I don't have the strength to do it anymore. *You love English words, don't you? Dyke. That's what you are. That's the word for you.*

He spits at me, a spray of shame across my face. It is too long before I can move my hand to wipe my face of his spit, but my face is dry. I am in the carriage house living room, and Rey is sitting so close to me that I can see the pecas scattered across her nose. *She has pecas,* I think. *Like me.*

"Are you okay?" Rey asks. I curl into a ball, pushing myself into the corner of the sofa as far as I can go. I want to disappear.

"Please," I beg her. "Just give me one night on my own." I wish I had more to give.

"When I touch you, it's worse for you? The way it's better for me?" She reaches her hand out to my shoulder.

I press my mouth closed so I do not speak, telling myself to *withstand* it, not to move, but I have no control over my body. I pull away, further into a ball. Just get through this now. And tomorrow I will do better.

"Tomorrow I will do better." I shut my eyes tightly against the pounding in my head, the pounding of my heart. What does Rey see when she looks at me? A small brown girl of no importance? A twisted girl infected with the wrong kind of love? A dog, a donkey, a broken bird? Every thought is like a shovel digging out my chest, making me hollow.

I open my eyes when she touches my leg, feather-light. Rey kneels on the carpet in front of me, her eyes on mine. I think of the way you watch an angry dog, keeping your eyes on its eyes so it does not surprise you.

"Don't," I whisper hoarsely. But I don't stop her when her fingers scratch at my ankle, finding the release button on the cuff.

"I never thought the cuff would work." I don't move when

she opens the cuff and slides it off my leg. "The only reason I put it on was because of you. You said I wasn't alone anymore and I believed you." The cuff clatters loudly when she places it on the glass table. A moment later, her cuff is next to mine.

"Now you have to believe me." Rey sits next to me again. "Can I?" she asks. I am confused until I see that she holds her arms open. She holds them for me. I don't trust myself to speak, only nod.

I tense as she pulls me into her arms, waiting for the wave of pain, the memory of terrors. Slowly, with her breath in my ear, and the warmth of her body surrounding me, I relax. She pulls me closer, putting my head on her shoulder. In the center of my body, I know I am still waiting for La Mala Suerte, for the bad luck to come.

"Is this all right?" she asks.

I don't know if it is. I am afraid for both of us. But I don't want anything to change. The house is asleep around us; I can feel each room, each person sleeping deeply in the night. My breathing slows down. I let myself be held, then reach my arms around her and hold her too. This is the most dangerous thing I have ever done.

"We'll work it out tomorrow," she says. "Try to sleep."

And I do.

# Chapter 27

The sunlight wakes me. I'm under a blanket I don't recognize and my neck hurts from being curled into Rey's side. I sit up quickly, taking most of the blanket with me.

"You're a blanket hog, you know that?" Rey says sleepily.

We're in the living room where we fell asleep last night. I hear Olga in the kitchen, making breakfast, listening to Celia Cruz on the radio.

I don't feel anything. No rise of anguish, no fall of despair. No tears. And then I feel something that is almost sweet. Relief.

Rey is wearing a sweatshirt and pants with Mickey Mouse on them. She must have changed last night, and covered us with a blanket. She must have taken care of me.

"You have a look on your face," she says, studying me. "Are you freaking out?"

"No. I don't know."

"Okay, because you have this kind of funny thing going on with your eyebrows."

My hand covers half my face automatically. I want to hide whatever the funny thing is.

She laughs. "No, I mean, it's cute. It's like your eyebrows are trying to talk, but they're only saying 'surprise!'" She laughs harder.

"I can't raise one eyebrow like Gabi," I say.

She raises her left eyebrow, sharp as a bird's wing.

"Or you."

"How are you feeling?"

Her face makes me want to cry, but in a pure, hopeful way. Esperanza. It is so fragile.

"I don't want to die today," I say.

"Me either." She pulls the blanket back from me so we are both under it, huddled like little children. Under the covers, she reaches for my hand.

"Is this okay? Does it hurt?"

I'm too overwhelmed to speak. Her long fingers are bony and thin, but her grip is strong. She holds me like she means it.

"This isn't bulls' shit. Right? You and me?" I have to ask, even though I'm inviting disaster by putting it into words. She could drop my hand and turn away. She could tell me we're just good friends.

Rey shakes her head gravely. "No bullshit," she replies.

Olga sets a tray of breakfast on the glass table. When she sees the two cuffs sitting side by side, she looks at me sharply.

"¿Qué pasó aquí?"

Rey rolls her eyes. "Why the hell did I take German?" she mutters, reaching for the plate of eggs and bacon. At the first bite of bacon, a blissful smile spreads across her face.

Olga tsks. "Don't say bad words," she tells Rey. She casts another worried look at the cuffs.

"¿Vas a estar bien? ¿Sabes lo que haces?" *Will you be okay? Do you know what you are doing?*

"Está todo bien," I say, hoping it will be. "Is Gabi awake?"

Olga snorts. "She left already."

"Where did she go?"

"The party for the friend, la Filipina, ¿cómo se llama?"

"Her name is Juliette," I say.

"Yes. Mr. Guinto left me a note. The party is later today, and Gabi is helping with the decorations." Olga counts off the things my sister will do on her fingers. "They go to the mall for shopping and getting nails done with Mr. Guinto . . ." Olga stops to check the notes.

"Luego, Mr. Guinto will drop the girls off to the movies for to see *The Granny*." She frowns. "It's either a comedy about abuelitas or about abuelitas who kill." Olga continues, "After sleeping over, and then breakfast, the girls will do algo para la escuela." She snaps her fingers, trying to come up with the right word. "You know, la feria de la ciencia?" I nod. "Then, Mr. Guinto will bring Gabi home."

Rey tries to follow the Spanglish conversation. "What's *feria*? Haven't heard you say that before, Olga. Does it mean *fierce*?"

Olga frowns. "You don't listen. I try to teach you, but you never listen."

"It doesn't mean *fierce*. It means *fair*, like a science fair," I say.

Rey reaches for her phone. "So, how do you say *fierce*?"

"Feroz. Like, you are *so* not feroz." I smile.

"Watch yourself, Aimee."

"Okay, ¿algo más, chicas?" Olga says.

"I'll be right back," Rey says before leaving the room.

"Are Gabi and Juliette going to the movies by themselves?" I ask Olga.

She squints at me over her reading glasses. "Mr. Guinto will be in the mall where el cine is, and his daughter has a phone with the thing on it so he knows where his child is at all times."

"What thing?"

Olga's thin shoulders bunch up. "I do not know what it is called. One of those things on the phone, like a button."

"An app."

"An app. Okay." Olga looks at me. "Cuidado, ¿okay, chiquita?" she says before turning to go back to the kitchen. I appreciate that Olga wants me to be careful—careful of taking the cuff off, careful of being with Rey. But I want to be more than careful. I want to be happy.

Rey walks back into the room slowly, balancing a plate. "Now we do shots, remember?"

On the plate are three little pills and tiny paper cups of the bitter liquid medicine.

"But why? I don't need it now."

Rey opens my hand and places the pills in my palm. "Yeah, you do. You took them before, and you take them now. That's a rule. You can't stop cold turkey. How do you think I ended up at the VCU ward last time? Stopped taking my meds. And how did I end up puking butterflies?"

"You listened to Pixie."

"Exactly. I am sometimes stupid, but I can learn."

I take the pills and drink the liquid medicine. Then, I eat a little toast to get the bitter taste out of my mouth.

"So. Since we're feeling good, and, you know, we're—" She takes my hand. "Feeling good," she says, drawing out the words.

My face must look confused again because Rey becomes serious.

"You know I like you, right?" She pauses, biting her lip. "*¿Como una novia?*"

I hold still, waiting to see what kind of suerte this will be.

"Did I say it right? *Like a girlfriend?*" Rey asks anxiously. When my expression doesn't change, she starts to pull her hand away. I hold on tightly.

"You said it right."

She smiles. "Okay. So. This is okay?" She holds up our clasped hands.

How can I know? I only know that I don't want her to stop holding my hand.

"Yes," I say. "This is okay."

"Good. Then let's go out."

"What about Indranie?" I ask. I don't see her car in the driveway.

"She's with Dad at a reelection fund-raiser for some senator," Rey answers, adjusting the mirrors on the sides of the car.

"On a Saturday?"

"My dad is ready to deploy his checkbook whenever and wherever he can buy votes. Corrupting the government isn't a nine-to-five job, you know."

"You're kidding around, right?"

"Mostly."

We sit in another of Mr. Warner's cars. A small, funny car painted dark green and white, new and shiny like a toy. "The Mini was supposed to be Riley's. He failed his driver's test too many times, so Dad said he couldn't have the car until he re-took the driving course."

I watch her face as she talks about her brother. I can't feel her emotions anymore. I can't sense when she is stopped by grief, when it eats her up. I can only watch her face and try to figure out how she feels.

"Was he terrible at driving?"

She turns down the driveway. "Yeah, he sucked," she says, smiling sideways at me. "He felt it was unmanly to be so bad at driving. I think he psyched himself out watching the driving shows Gabi loves so much, with those idiots doing spinouts in parking lots. He thought driving would be like that." Her voice falters, and I think I almost feel it, the wave of grief that passes through her. But it is only what I think is happening, not what I feel is happening.

"What's a spinout?" I ask.

Rey looks at me with a devilish smile. "You want me to show you?"

"Is it dangerous?"

"Hell yeah."

"Then no."

"I thought you'd say that," she says, putting her foot on the gas pedal and making the car leap forward. She laughs at my expression. "I'm just kidding. I don't even know how to do that. I'm the good twin, remember?"

"You're mostly good," I say.

"But you like mostly good," she says, driving out through the black gates.

"I like a little bad too," I say. I keep my face turned to my window so she cannot see my cheeks flush. But we are both smiling, I know.

"Where are we going?" I ask.

"Where aren't we going?" she says teasingly.

It's like she is inviting me with a joke. "Okay," I say, trying to sound innocent. "Where aren't we going?"

She laughs. It's a joy to hear her laugh like this when we are both ourselves. I think I am myself. I am still confused by the lack of weight on my leg. By the lightness of my heart.

"Pixie says she's sorry."

"She said that?" I can't imagine the sour girl saying those words.

"No. What she said was, *Whine, whine, whine, we used to be so close. Why don't you want to be my bestie forever and ever. Cry.*"

"What does that mean?"

"It means she was jealous and acted like a little bitch because of it. I told her to cease and desist."

I shrug, as if it isn't a big deal, even as I think of all the terrible things Pixie said about me. How she wanted to make me feel small. "Well," I say, "Pixie should be sorry."

Rey's mouth opens in shock, but there's a smile there too. "Why do you say that?"

"Because she wanted to fit me into a box. To say I was one thing, not another. She didn't like to see me as a person. That was why she was such a bitch." I probably shouldn't enjoy saying that word as much as I do.

Rey laughs, then smacks the steering wheel for emphasis. "Poor Pixie is no match for you. No wonder she was so pissed I couldn't stop talking about you."

"You couldn't?"

"No. I honestly couldn't." She glances sideways at me, then quickly looks away. We speed down a highway, past stores and cars. Everything seems so big, bright, and clean. I can almost guess what Rey would say if she could read my mind. *Give it time; it'll get dirty soon enough.* I don't care. I like seeing the world this way.

"Wait," I say. "Does Pixie, um, like you?"

"Everyone loves me."

I wish I had a pillow to throw at her. "I'm serious."

"You can be Sirius Black, if you want," she says.

I groan. I have to remind myself to ignore what I don't understand. And then, I do understand. She is making a Harry Potter joke. And I understand it! I grin madly at Rey, and she grins back.

"I knew you'd get it," she says. *Getting it* feels like warmth spilling through my chest. *Getting it* is me and Rey in a tiny car, and the rest of the world doesn't matter.

"Does Pixie like you?"

The light we are at changes to a green arrow, and Rey turns left. "No. I'm not saying she couldn't be convinced to like me. Pixie can be convinced of a lot of things. But that's no reason to do it."

"And you don't like her?" A little boat on rough waves, that's me. I have to hold on.

She shakes her head. "I'm way too busy liking you," she says, and her smile is full of secrets. A secret smile can be a lie. I know that. It can be a real smile or a slap. I don't trust myself to know the difference.

"How do you do that? How can you be so confident, so sure?"

"I'm not. I'm just faking it. I'm shit-scared, obviously. Did you see how many times I changed my clothes?"

She did change a lot. I put on a red shirt and a new pair of jeans and the boots Indranie bought me, a pair that I couldn't wear with the cuff on my leg. Then I sat in the kitchen of the main house with Olga, listening to Rey get dressed.

The first Rey came down in was a long-sleeve shirt, a pair of shorts, and boots like cowboys wear. She grabbed a bag, walked to the door, then turned around and headed back upstairs, mumbling.

"Esa chica está loca, ¿sabes?" Olga said.

"I think it's okay," I said back.

The next one only made it halfway down the stairs. Olga and I bent our heads to try to see the whole outfit, but Rey turned around before we could.

"A dress, I think?" I said.

The clothes she finally chose—jeans that end at the calf and a green T-shirt with a rainbow and a frog on it—remind me a little of what Olga would wear. But in a nice way. I wonder if Olga wears Rey's old T-shirts. Or if they go shopping together. That thought makes me laugh.

"What's funny?" We're driving near water, away from the stores and traffic.

"Nothing."

"Come on. You laughed and it wasn't something brilliant I said. I need to know what caused it. I'm taking notes." I look at her hands on the wheel. "Mental notes." We slow down, pulling into a wooded area. In front of us, a car with a bright yellow boat tied to the top of it stops at a little wooden house to pay a ticket.

"I thought of you and Olga shopping together."

It takes her a moment. She looks down at her T-shirt and then gasps. "I'll have you know, I look amazing. My T-shirts are ironic. I'm making a statement."

"It's a very nice T-shirt. The color green is nice with your eyes," I say. When it's our turn at the little wooden house, Rey shows the woman an orange card, and she waves us through the gate.

"Are you messing with me?" Rey says as she looks for a parking space.

"Probably," I say, smiling. We find a parking space near a path in the woods. I'm excited to be outside, free and with Rey. Excited and a little scared. I have to remind myself that Rey isn't Liliana. And the past can stay in the past—if I push it away hard enough.

Chapter 28

At mi abuela's house, before she sold it and moved to the casa para ancianos, there was a lake. Pablo and I learned to swim there. All summer, we lived like kings, playing on the lake's beach until our strength gave out and we needed food and sleep. Until Abuela shouted for us to come home. Only to wake up the next day and do it again. When I can't bear to think of Pablo and what he became but I can't help but think of him, I try to remember him at the lake, sitting on a sun-hot rock and telling me stories about ancient warriors and the monsters that lived at the bottom of the lake. It never made me scared. It only made me want to find those monsters for myself. Fight them with Pablo on my side.

This beach is nothing like the lake at Abuela's. We're in the middle of a city. Smooth, warm rocks lead to the water while on a nearby bridge, cars zoom past. Rey tells me this place is called Belle Isle.

"The rocks look like lava flow from a volcano," I say. "Do you have volcanoes here?"

Rey has taken off her shoes and put them in a little dent in the rocks. Her feet are already in the water. I haven't taken off my shoes yet.

"A volcano? In Richmond? Nope. At least, not in this geological age. But Dave would know that kind of thing. He's crazy about this place."

I sit next to her. It's only spring, but I could see the rocks getting too hot in summer. The bridge we walked across to get here was a bridge for people hung under a bridge for cars. It swayed as we stepped across it. "It's an adventure," Rey said when I hesitated to cross. From the moment I opened my eyes this morning, this has been an adventure.

There aren't that many people here yet, but I see them walking across the bridge with bikes and dogs and picnic baskets. I point to the walkers' bridge.

"It looks like they're going to work. I know it's Saturday. But they don't look like they're going to have fun."

"Yeah. People take their fun very, very seriously around here," she says. "Hey, why are you even looking at them? You're supposed to be looking at me."

My face must do something funny, or maybe it's my eyebrows again, because Rey laughs at me.

"Oh man, I'm sorry. I am so teasing. And your face was like, *Who is this psycho?*"

"No. I wasn't thinking you are psycho."

I know the word *psycho* because Mrs. Rosen made me watch that movie with her. I thought about that movie every time I helped Mamá clean Mrs. Rosen's bathtub.

"I just mean, your face is, like, inscrutable."

"I don't know that word."

"It means I can't read it," Rey says.

"You aren't supposed to be able to read it."

"It would help." She sounds a little sad. As if my face not being easy to understand is a problem.

"I'm not trying to be mysterious," I say. "I don't always know when you're joking. I like to wait until I understand what you're saying."

"So, you're always waiting and thinking, is that it?"

She's stretched out on the rock, her sunglasses hiding her eyes, her pale toes wet from the river. The James River, she told me.

"Yes," I answer finally.

"Man, I wish I knew Spanish."

"Why? I speak—"

Rey groans. "I know . . . excellent English."

"But I do."

She sits up. "You totally do. But you think too much about what you're saying. I have a theory about you."

"A theory?"

"Yeah, an idea about what's going on in your head."

I don't speak.

She points a finger at me, but at least she's smiling. "See, you're doing it now! You're not talking because you're getting the lay of the land. Trying to figure out what I'm thinking first so you can respond to that."

Still, I don't speak. Not because I don't want to, but because I don't know what the right thing to say is. I guess that means what she's saying is true.

"Any other girl, man." She shakes her head. "Any other girl, and I'd think you were perfect—totally into me, wanting to know my every thought. You'd be like catnip to my ego. But you? You go fathoms deep."

"You're doing it again! Using words you know I don't understand!" *Any other girl would be perfect.* Does that mean I'm not perfect? Wearing the cuff was terrible. I thought about dying more in the last week than I have in my whole life. But it was bearable because I knew I was helping to save Rey's life—and because I could *feel* how she felt. Now I struggle with every word, turning them around in my head, trying to understand her.

She nudges me with her shoulder. "I'm trying to be annoying, get under your skin. So you'll talk to me."

A tiny smile crosses my face. "Because sos una peste," I say.

"What's that mean?"

"You're a pest. Annoying. I call Gabi that all the time." I say it like a joke, thinking that she'll laugh. But she doesn't.

"I want you to say what you think, without being afraid," she says.

All the things that have happened from the moment I went to the feria with Liliana to this moment sitting on a rock with this girl—they are a country between us. I don't know how to put that into words, how to explain to Rey that, for me, being afraid is like being awake. "It's not that easy," I say.

She pushes her sunglasses onto her head, her expression an invitation.

"I've been afraid for Gabi a long time. For myself, too." *And you*, I almost have the courage to say. "It's going to take me some time."

She nods. "I understand. But I'm about as subtle as a stick of dynamite. I'll be una peste a lot. Probably on an hourly basis."

I laugh because she is so ridiculous.

"I wish I could hear you laugh more."

"Do I have a funny laugh?"

Her face is perfectly serious. "You have a beautiful laugh."

I look away. A person—maybe a man, maybe a woman, I

can't tell—in a pointy blue boat only big enough for one lifts a paddle to us in greeting.

Rey waves.

"Are you hungry?" she asks at the same time I say, "I talked to Indranie yesterday."

"Oh, so you're thinking about people and I'm thinking about food. That sounds about right." She takes a handful of almonds out of her pocket. She gives me the bag, and I take a few. They're salty and smoky. They make me feel hungry for the first time in a week.

"So, what did Mommy Dearest have to say for herself?" Rey asks. I carefully review her words to see if I understand their meaning. I shake my head slightly.

"Who is Mommy Dearest?"

She smiles crookedly. "I swear, that time I wasn't doing it on purpose. I just forget sometimes that you might not get all my little jokes. Mommy Dearest is Indranie." She waves her hands above her head. "Too complicated to explain why right now, except to say that I don't mean it in a bad way. Indranie's all right. She's been hoping to be my stepmom for a long time."

"She does spend a lot of time at your house. But I wasn't sure why."

"Yup. Beast with two backs." She winces. "Sorry. I have to stop the verbal acrobatics. It's a sickness." She clears her throat. "She basically lives with us. Only keeps her apartment in Alexandria so her hundreds of gray suits have somewhere to hang. Dad and Indranie have been together for years."

I remember how Indranie's voice was full of self-hate when she told me about all she'd done to me and Gabi. All she'd done *for* Rey. "She loves you like a daughter."

"I guess," Rey says, ducking her head down a little. "So, what did Indranie say?"

I hesitate. Indranie's story isn't mine to tell. "She wanted me to take the cuff off. She didn't want me to suffer so much."

Instead of making Rey happy, my small admission causes her to frown.

"Did they know what they were doing to you? Did they understand?" she whispers. Her questions hang between us, painful.

"I don't know. I only know that Indranie didn't want you to suffer. And now she doesn't want me to suffer either."

Rey's expression blooms into anger. "Who the fuck are they to decide who suffers and who doesn't?" I don't know if Rey expects me to answer. When I stay silent, she continues, her voice rising in disgust. "They were fine letting me be a vampire? Sucking you dry of your good feelings and leaving you with just the black stuff? The stuff no one wants?"

I think of how I felt after the cuff worked for the first time. Empty yet still filled with pain. Un vampiro, a creature that takes and takes. That's not who Rey is. "It wasn't like that."

"I thought you were doing this with me, Marisol, I swear. I didn't know I was the one hurting you like that." She hugs herself into a ball, closing her eyes against tears. "I should have realized what was happening. I'm so, so sorry."

If I say it's okay, she won't believe me; we both know it's not true. I don't want any more untrue things between us.

"You were a wolf," I say.

"What?" She sniffs.

"You were in the dark, a hurt wolf. You know."

"A rabid animal." Her lips twist bitterly.

I put my hand on her arm. It's the first time since the cuffs came off that I've touched her first. "Not rabid, hurt."

"I was the one who hurt you."

I shake my head. "No. That makes me sound como una víctima."

"You aren't a victim."

"See?" I smile. "You do know a little Spanish."

She rolls her head toward me, looking up with a smile.

"I could learn." Her grin stops my heart. It must stop every heart around us, every person sunbathing and playing on the rocks. It is that strong. "You could teach me."

"Yes. I could," I say.

I tell myself that I won't be the first to look away from Rey's eyes, I won't be a coward, but I hear a bell and turn to look. On the dirt path that runs along the smooth black rocks, a man with a bicycle and a big silver box strapped to the handlebar rings a bell.

"¿Paletas?" I ask.

"Ice cream," she agrees.

Chapter 29

Why do you like me?" Rey asks as she bites gumballs out of a square yellow ice cream. I think the ice cream is supposed to be a face.

"What do you mean?" We walk along a path in the woods that leads to a ruined building Rey wants to show me. It's cool here and smells wonderfully of tierra y arboles.

"You've seen me try to throw myself from a balcony. You've seen me unshowered and crazy."

"You've seen me that way too." I was disappointed in the ice cream the man was selling. They weren't paletas, freshly made, packed with fruit. They were more like frozen cakes on a stick. But the one I picked—no faces or gumballs for eyes—is delicious, strawberries and crema.

"Fair, fair. But still. Why?"

I think back to the first moment I saw her. It would be stupid to say that I liked her then. She was crouched against the door to her balcony, her long golden hair in knots, her face a map of devastation. When her eyes found mine, I didn't see her beauty at all. I saw her pain. And I thought I could understand her. But I can't say any of those things.

"You're funny," I say, and I cringe at how lame I sound.

She breaks a twig off a nearby tree and smacks me with it.

"I'm not funny. At least, not lately."

"But you can be now?"

Rey pauses, chewing. I wonder how she can chew gum and eat ice cream at the same time.

"A little. It's not like, Praise be! I'm healed!" She gives me an exaggerated smile, wiggling her fingers by her face. "It's more like, I'm going to keep going, no matter how heavy I feel."

"So, the experiment worked? A little?"

Rey finishes her yellow ice cream.

"I don't know if the cuff worked. Wearing it did give me the chance to breathe. I'd nearly convinced myself I wanted to stop breathing altogether."

"So, it did work." It's stupid to keep asking, but I want to know that what I went through was worth something.

"Doesn't matter if the experiment worked a little or a lot. It was heinous what that cuff did to you." She finds my hand and squeezes. I love and hate how she will take my hand, will touch me before even I know it's what I want. I love the pulse of electricity that shoots through me. I hate being scared of what happens next. I'm waiting for La Suerte, and I don't know if she will be good or bad.

"Here it is," Rey says, stopping in front of a brick wall the color of red clay and gray dust.

"What is it?"

"Well, it used to be a factory. To make buttons. No. That's not right. I should text Dave."

"Is Dave your best friend?" I ask.

"No. He's a good friend, though."

"Was he your boyfriend?" I follow Rey as she walks through the arched opening to the ruined building. On the other side, most of the building is missing, crumbling into the parts of nature surrounding it. Wooden boards rot into dirt. I wonder what the blocks of stone, the old pieces of rusted iron were used for.

"In junior high. For like a week. He bought me a book on growing mushrooms. That was kind of the end of romance with him."

"So, you liked boys?" I am careful not to look at her when I ask.

"Not really. I went out with Dave because he asked me. It seemed like the thing I should do, you know? It was seventh grade, and suddenly everyone was pairing up like the freaking Ark. Dave asked. And asked and asked. And I couldn't think of a good reason to say no. So I said yes. Beside the mushroom book, I knew pretty quickly that boys were not for me."

I don't speak.

"Does that seem weird to you? You've only ever dated girls?"

It takes me longer than I like to find my words. "One girl."

Rey stops on the small hill we're climbing behind the ruined building. "You've only ever dated one girl?"

My face feels like it's on fire. "Before you. At home. A girl. I liked girls on TV before. Not real girls, girls on TV."

A horrified look comes over Rey's face before melting into a grin. "You liked AMBER!" she almost screams.

"Shush!"

"You did! You had a crush on Amber from *Cedar* freaking *Hollow*!"

I keep walking up the hill. "How do you know I didn't like Aimee?"

Rey catches up to me. "Because Amber's the hot one. No question."

"They are both very pretty."

She rolls her eyes at me. "Come on. Amber is the one always conveniently wearing short shorts and forgetting her sweater. She's the one who goes skinny-dipping while Aimee fumes about it in the car." She shakes her head, her smile even wider. "Of *course* you liked Amber."

"Did you like Amber?" I ask.

Her grin turns fierce, and it ignites me. "Like a beast. Oh, man. The times I'd slo-mo those DVDs—it's not for polite conversation."

I blush hard as we laugh together.

At the top of the hill, we can see the water and the gray-black rocks. The ruin is on the main part of the island.

"Why don't you say the *s* in *island*?" I ask Rey.

"It's not just me, you know. Everyone skips the *s*."

I smack her lightly on the shoulder. "I know that. I just mean, why not?"

"I don't know. I don't question words. Probably because I only know one language. You're always comparing and contrasting how things work. I just talk."

Beyond the beach of rocks, I can see the bridge we walked across—it is farther away than I realized. We must have walked a long way. On the other side is a cemetery with pretty white stones and tall trees. Rey points to it.

"That's why I keep wanting to text Dave. He's got illustrious dead buried there. Old southern family, full of pompous asses."

"You are lucky to have good friends," I say.

"Fuck yeah, I am. And I kept them away for too long. They hurt too much. Their faces reminded me of Riley. If it wasn't for you, I wouldn't have been able to see them again."

"Is that why you like my face? Because it doesn't remind you of Riley?" I don't know where I find the nerve to say it.

"I like your face because it's attached to the rest of you." My face gets hot again, like I have a fever that comes in waves.

"And anyway, I don't think anything could keep me from thinking of Riley for long. Even while we wore the cuffs, I think he was trying to break through, you know?"

"What do you mean?"

She blows out her breath. "I don't know. I felt better, lighter, and that was amazing. But I knew the grief was out there, that *Riley* was out there. I sound sketchy as fuck, I know, but I felt like Riley was a ghost I had to reckon with. Sooner or later." She looks at me as if I won't understand. But I understand her too well. "Do you ever think of your brother?"

I give one quick shake of my head. "I don't want to think of him."

"Too painful?"

"Yes."

"And if you think of the girl who you liked? Is that better?"

"Worse."

Rey steps closer to me, placing her long fingers along my cheek. "And if you think of me? Is that better?" Her face is so close. If I moved my head up, only a little, I could touch her lips with mine.

She doesn't smell like Liliana. Not at all. Rey smells like hot rocks and sweat and sweet like pan dulce. "It's better," I say. My heart is painful in my chest, dreading the moment Rey will pull away and laugh. The memory of Liliana's laughter makes me step back, but Rey is faster than I am. Her lips are on mine before I move.

I have never kissed a girl, not really. I have thought about it and thought about it. One time, I drew a picture of how I thought it would look. I thought about where I should put my hands, the problem of noses. I thought about how long lips stayed together, how long until they parted. And then? I am not a good artist, so my drawing was mostly lines and thinking. When I got frustrated, I ripped up the scribbled drawing and burned it en la estufa. But I never thought about how soft a girl's lips would be. I never felt my own to be soft. I had everything wrong.

"Are you okay?" Rey asks against my lips. She pushes her cheek gently against mine, nudging me. I notice for the first time the tiny blond hairs across her cheeks. I think about her pale pink cheek against my brown one. Café y crema. I smile and that is my answer.

Chapter 30

I want to tell Gabi about Rey, but I don't think I can. It isn't that I don't trust Gabi—I trust her with my life. But Pablo's words dig like a worm through my mind. *Do you think I would let you infect our little sister with your disease?* Not everyone thinks I am a twisted thing. Not everyone thinks a girl can't love another girl.

But Pablo and Antonio did. Maybe Liliana wanted to think differently. I still don't know if her attention was real, or if it was because of Antonio. I don't know what Mamá would think. I never thought further into the future than getting Gabi safe to wonder if I would tell her. Then I think of my tía Rosa. Tía never married. She has lived for many years en el campo with her friend Carola.

"What are you thinking?" Rey asks. "I tried to decipher what your inscrutable highness was thinking all on my own, but I admit defeat. Defeat! Also, I can't keep looking at you and driving. I'm afraid I'll crash." Her grin widens in the afternoon sunlight. We have been out later than I thought.

"I was thinking about Tía Rosa. Uh, my aunt Rosa. She lived with her friend Carola for years, and I never thought about it."

"Did she wear men's boots and very thick sweaters?"

"What?"

"I'm kidding. But did they have a lot of cats?"

"No. They had one or two. But they mostly had goats."

Rey nods wisely while turning off the highway. "Definitely gay."

"You're just kidding?" I ask, unsure.

"Sure I am. That's just one kind of gay. The book says there are many kinds." Rey keeps her eyes on the road, her face unreadable. We are almost at the house. I have an exhausted feeling in my bones, the feeling of too much smiling and too much kissing. No, there can't be too much kissing. That's not possible, especially when I wish I had the nerve to ask Rey to stop by the side of the road, just one more time, so we can kiss again.

"I can lend you the book if you want," Rey says.

I pull my thoughts away from kissing Rey. "Wait, there really is a book?"

"The gay book. Of course, I only have it in English. But maybe we can get a translation in Spanish. Amazon probably sells it."

"There is a gay book?" ¿Será posible?

"Oh, yeah. You get it when you graduate gay school." She pats my knee, as if to reassure me. "I know you haven't been to gay school yet, but when you go, you'll do fine. You're already *really* good at the girl-kissing."

She tries but can't keep the smile off her face. The smile turns into giggles the longer I stare at her in disbelief. I have trouble finding the right thing to throw at Rey—something that punishes her for making fun of me but that doesn't distract her from driving—but finally, I find a small bag of candy.

"You could have opened the bag first and thrown the jelly beans actually into my mouth," she says. We're at the gates of the house when Rey stops the car suddenly. The gates are closed.

"Oh, sweet baby Jesus," Rey sighs.

"What is it?"

"It's probably Dad and Indranie, and they are probably going to lose their shit." She digs under her seat until she finds a little remote. She pushes the button and the gates open slowly, reluctantly.

"I haven't ever seen the gates closed," I say.

"Yeah," Rey says distractedly as she parks the little car next to Indranie's car. We walk to the carriage house, and the door opens before we get there. Mr. Warner stands at the door, a terrible expression on his face.

"Thank God," he says, hugging Rey to him as fiercely as a punishment. I stand behind her, wishing I could escape to my room unnoticed. Behind Rey's father, I see Indranie. And the expression on her face is so painful I cannot move.

We sit around the glass table where the two CTS cuffs still sit like accusations. Everyone has cups of coffee in front of them, but no one is drinking. I hear Olga in the kitchen, trying to be quiet enough so she can listen to our conversation. But no one has been talking.

Mr. Warner clears his throat. "Reyanne. I'm glad you're home and safe. I was worried about you."

She traces her fingers behind her ear, and I remember

placing a kiss on that ear only an hour ago. I want to go back to that moment—or any moment today when I could look at her and feel breathless.

"I'm sorry, Dad. I thought you and Indranie were at that fund-raiser."

"We were. But when we got home, you were gone. Then we saw the cuffs." He gestures at the glass table. The living room is clean again—the breakfast tray, the extra blanket, everything has been put away. But the cuffs are exactly where we left them last night. "You didn't answer your phone. We were worried about you." He looks at me. "Both of you," he adds.

Indranie sits next to Mr. Warner, her body leaning toward where Rey and I sit on the other couch. "The experiment—"

"The experiment was bullshit, Indranie, and you know it!" Rey bursts out.

"Reyanne!"

She turns sharply toward her father. "Dad, do you even know what the cuff does? Do you know how it works?"

He looks uncertainly to Indranie for an answer, and she places her hand on his knee.

Indranie uses the soft, low voice she's used with me and Gabi so many times before. She has used it to encourage and explain, to convince and reassure. "Rey, it's very complicated technology, cutting edge."

Rey interrupts her. "That's not what I'm talking about. You told me *we* were the lab rats."

A spasm of pain crosses Mr. Warner's face. "Reyanne, please don't talk about it that way."

But Rey continues. "You told me Dr. Deng would give us a

way to take the grief away. A medical device to make me feel a little less like dying." Mr. Warner covers his eyes with his hand, squeezing his fingers into his eyes.

"Marisol and me, we were supposed to get over our grief. This was supposed to help *both* of us."

"It's not that simple," Indranie says.

The more upset Rey gets, the more I wish she would hold my hand, as if that could still help her feel better.

"It's exactly that simple. Except you didn't tell me that Marisol was acting like some kind of grief keeper. Like she was a dump where I could safely throw all my privileged-ass pain."

Mr. Warner looks away. Indranie's lips go pale and tight.

"Don't you see, Dad? We used her."

"That's not fair," he says, anguished.

"She wasn't used." I don't know how Indranie keeps her voice so calm. Her face is a smooth mask, totally different from the broken one she showed me yesterday when I left her sobbing in her car. "Everything was explained to Marisol." Indranie darts a look at me.

Somehow, I find my voice. "I was told everything. I just never imagined how terrible it would be." I'd be angrier if I didn't understand Indranie so well. I did a terrible thing to protect Gabi. Indranie and I aren't so different.

"Well, I wasn't told anything!" Rey's anger rises with every word. "Did you think I'd be okay with this? That because she's an immigrant, I wouldn't care? As long as I got rid of my grief, I'd be okay with ruining another girl's life?" She looks from her father's face to Indranie's.

"When my parents first came to this country," Indranie says patiently, "they took any job they could. Sometimes two or more. They did whatever they had to do." Again, I find myself understanding Indranie more than I want to.

"Do not fucking compare this with cleaning bathrooms and being a nanny. This could have *killed* Marisol."

Indranie's calm finally snaps; her mask disappears, revealing a face full of anguish.

"*You* might have died without this treatment, Reyanne. Your father, me, we couldn't have—" Her words choke as she struggles to regain her composure. Mr. Warner puts his arm around her.

"The experiment is over," he says finally. When Indranie tries to speak, he cuts her off with a gentle hand on her arm. "We can't."

Indranie lowers her head, and I think she is crying. "What if we try with someone else? Someone older?"

Rey's face is horrified. "Absolutely not!"

"What if something happens to you?" Indranie says, her voice breaking. "What if you try to kill yourself again?"

"I don't feel like dying," Rey says. "I know my life isn't over."

"Indranie, she's getting better," Mr. Warner says. "You can see that."

She turns her anger on him. "How can we know? What if we can't stop her next time?"

"Okay, so we can't know!" Rey throws up her hands. "No one can know. Maybe one day I will feel so bad that dying seems like the only sane thing to do. Even if that happens"— she takes a deep breath, and I feel like I'm taking one with her—"I won't make someone take my burden for me. That's no way to save anyone."

We leave Indranie and Mr. Warner to argue and go to

my room. Rey stands by the door, trying to listen in on their muffled conversation.

"She must love you very much to do this for you," I say.

Rey sits next to me on Gabi's bed, propping a giant banana up behind her as a pillow. "We made fun of her at first, me and Riley. She was always so serious, always worried something bad would happen. Then it did and I think she lost her mind. It's the only explanation I can think of, why she would be okay with what we did to you."

Rey's anger *for* me, on my behalf, lights me up.

"It broke her heart when Riley died. It broke all of us. But it's Dad she can't stand to watch suffer. I don't forgive her, though. Not a fucking iota."

"Will it end now? Or will they find someone else to experiment on?" I ask.

"Jesus, I hope not. I hope they find some moral courage," she says, closing her eyes.

I take a long time to say the next thing, because I don't know how to say it, and I don't want to get a wrong answer. But it's at the top of my mind.

"Rey? Does this change anything?"

"What do you mean?"

"I mean, now that the experiment is over, I won't feel things about you—I won't know things about you."

"We'll do it like normals. We'll talk and fight it out and just do it. Like we would have before this Frankenshit took over."

"But without this frank or shit, we wouldn't have met," I say.

She leans close to me, urgent. "I don't know nearly enough about you. I don't know your favorite color, or what you like to eat, or even if you think coffee is a sacred beverage." She closes her eyes. "What if Indranie can't get you a green card? What if they send you back?"

It's the answer I wanted. I wanted her to care. "Kiss me." There's only a few centimeters between us.

"I can't. I'm too mad." She blinks back tears.

"I know, but maybe you won't be so mad after you kiss me."

It's sweet, every kiss sweeter than the last, but Rey cannot stay still. She pulls back.

"You should be able to stay," she whispers against my shoulder. "You paid for the right to stay in blood and guts." I've seen her cry so much in the short time I've known her. But now she is crying for me. I feel happier, lighter than I have ever felt. It is ridiculous to feel so frightened and happy at once.

"No llores," I say, hugging her close. "Indranie says I have a good chance now. And as long as Gabi can stay, it doesn't matter."

"Well, it matters to me. And you don't really mean that."

"Of course I don't." I sigh, and she settles against my shoulder. "It doesn't matter what I paid, or how much I suffered. I'm an illegal."

Rey lifts her head away from me. "You know that's not a thing, right? You can't use it like a noun, like an *illegal* is a thing." She spits out the bad taste the word leaves in her mouth.

"I heard it used that way. At the detention center. I thought it was right." I shrug.

"You aren't an illegal. You are a person. A girl." She lifts my hair off my shoulder and gathers it in her hand. "You have a right to live and love. And to not be afraid."

"I don't," I say. "No one has that right."

She sits up. "I'm going to talk to my dad. I can't stand this."

I grab her hand, pulling her back to me. "Wait, Rey. Don't get worried before we know what's going to happen."

She curls into a ball, facing me. I hold her hands.

She's crying and it hurts to see it. "Today was the first day I didn't feel totally numb. Even when the fucking evil cuff was making me feel better, I wasn't myself, not the best part of myself. When we were at Belle Isle, I felt as good as I did when Riley was alive. How can you make me feel better just by being here? No cuff, nothing but you." She traces her fingertips along the inside of my wrist and down my palm.

I shiver. "It's not me," I say quietly. "It's us."

There's a knock at the door. Rey and I scramble to sit up. Indranie opens the door. It is clear from her eyes that she has been crying. I watch her gather her calm around her like a coat.

Rey's body stiffens.

"Your father and I have agreed. I called Dr. Deng. We've suspended the experiment."

"*You* agreed? You can't fucking agree. You aren't anything to me," Rey spits.

I flinch at how hard the words are. If Indranie is upset by them, she doesn't show it.

"That's fair enough." Indranie nods. "But I want you to know, whether you believe it or not, I did this because I thought I could help." She looks at me, and I wish I wasn't here to watch. It's too private a thing.

Indranie moves to sit on the bed, but Rey doesn't make room for her. I stand up instead. "Rey," she says, "I saw you and your dad hurting. Riley's death was like the death of this family. I didn't want you to suffer. When the opportunity for testing came up, we jumped at it."

"I know Dad did this too—if that's what's worrying you. He's just as much to blame as you are."

"Your father got the funding for the clinical trials. He approved the budgets. But he didn't know how it worked. He didn't . . . want to know the details. I tried—"

Rey's expression stops Indranie's next words.

"I'm sorry I lied to you, Rey. I hope someday you'll trust me again. I only wanted the best for you."

"Those are probably the most useless words ever uttered. Does anyone believe them anymore? And don't you think it's Marisol you should apologize to? She's the one you made suffer."

Indranie turns to me, her eyes filled with so much emotion that I'm not surprised she doesn't speak. She took us, not knowing if she could protect us. She didn't know if I would even survive the experiment, but she did it anyway.

"I am so sorry, Marisol."

I should hate her, but I only pity her. I won't tell Rey that Indranie lied to me about asylum. I don't want any more bad things between them. There have been too many lies already.

"It's over now. There's nothing more to say."

Instead of looking relieved, Indranie looks more upset. "There's every chance your asylum request could be approved. You've got a solid case for fear of torture and death in El Salvador. It's not easy, but there's a lot we can do to get you and your sister the legal right to stay. Certainly, while your case is being reviewed."

"They can stay?" Rey's words echo in my ears.

"Yes, for now. And hopefully for the future. Nothing is certain. There's so much upheaval in the system. But I think we have a good case. I'm sorry I—" Her expression is full of sorrow but not regret. If she had to do it all again, I think she would. "I didn't want Rey to suffer. I'd do anything for her," she says.

"I understand," I say. Because if I could go back in time, I am sure I would do everything again. Even being with Liliana. Even pulling the trigger of the gun.

Chapter 31

"Dad and Indranie have gone out to another meeting," Rey says, pocketing her cell phone. We stand at the kitchen's glass door, holding hands and watching the sky change color for the last time today. I think of what Mamá would say if she were here. *Cuidado los mosquitos,* probably. Then she'd take something for the pain in her cadera and shut the door to the bedroom. I will have to think about my mother next. About how to keep her safe. And if she will be disappointed in me when she finds out I'm gay. Maybe she already suspects. I push the thought away. I'm not ready to end the day with Mamá and all she expects of me.

"How did Indranie sound when she went out? Is she okay?" I ask.

Rey lifts an eyebrow in question. "Why do you care?"

I shrug. "She was good to us."

"She practically kidnapped you and Gabi just so she could lab-rat you almost to death," Rey says, exasperated.

I don't know how to explain things to Rey without admitting my own guilt. I'm not so different from Indranie, and what I did was so much worse. "She wanted to keep you safe. She didn't want your father to suffer. Everyone has reasons for what they do."

Rey looks at me closely. Maybe she doesn't believe that I forgive Indranie.

"Indranie's always so calm. I think it's a Jedi mind trick," Rey says.

I poke her in the arm.

"Ow!"

"I'm going to do that every time you say words I don't understand. That way, you can know that you need to explain, and I don't have to say it."

She rubs her arm. "I'm going to have to find some sort of armored shirt."

We watch a bird, blue with a long white tail, hop along the back of a wooden bench.

"When does Gabi get home?" Rey asks.

"She's staying over. It's her friend's birthday party."

"The boy-girl one?"

"She told you about that?" I didn't know Gabi talked to Rey. But I guess there are many things I've missed while wearing the cuff.

"She told me you were overprotective. I told her *I'm* still not old enough for girl-boy parties."

I laugh. "Well, I already said yes to the killing abuelitas thing, so I can't be that protective."

"The what?"

I point my finger at her. "Ha! Something you don't understand! How do you like the feeling?" I say with triumph.

She kisses me so fast I barely realize it's begun before it's over.

"I like the feeling pretty good," she says.

My face flushes. "Pretty well," I correct her.

She looks horrified. "You're one of those grammar nutters, aren't you?"

"No. I'm not a nut-er. I just want to speak properly."

Rey takes a cookie from the pocket of her sweatshirt.

"Where did you get the cookie from?" I ask.

She gives me a side smile. "From my pocket," she says, taking a huge bite.

"Did Olga give it to you?" Olga is very fair—she would never give Rey a cookie without giving me one.

She shakes her head, swallowing her bite. "No. Olga's out. She wouldn't let me have cookies before dinner. I took it. From the cookie jar."

"There's a cookie jar?" The cookie is covered with stripes of chocolate. Olga tried to get me and Rey to eat when we were ill, trying everything she could think of to tempt us, so the kitchen is full of many kinds of colorful, candy-filled cookies. I just didn't know where they were.

"You don't know all of Olga's secrets," Rey teases.

I reach for the cookie, but Rey pulls it away. I reach around her, grabbing it, and she leans against me. "Say the magic word." Her nose touches mine.

"What's the magic word?" I ask.

"Just kidding. There's no magic word," she says, then kisses me again. I light up. Like the string of lights in the hall my parents rented for my quinceañera. Like the dancing and laughing and eating of that night. Like the flushed cheeks of all my cousins, my tía, my mother and father, dancing together for the last time. I light up with esperanza.

When we part, because I am out of breath or because we

heard a sound somewhere in the house, Rey puts something in my hand. It's a cookie.

"I promise to keep giving you cookies so long as you keep kissing me."

I smile and hide my face against her chest. It is too much to show. Too much when I want more all the time.

There's a knocking sound and we both look toward the front door. After a moment, the knocking gets louder. When no one else gets the door, Rey moves down the hallway. "Duh," she says, turning back to me. "We're the only ones here."

Rey opens the door and a thin man with dark hair stands there, clutching a paper bag.

"Is this Mr. Warner's house?"

"Yeah, well, sort of," Rey says. "I'm his daughter. Can I help you?" I stand behind Rey. The feeling of dread grows in my stomach. *No,* I say to myself. *Nothing bad has happened.*

"I'm Arun Guinto. Juliette's dad."

"I'm Marisol. Gabriela's sister," I say. Mr. Guinto shakes my hand with a smile.

"Oh, good. I wasn't sure which building was the right one!"

"We get that a lot," Rey says with a grin. "Do you want to come in?"

"No, thank you. I just wanted to drop this off for Juliette. She's terrible. Always forgetting to take her EpiPen with her." At our blank expression, Mr. Guinto looks a little annoyed. "Of course, she probably didn't tell you that she's allergic to cashews? I know it's not as common as peanuts, but it's still dangerous. And she's not taking it seriously." When neither Rey nor I move, Mr. Guinto steps inside the entryway.

"Maybe I will come in. I should talk to Juliette about this." He turns to look at his car, which is still running. "I've got my younger daughter in the car. My wife is out of town, so I'm on kid duty. Can you call Juliette for me?"

I believe in luck. I know what it feels like when La Mala Suerte visits.

"She isn't here," I hear myself say.

"Excuse me?" Mr. Guinto's face must look the way I feel. As if the ground is slowly disappearing under our feet.

"Gabi said she was going to Juliette's birthday party tonight. At your house," Rey says when words fail to come out of my mouth.

"There was no party. We took the girls to the movies, then dropped them off here." The shock on Mr. Guinto's face has evaporated, replaced by fear. "I don't understand," he says, though of course he does. "Where are the girls?"

"How tall is Gabi?" Rey asks me. She is on the phone with the police.

"Un metro y medio," I say, then repeat in English, "a meter and a half." I sit on the sofa, a pillow against my aching stomach.

"Crap. I don't know the metric system. I'll guess."

Rey told Mr. Guinto it must be a misunderstanding. That she'd call him as soon as she talked to her dad.

A misunderstanding. A missed understanding. I can't think. I hear Rey getting upset with the police officer, but it washes over me, too much noise. Gabi would never leave with a stranger. That means it must be someone she knows.

Rey sits down heavily beside me. "I can't report her missing because I'm not her guardian or parent. Asshole probably thinks it's a prank. Jesus." She presses her hands into her head. I don't move and I don't speak. I'm afraid I'll break.

"Listen. When Dad and Indranie get my messages, they'll come right home." Rey called her father; I called Indranie and Traci. We have left messages everywhere we could. I don't know how long Gabi has been missing, but I have known about it for ten minutes, and already I cannot breathe properly.

"Dad will call the police and get shit done. It's not completely useless being a pillar of society."

"It doesn't matter. No one will care about one more illegal girl," I say.

"Don't say that! That's not what she is." Rey's voice is so sharp I know she doesn't believe it. The sharper the protest, the less the faith.

"Who is going to find her? Care about her?" I ask.

Rey's agitation grows, mirroring mine. I can feel her shaking beside me—can she feel me falling apart? "If we could just figure out what happened."

"I know what happened."

Rey searches my face. "You do? What happened? Who took her?"

"La Mala Suerte."

"*La* what?"

"Bad luck." I make a face. It sounds silly when I say it in English. Bad luck. As if I've only lost a key or missed a bus. "La Mala Suerte is always taking things from my family. Now she's taking Gabi." I hold my head with both hands. When that does not help, I dig my fingernails into my scalp.

Rey sighs, leaning into me. "No, no, no, Marisol. That's

just your head playing games with you. Believe me, I know." She reaches her arms to me, but I cannot be still anymore. I stand, exasperated. Where before I could barely move for fear of breaking, now I feel if I stop moving, the earth will stop turning.

"You don't understand. La Mala Suerte is real. I don't mean she has a body and arms and legs. She works through real people. She makes things happen."

"Why?"

"There is no why! It just happens." I double over, forcing the air from my lungs. Family. Home. Love. Nothing can be mine. I gasp and gasp, falling to my knees.

"Marisol!" Rey's voice is farther away than it should be. I can't see Rey's face or the Warner house anymore.

Liliana opens the door, her face as cold as the moon.

"Where's Gabi?"

I stand at the open door to Liliana's house. I didn't think I'd have to see her again. Her little dog, Bonbon, yips at her feet.

"She's not here," she says, turning away from me.

"Mamá said she left with you. What did you do to her?" I follow her inside her house. She hasn't invited me in. She never has. I was too stupid to wonder why. Why we stayed in public places, why she didn't want to be alone with me.

Liliana's hair is tied back, her face clean of makeup.

"I did Gabi a favor." She clutches un trapo to her chest, a bottle of Actichlor in her hand.

"My mother is scared, Lilí. I'm scared. What did you do to Gabi?" My voice is too soft, too fragile, when I want to sound harsh.

She puts the cleaner and rag on the table, and leans against it for strength. I don't recognize this defeated person. "Your sister won't be confused like us." *Liliana looks up at me.* "Don't you want that? Don't you want her to be happy?"

"I want her to be herself."

"You mean, you want her to hate herself."

"Is that what you do?" *I step closer to her, but she pushes back, knocking over the cleaner. The smell of bleach spreads through the room.*

"Yes! Don't you?"

I thought I knew her. I thought she knew me.

"No."

Liliana is on her knees, putting the cap back onto the bottle of Actichlor, wiping the spill with the rag. "You should," *she says bitterly.*

"¿Qué hiciste?" *I ask. My body seizes, hot and cold.*

"I made her beautiful. I dressed her and did her makeup. I gave her tacones, un brasier como la gente."

I can't imagine it. My little Gabi dressed in Liliana's clothes, her shoes, and bra.

"I turned her into a woman."

"She's just a kid," *I spit.* "You turned her into una puta."

"Better to be a whore than to be dead," *she shouts.*

I freeze.

Liliana stands, her pants wet with bleach.

"Marisol, don't you see? Antonio wants her. It means she will have everything. Clothes. Money. Protection. Don't you want that for her?"

I shake my head violently. "No. Pablo would never let it happen."

"He already has. Pablo no quiere dos lesbianas en la familia.

*One in the family is enough. He's going to make sure Gabi isn't
like you."*

*I look at her. She is more beautiful than ever. It makes me hate
her more. ¿Quién dice que la vida es justa?*

"Like us," I say.

*"No. I'm not like you. Not anymore." She wipes the tears from
her face with her fist. I almost pity her.*

*"Where is she?" I grab her by her ponytail, finally finding my
rage. Her gasp of pain means nothing to me.*

"Pablo took her. I only dressed her."

"Where is she, Lilí? Where is Gabi?"

*"It's too late. They took her to el Club. She'll be better off in the
end." She smacks my hand away, then holds it. To stop me or to
pull me to her, I don't know. "If I were you," she says, "I'd worry
about myself."*

I snatch my hand away and smack my elbow into the glass
table so hard I'm afraid I broke it.

I blink back tears. When my blurry eyes clear, it is Rey's
startled, worried face I see. I know I have been caught, tangled
in the past. My heart races as it did that day.

I pull myself back, sitting on my heels. I try to mimic calmness.

"Antonio's men took Gabi," I say between struggling breaths.

"Who?"

I close my eyes. I don't want to see the judgment on her face.
"Antonio. He was the leader of a gang in my hometown. He
killed my brother."

"Shit."

I cannot afford to fall into the past again. When I try to

forget, to pretend it didn't happen, the past comes after me like a nightmare.

"And I killed him."

Rey's voice is soft. "You killed a gang leader?"

I open my eyes. "It was not because I wanted to. I had to."

"I believe you." Where's her judgment? Where's her disgust? "Jesus," she says with a tiny lift of her lips. "You are a badass."

"Because of me, we had to run away. I had to take Gabi, or they would have killed us. My mother went to her sister's house far in the country to hide."

"The one with the goats?" Rey is beside me on the floor. We're crammed between the sofa and the glass table. But it feels safe here. She holds my hand.

"Yes. Then we left with the coyotes."

"What?" Rey's face is tight with concentration.

"The men who take you into the US. The ones you pay for a chance."

"But how would they get here? The gang, I mean? When it was so hard for you to get here?"

"Nothing is hard when you have money and guns. They come for la revancha, to take the one thing away from me that I can't live without." Every organ in my body is waiting. Every thought in my head is frozen. There is no reason to go forward. I want to die.

Rey shakes my shoulders. When I don't look at her, she grabs my face in her hands, forcing me to pay attention. "Stop, Marisol. Just stop."

I stare at the purple smudges under her eyes. The way her lips almost don't meet. She is here with me.

"You're freaking out," Rey says. "Not that I blame you. With the shit you've had to deal with, I don't blame you for thinking the worst. But maybe this time, it's not the worst."

I feel like I'm blind, even though I can see Rey's face, see the room we sit in. What could this *be* if not the worst?

Rey gently strokes my hair, holding me tightly to her shoulder. I think she is afraid I will fall away if she doesn't hold on. She is right. "Didn't you tell me Gabi wanted to go to a party?"

I am slow to answer. "Yes. This party of Juliette's that wasn't real."

"No. Before that. She wanted to go to a boy-girl party. Some kid named Justin or Julian, remember?"

I remember arguing with Gabi when I barely felt like myself. I remember her being so angry with me.

"Jake," I say. "His name was Jake. He was in high school. A freshman."

"Okay. So, what if they just went to a party?"

I shake my head. It can't be that simple. "Gabi would never do that." But there is a doubt in me. I'm not sure anymore of what she would or would not do. I've spent too long pretending she's a baby. "What if she did? How can we find her?"

"Okay. Stay here. Don't move. Don't think. *Do* breathe, okay?"

I nod.

She crosses to the kitchen and starts opening drawers. "There's usually a directory or something that the schools send home. So you can call other parents and invite them to parties, that kind of thing."

I did not know this. "I should have done that," I say.

"No. You're done with blaming yourself. You have reached your maximum quota. Try again tomorrow."

In a moment, Rey settles herself next to me again with a little orange book in her hands. She opens to the back, where the older kids' names and numbers are listed.

"Well, shit. Every kid is named Jacob that year." She turns a page. "But this guy . . . he lives less than a mile away." She looks at me. "Could Gabi and Juliette have walked there?"

"Walking is nothing to Gabi," I say. I'm getting hopeful, and I know I shouldn't. Could it be true that Gabi is only at a party?

Rey calls the number listed in the book but only gets a voicemail.

"That could mean they're not home, or it could mean they don't want anyone to know they're home." She taps the booklet against her lips. "Okay, let's go." She pushes against the table to stand up.

"Go where?" I am bewildered by too many emotions, as if I am wearing the cuff again. As if I'm being hit with waves and I don't know where I am. Rey holds out her hand to me. Not to hold it but to help me up. My legs tremble as I stand. I fear I will fall.

Rey hugs me hard. "Let's go get Gabi."

Chapter 32

I barely remember getting into the little car, or leaving the carriage house. Rey's hand tugs on my shirt, and I take it gratefully.

If Rey is right and Gabi and Juliette walked to Jake O'Brien's house, they walked through private gardens and climbed over fences. We have to drive a long way around. Not all the houses in this neighborhood are as big as the Warners'. There are a few that are, incredibly, bigger. Jake O'Brien's house is one of them.

We park in front of a fountain. It is like el Museo de Arte, with statues on either side of a huge wood and glass door. The door is unlocked.

I don't know what I expected, but it was not this quiet entryway of marble and polished wood. Beautiful flowers in a vase almost as tall as Gabi. It looks nothing like the time on *Cedar Hollow* when Aimee's parents went to Switzerland and Amber threw a party in her friend's house without her permission. Amber's friends broke things, no, *trashed* things. *You trashed the place,* Aimee angrily accused Amber. I remember because I wrote the word down, surprised that it could be used as a verb.

Nothing in America is like *Cedar Hollow*. It was a fantasy I kept alive for too long. I never realized how much I needed it to be real. Aimee and Amber with their containable drama, their incredible *safety*. How I wanted it to be real.

"She isn't here," I say, heartsick.

"Hold up," Rey says. She's listening intently, and I listen too. Far away, as if it is in another house, I hear music.

Rey's smile is a satisfied line. "Looks like Jacob O'Brien has a basement lair. Come on," she says, pulling me toward the faint music.

In a kitchen twice as large as Mrs. Borges's kitchen, Rey opens a door to a stairway. The music becomes much louder.

"Have you been here before?"

"No. I've been in places like this. Brace yourself. Jacob O'Brien has terrible taste in music."

"Don't make jokes," I snap. My stomach feels full of víboras, a ball of them, sliding over each other, biting me from the inside. If she isn't here—

"It's going to be okay," Rey says, and pulls me down the carpeted steps, not letting me give in to the snakes in my barriga.

This basement is not like any sótano I have ever seen. I didn't expect it to have a dirt floor, to have barely enough space to stand, to smell of mold and spiders—I knew it would be different, from the pure white carpet on the steps, but it is even more than I could have imagined. It looks like a hotel. There are people everywhere—not puking in corners or breaking vases like on *Cedar Hollow*. They are playing games. Video games in one corner, with a TV as wide as the wall, and card games at a large table in the middle of the room that looks like it belongs in a casino. A long bar runs the length of the room. Girls in silvery dresses sit in high leather chairs drinking cloudy pink drinks. And everywhere there is music, murmurs, and laughter.

"This is not the right party," I say. "We made a mistake."

"No. This is right. I know some of these kids. A few are twelfth graders slumming it," Rey says.

The basement is as large and as wide as the house above it. And beyond this room are smaller rooms, each full of people. I don't even know how I would find Gabi. Most of these kids would look right at a bar in a city, or at a dance club. My Gabi should stand out like a thumb. But I don't see her anywhere.

"We need to split up," Rey says as she scans the room. "I'll check those rooms over there. You look here."

I grip her hand reflexively.

"You'll be okay. You have your phone. I put my number in it."

"When?" I reach in my pocket for the phone.

"This morning. When you were sleeping." A quick smile warms her face. "When I was worried you'd freak out and run. I wanted you to be able to call me."

I look at the phone. Rey has put a picture on the screen. Before, it was a simple blue screen. Now it is a picture of Gabi, grinning up at me.

"*No llores,*" she says awkwardly, her terrible accent beautiful to me. She presses a kiss to my lips before moving through the crowd as if she belongs here. I feel like I've fallen through a hole into a strange world. Like Alicia in Wonderland. Any moment someone will notice the mistake of me and ask me to leave. I put my head down and keep my phone clutched in my hand. *Find Gabi. Find Gabi.* That is all I need to think about.

I walk around the largest room, peeking into groups of people, boys and girls, sometimes two or three sitting on each other's laps, laughing. Sometimes there are couples kissing, but mostly they are pushing at each other, teasing. I look for

Juliette's shoulder-length hair, for Gabi's dark braid. I look for kids in a grown-up world.

"You want a drink?" A boy stands in front of me holding up two bottles of beer like they are fish he's just caught. He has a messy grin, and his blond hair is smeared with sweat. He tips from side to side, as if the room is spinning. I suppose it is for him.

"No, um, no, thank you." I try to move past him, but he steps in front of me.

"You sure? I've got an extra for a pretty girl like you."

I scowl at him.

He pulls back, unsteady. "Cold bitch, huh? Okay, whatever," he says, and turns away. I push him as I pass, hard, just for the pleasure of seeing him fall down.

I am terrified that I have made a mistake. That Gabi isn't here and we're wasting time.

Then I see her boots—the ones that Indranie bought her and that she's worn almost every day since—in a heap with other shoes.

"Gabi!" I yell. One girl, in a T-shirt and high heels, turns to look at me. No one else notices. I scan the group of people near the discarded shoes.

Am I losing my mind? Are these boots very common and I'm seeing the things I want to see?

I open a door near the boots, but it's a bathroom. I try the next. It's a room with a washing machine, warm and smelling of soap. I feel worse than ridiculous. I am wasting time. I look for Rey. Maybe she has found Gabi. Or maybe Gabi was never here.

"GABI!" I scream. The girl with the high heels turns to look at me. I turn away, my face on fire, and bend to look at the black boots.

"Hey, you okay?"

I whirl around to find the girl with the high heels looking at me. I take a deep breath to find my words. "My sister. I can't find her." This girl has long black hair with dyed blue ends.

"Who's your sister?"

"Gabriela. Gabi. She's only twelve. She ran away from home." That is a little true.

"Ahh, I get it. She snuck out and came here, huh? Jake is not the most discerning host."

"I don't know Jake."

"Really? I thought my little brother knew everyone. Have you checked the game room?"

"Where is that?"

She points to another door. "My dad's a freak about the Persian in there—no-shoe policy."

Why does a house need so many doors? This one doesn't open. It's locked. I knock, hoping it isn't another bathroom. Someone behind the door giggles.

I pound and pound and pound on the door, desperately willing it to open.

Until, suddenly, the door to el Club opens, and Antonio's grinning face emerges.

"I knew you'd turn out pretty," he says, self-satisfied. "I am never wrong." He opens the door wide to let me pass. In the years since I first saw him, Antonio has aged more than anyone. He is just as tall but much fatter, much more wrinkled. As if the weight of so much power has settled into his skin. He's impeccably dressed in fashionable American clothes, the picture

of a gentleman even with a gun tucked into the waistband of his pants.

"Where is Gabi?"

Antonio's mouth turns down in disappointment. "No pleasantries?" *He shakes his head sadly.* "No, you have never been pleasant. But I was right about you!" *He circles me like a cat he wants to play with before killing it.* "You did turn out pretty." *He trails his finger down my cheek. I don't know how it doesn't leave a scar. How I am able to withstand it.*

"But your little sister is much prettier," *he says with a bellowing laugh.*

I dig my fists into my sides. She's not here, I think, he's playing with me as he has always done. I turn to leave while I still can.

"Pablo!" *Antonio shouts.* "Bring out your lovely sister!"

I turn back to face him, feet pinned to the floor.

From the tiny bathroom of el Club Atlético, Pablo—the only boy I have ever looked up to—pulls Gabi by the hand. As if it's a natural thing, Pablo holds una pistola loosely in his other hand. When Gabi sees Antonio and me watching her, she trips in too-big heels. She hides behind Pablo, covering her face with her hair.

"Gabi," *I whisper.*

Her thin body is wrapped in a skintight skirt, her arms bare in a blue tank top with sparkles on the straps. A pink bra peeks through the tank top. They have put her en un disfraz, a costume of a grown woman. Gabi's eyes dart to mine. It's okay, it's okay, I say with my eyes. She tries to walk to me, but Antonio grabs her in a sickening embrace. My sister stands in front of me, and I can't touch her. She cries, the makeup running down her face, and I can't reach her.

My brother walks behind me, leaning into my ear, a snake spitting poison.

"Did you think I would stand for such an insult to our family? That I would let you infect our little sister with your disease?" His mouth is so close, I can smell the beer and cigarettes on his breath. In the shower room, El Flaco, Tato, and other boys I grew up with laugh, the sound echoing like gunshots.

"Sos nada. Menos que nada. Sos una mancha."

I could not argue with him. It is how I felt. Unclean and guilty. If I had not been with Liliana, if I had been paying attention, would they have taken Gabi? It's my fault she's being held by this monster.

"No te preocupes, Marisol, mi amor," Antonio says. "I'm going to make sure Gabi never catches your disease." He squeezes Gabi so tightly that she yelps like a whipped dog. He lifts her up to his face, her body like a rag doll, and kisses her with no pity.

"Pablo! You have to stop him!"

The smile fades from Pablo's face, as if there is some mistake, as if this isn't the movie he wants to see.

"Do something!" I scream.

"Cálmate," Pablo says, his voice high, unsteady. "Okay, Tonio, that's enough." He forces his words to sound teasing, light.

"¿Qué te pasa, Pablito?" Antonio says, tightening his hold on Gabi. "You said you didn't want otra camionera in the family. You said you would die of shame, remember?"

We both watch, frozen, as Gabi cries and Antonio crushes her to his side. It's a parody of love, of closeness. I can see Gabi shaking from where I stand.

"But I thought you said you would show . . ." Pablo's hand loosens from my arm, and I pull back, not wanting him to be able to grab me again. "You said it was to show, to show

Marisol." He steps closer to Antonio, confusion on his face. In the shower room, one of the boys puts on a radio and loud music fills the room. I imagine that Antonio told them to put the radio on loud so no one would hear the screaming.

"I will show her," Antonio says with a nod. "The Morales family is a good Christian family." He turns to me and enunciates in English, carefully, as if he has been practicing, "No. Faggots. Here."

Antonio digs his hands into Gabi's sides, making her whimper. I scream, stretching out my hands, as if I have any power to save her.

Pablo runs to Antonio, pulling on his jacket to get him to let go. When that does nothing more than earn him a slap, Pablo puts himself between Antonio and Gabi. She falls to the floor in a heap by his feet.

Antonio, with a growl of rage, pushes Pablo. But Pablo locks an arm around Antonio's neck, trying to bring him to the floor. A bang, sharp as a scream, echoes in the room. Antonio shoves Pablo away, kicking him when he lands on the floor. We stand frozen, me and Antonio, his heavy chest heaving.

I wait for Pablo to get up, to wipe the blood from his mouth. To use his charm to get us out of this horrible pesadilla. But he doesn't move. Antonio's gun hangs from his hand, as if it's a harmless toy.

I stumble to where Pablo lies on the floor. Gabi's cries get louder, shrieks of a bird. Pablo's light blue shirt, from his favorite equipo de fútbol, turns purple as the blood soaks through it.

"Marisol?"

The music from the shower room, the laughing, gets even louder. It crowds every thought out of my head. I pick up Pablo's gun, cold in his hand, and turn it on Antonio. I don't wait for the *words that form in his mouth to come out. I shoot him. I want to destroy his mouth, his hands, so he can never use them against someone again. I'm pretty sure my bullet hits the soft underside of his large belly. When he falls to the floor, I drop the gun.*

A hand grabs my arm. My fist is raw from pounding on this door.

Rey's worried face meets mine.

"Marisol?" she repeats. Her voice pierces through the fog of my mind. I am not in el Club Atlético. Antonio is dead. All should be fine, but it's so far from fine. I lean both hands against the closed door, nowhere for my rage to go.

Pablo and Antonio dead on the floor and *corre, corre, corre* driving like a train in my head. The images of what happened weeks ago and what is happening now bleed together, and I can't place myself anywhere. Rey's hand—I am sure that I would recognize the feel of her hand no matter where I am—clasps mine.

The door opens suddenly. A confused-looking boy opens the door. I blink and he blinks.

"Sol?"

Gabi's hair is messy—what's left of it. It's been cut to just below her ears, a shiny black cap. She has a game remote in her hand—like the ones in Rey's room. She squints at the brightness flooding the dark, little room with the huge TV screen. I see my sister's bare feet, her toenails painted pink. Her feet have always been so small. *Pata de pájaro*, Pablo used to call them. Bird feet. The boy looks from Gabi to me and laughs. "What the hell is this—"

But he doesn't get to finish his sentence because I push him away. I grab Gabi as if she is an apparition, as if she will melt away. She is real and safe. That is all I need.

Chapter 33

My name is Carla Manzo, and this is a credible fear interview. Your name is Marisol Morales, correct?"

I answer the woman's questions slowly and carefully. I am not in a detention center. Gabi is at school. Olga will pick her up at 3:00 p.m. People who love her will make sure she is all right.

"You have claimed that you are seeking asylum in the United States of America due to your belief that you are in physical danger of torture or death, is that correct?"

"Yes," I say, aware that every answer is being recorded.

"You have stated that you and your sister have been targeted by gangs in El Salvador and that your lives are threatened by violence and torture. Is that correct?"

"Yes."

"What is the nature of these threats?"

I hesitate. After all these weeks that have turned into months, I still hear Pablo's and Liliana's voices in my head. *Tortillera. Dyke.*

Carla Manzo clears her throat when I don't answer. "Are these threats political? Religious? Based on ethnicity?"

"No. They are because I am gay," I say. I feel as if I have dropped a bomb. As if the room should shake and dust should fill the air. But all that happens is that Carla Manzo writes something down.

"And your sister? Is she also being persecuted because of her sexual orientation?"

"No!" I say. Then, "I don't know."

Carla looks to me. "And what is the nature of the threat against her? I have to specify for each asylum request."

I shift in my chair, uncomfortable in my new dark blue suit. Olga bought it for me along with the black high-heeled shoes that pinch. *I am not in a detention center,* I remind myself. I can leave this lawyer's office whenever I want. The lawyer Indranie hired sits next to me, taking notes.

"Would you like some water, Marisol?" she asks. I nod, and my lawyer, Irene Sagasti, crosses her office to a little fridge and brings out three bottles of water.

After a long sip, I answer Carla's question. "They were threatening Gabi because they thought she would turn out like me. They wanted to . . . make her . . . force her . . . to not be like me."

Carla Manzo's mouth turns down at the corners, but she does not comment, only writes more notes.

She asks Irene some questions about my legal status, questions that I don't understand, and then it's over.

"I can go?" I ask when Carla Manzo stands and gathers her things.

"Yes," she says, holding out her hand for me to shake. "It was a pleasure to meet you. We'll be in touch with Ms. Sagasti's office throughout the process. Thank you for your time."

Rey is waiting for me outside the lawyer's office. "You look amazing in a suit," she says.

I hug her tight, my fear and elation mixed like sweet and sour on the tongue.

A man walking past with a newspaper looks at us, and I pull away from Rey. I don't know if he was looking because he liked my suit or if I reminded him of someone or if under his breath he was saying "tortillera." I'll never know. But it doesn't matter anymore.

"I thought Indranie was picking me up," I say once we reach Rey's green-and-white minicar. "Not that I mind. This is better."

Rey grins and pulls her seat belt on. "She and Dad are making plans. They have an idea."

"Good idea or bad idea?"

"Interesting idea," she says. "Dad thinks he can set up a hearing with a senator he knows. On undocumented minors."

"What does that mean?" I click my seat belt into place. Now that the interview is over, I can finally relax. It doesn't mean everything is fine—of course it doesn't. But it's a start. And I'm not alone.

"It's when expert witnesses talk in front of lawmakers about a specific problem. It's called testifying."

"Like in court," I say, remembering Mrs. Rosen's crime shows about law and order.

"Actually, it takes place on Capitol Hill." I look behind me. The lawyer's office is a few blocks from the Capitol building. I can see the dome clearly through the back window.

"Your father is going to talk to senators about undocumented illegals and minors?" I ask. I say *illegals* because I know she gets a little mad when I do. But she doesn't react.

Rey grips the steering wheel, even though the engine is not turned on. She looks tense, like there's something she wants to say and she's not sure I want to hear it. "No," she says at last. She looks over at me. "They thought maybe you could do the talking."

My mouth hangs open. "Me?" I finally manage to say.

"You're the expert," Rey says, a half-worried, half-expectant look on her face.

Strangers asking me questions? Knowing things about me my own family doesn't know? It wouldn't just be about Antonio and Pablo. It would be the weeks on the carretera. Every remembered face, everyone who was not as lucky as me and Gabi.

"It would be terrifying," I say to Rey. Which is not the same as no.

She grins. "Yeah, but you're brave. Gabi says so." She turns the engine on and waits. "So," she says. "Where are we going?"

I take a deep breath, for courage. For me.

"Where aren't we going? That is the question."

ACKNOWLEDGMENTS

The Grief Keeper would not have been possible if not for the support, creativity, and sometimes intervention of so many good people. In 2015, when I first imagined two sisters crossing the border—the older willing to do anything to protect the younger—I wasn't sure I could write a book like this. I thought I wasn't a good enough writer, that I didn't know enough. I thought it would be too hard.

My agent, Barbara Poelle, told me in no uncertain terms to *write the hard book*. Without Barbara, I wouldn't have had the courage to try. The first thing I said to Barbara after she offered me representation was, "I love you!" That hasn't changed. Thank you for being the absolute best.

My thanks to everyone at Irene Goodman Literary Agency, who put up with my kids visiting for Bring Your Kid to Work Day—and who are unfailingly supportive.

Shout-out to my fellow Poelleans—a posse of excellent and talented writers who have supported me, counseled me, and held my hand through this amazing experience. Looking at you, James Brandon, Traci Chee, Sarah Lemon, and Renée Ahdieh.

Stacey Barney, my editor, is a magician. She can turn leaden words into gold. And she calls me out on my BS without mercy, but with infinite kindness. She is that smart, that good, that gracious. Thank you for loving these characters and bringing forth the depth and sweetness of the story.

G. P. Putnam's Sons/PRH is a *family*. From the kind (and hilarious) VP and Publisher, Jen Klonsky; to Caitlin Tutterow, who made sure I got my edits done on time; to copyeditors Nicole Wayland, Kathleen Keating, and Cindy Howle, who worked hard to get every palabra right. Thank you for welcoming me into this family with open arms.

The beautiful illustration on the cover is by the incredibly talented artist Kaethe Butcher. The book was designed by Kelley Brady and Dave Kopka. I still can't believe how perfectly they captured the connection and emerging love between Marisol and Rey. I am so thankful.

Jennifer Herrera, Lynda Gene Rymond, Kerri Maniscalco, Sarah Jude, and Becky Levine have been critique partners and beloved kindred spirits for many years. Through countless drafts, your support and creativity have made this book (and oh! The books that came before!) the best it could be. Thank you for keeping me honest and making me better in a million ways.

A huge abrazo y beso for mi hermana Anna-Marie McLemore. Your beautiful words showed me the way, and your encouragement and mentorship are a continuing joy. I can't wait to see what we get up to in years to come.

Maribel Fernandez DeLeon—who, from our first bus ride together freshman year of high school, has felt like family—thank you for reading a very early version of *The Grief Keeper* and encouraging me to keep going.

My thanks to Norma Gorrochotegui for her friendship and

for helping me make up for my deficiency with los acentos en español.

My sister, Anamari, was unabashedly my model for Marisol. As the older sister, she took care of me and kept me safe (and sane!) with equal parts exasperation and love.

Thank you to my parents, Gladys and Armando, who came to this country looking to create a better life for themselves and their family. You worked tirelessly and you instilled in your daughters an appetite to do more, be more. I am grateful beyond what I can say for your example and your love.

Thank you to Meredith Kneavel, Associate Dean and Professor of Public Health, La Salle University, for sharing her expertise on neurotransmitters, PTSD, and anxiety disorders.

And to Elizabeth R. Blandon, Esq., a wonderful and passionate immigration lawyer based in Florida. Elizabeth answered all my questions about immigration law and how the current administration applies the law—and all the ways that is shifting.

Thank you to Laura Pegram, editor of the *Kweli Journal* and founder of the Color of Children's Literature Conference, for her love and support. The work *Kweli* does to empower and lift voices of POC, Native, and marginalized creators is vital—and Laura does it beautifully.

So much gratitude to the Highlights Foundation (where parts of *The Grief Keeper* were written and revised) for serving as a refuge and safe place for writers seeking community, quiet, and inspiration. George Brown and Alison Myers, you turn the lonely, difficult job of writing into a communal act of generosity (with great food!). Thank you!

So many people have supported me throughout the years

in ways that seem invisible but have actually been monumental. Abbey Luterick, Rebecca Nellis, Michele Fecher, and Joyce Stewart have all heard me whine about how hard writing is, too many times to count. The Pretty Bird coven—Brandy, Alina, Lisa, and Kate—thanks for keeping me company (and caffeinated!).

To my daughters, Rowan and Lyra, for being the realest, most wonderful example of sisters who love each other and sisters who get on each other's nerves. Thank you for being patient all those times I was writing instead of helping you make slime. And thank you for showing me that love has no finish line, it goes on and on.

Lastly, but in no way least, thank you to my husband, Timothy. From our first date at IHOP, you have been the best man I know. There isn't anyone more supportive, more deeply caring, or more generous. It is no lie that I couldn't do this without you. Gracias, amor.

Resources

For people like Marisol and Gabi, caught between discrimination and violence and facing a bewildering immigration system, **Immigration Equality** can help.

immigrationequality.org

The Trevor Project is the leading national organization providing crisis intervention and suicide prevention services for LGBTQ youth.

thetrevorproject.org

GLSEN is an organization dedicated to championing LGBTQ issues in education.

glsen.org

Galaei is a queer Latin@ social justice organization based in Philadelphia.

galaei.org